Joyce

A Spiritual Warfare Novel

This is a work of fiction. The characters, incidents, and dialogues are the products of the author's imagination and are not to be construed as real. Any resemblance to actual events or persons living or dead is entirely coincidental.

A special acknowledgement and thank you to my incredible editor, Abigail Rivera. Without her tenacious reading, questioning and counsel, I would not have completed this book. Anyone in need of a quality editor would do well to seek her help. Email the author at Blog@RobertECook.org

For Corrine

"For our struggle is not against flesh and blood, but against the rulers, against the authorities, against the powers of this dark world and against the spiritual forces of evi in the heavenly realms." Ephesians 6:12

Chapter 1

It came from nowhere. It was something but what? She had never seen this before. Not this, ever. Then, just as quickly, there was another. Not the same but another. It was different in an unnerving sort of way. Again, she did not know where it came from. One second nothing, then, there it was. She could not describe what she saw. She had words. Big, ugly, animal, alien, menacing, dark, ghoulish. None of them described what she saw.

There were other words. Scared, anxious, afraid, shocked. None covered her true emotions. Where's the bus?

The bus bench offered no protection. She was in the open just across the street from the decaying strip center. It was once the center of commerce on the avenue, but no longer. The government called it blighted.

Then another showed up. Out of thin air. They were the same yet not the same. The third to appear, and that is what it did, appear suddenly. It had a head like a cow or ox or something similar. It had horns, two, like a cow or a bull. It wasn't a cow. It wasn't a bull. The body was like a man. But it wasn't that either.

She held a hand over her mouth to stifle any spontaneous screams. She did not want them to know she was there.

She looked back at the first wondering if it might be female. It wore a long red robe. The face was of a man, or a woman, but it was clearly not. It wore a golden crown, but it didn't look like gold. No shine, it was dull, and there was no sense of value. Any value at all was missing.

She steadily became more and more uneasy as the three things moved about on the front walk of the failed shopping center. She did not know if they had seen her, cared about her, or if they would attack her if she were spotted. The bus was due in a couple of minutes. It was the last one tonight. She could not miss the bus. She had to wait.

She could not afford a fancy smartphone but her daughter could. It had been a gift. She dug it out of her purse, which was no easy task. She started to take pictures. As she did, yet another thing appeared. It was like they were there, but then they were invisible. Then she could see them again. It was a crazy idea, but everything she saw at the moment was crazy.

It did not make her any less scared. Crazy, scared, the feeling was the same. She could see the bus. I was two blocks away, an eternity of seconds. Then the cow head disappeared. She was lost for an explanation. The three still on the sidewalk became more agitated. It was not her word but it described what she was thinking. The bus was now only a block away. The female, if it was a female, maybe, with the red robe vanished. That's when she realized two had red robes. Different, completely different but they wore red robes.

The bus was just one hundred yards away when she saw them for the first time, three more on the flat roof above the sidewalk. These three were different, completely different.

They were white, majestic looking. Other than their size they were not at all frightening. She had seen them before. She liked them. But she had never seen them like this, out here in the world.

Displaying her card she hurried to board the bus. Moving down the aisle she leaned over the seats to look out the window. Nothing. All of them were gone.

Chapter 2

"You're not going to like this one." The uniform sergeant was quick, snapping his words. It was hard to tell if he was being sarcastic.

"Can't remember the last time I liked one." Joyce was not sarcastic. Murder was a fact of life, at least in his line of work. He had never come to like it. The big detective was a homely man, slow to speak and slower to move. He stood on the sidewalk of a nearly vacant strip center.

In days gone by, before the veteran investigator ever thought of police work the commercial center was top self. It was the place to go in the days before malls and Wal-marts and franchise restaurants and all that goes into being a commercial magnet for the hard-earned cash of the neighborhood.

Tommy Joyce did what he always does when arriving at a crime scene. There was no hurry. To work quickly now would not help the case. If the killer were known it would be different. With a known killer on the loose, time is of the essence. Not this time.

The victim was dead. The killer or killers were gone. Deliberate work now was important. Don't be in a hurry. Take your time and get it right.

The uniform men do good work. Some may actually enjoy calls like this. Joyce did not. He wasn't even certain that he liked his job. There had been a time when the work gave him a sense of satisfaction. Not anymore. People relied on him. The public expected results. Good work with the right outcome.

In Joyce's case file, homicide, the public tolerance for unsolved cases was non-existent. Joyce got it. He understood. He had his methods and for the most part they worked.

Inside the business, uniform officers were watching over the victim. The ME had not yet arrived. That meant that the men were watching a dead man. Nothing happens to the body until the medical examiner's crew arrives.

Joyce speculated about the conversations. Even as he made copious notes he wondered if the men were making jokes in hopes of lightening up the seriousness of what had happened. Others may be trying hard not to look at the victim. Finding other things to investigate or otherwise not be involved with the dead. He hoped none of them were looking at the stuff for which the store was known.

Joyce took in everything. He had his notebook open and was writing things down. At the top of the page were two times. The time he was first notified. Then the time he arrived on location. Both had come from his phone. It was all he had for a watch. The time notation was a little thing but something of credit if asked at a trial.

Now he wrote notes about the weather. He noted what vehicles were on the scene. An ambulance was parked along the curb. Three uniforms cars were parked irregularly in front of the storefront. An unmarked police car was parked in the lot in front of the store. Joyce surmised it to be the sergeant's car. The lot also contained two private cars. He imagined one belonged to the victim. It was a guess but the guy certainly would have a car, right? Tommy Joyce would find out. He didn't know if anything was parked in the back. He made another note.

Detective Joyce slipped back behind the wheel of his own unmarked patrol car. It was a tight fit. Joyce knew he was bigger than most, but the Dodge Charger just wasn't a Crown Vic. He allowed his left leg to remain outside, his shoe resting on the old worn blacktop that had been new decades ago. He stared at the storefront. It was glass. Four panes, two on either side of the door. The glass was covered on the inside with brown paper obscuring the contents of the business from anyone passing by.

It was a cheap disguise to prevent the innocent from seeing the wares of a depraved business. The idea of depraved applied to the owner as well as the clientele.

He knew what he would find inside. He expected it to be dark. Above the eave line was a cheap white plastic sign designed to be backlit. The letters were blue. ADULT. That was all Joyce needed to know. A seedy business, with a seedy owner done in by a seedy killer. His heart was not in this. He did not want to go in.

Chapter 3

"This one's not good detective." It was a uniformed officer.

Joyce had just heard the same thing from the sergeant. He nodded but did not answer. Privately he wondered if the uniform or the sergeant for that matter had ever seen a 'good' one. Joyce signed in on a clipboard held by an officer just inside the front door. The officer pointed.

Joyce removed a pair of blue latex gloves from his pocket. He pulled them on as his eyes took in the interior of the business. He then grabbed a pair of white paper footies from a box just inside the door. He stooped to slip them over his dock sider loafer style shoes. Joyce moved a few paces into the store and looked to his right. The subject of his presence was behind the checkout counter along the wall.

Joyce nearly retched. "This is not good." The words just slide past his lips. At first, he did not even realize he had said them. He stared at the corpse.

"Who's got a theory?" He considered it a dumb question but it was all he could think of as he collected his own thoughts.

"I've looked around. There's nothing here that would explain how this happened."

"Yeah, but what happened? What am I looking at?"

"Burns. Looks like he was…I don't know….somehow…incinerated." It was a uniformed officer speaking.

Joyce turned to a cop that had looked over the business. "Any sign where this may have happened?"

"None detective."

"So how does a man get burned up like this and there is nothing else that is so much as singed?"

"Blow torch?" The uniformed officer said it without any confidence.

"Did this happen here? I mean, is this our crime scene?"

"Would you carry him in here like that?" The officer pointed to the body.

"Okay, who called it in? Have you talked to them? Are they a witness?

"9/11 call, not an emergency. Supposed to be a disturbance. We pulled up and no one was here." The patrolman stopped.

"What made you look in here?"

He shrugged, "Gut I guess. Only place around. A call could have come from here." He motioned around with his arm. "With the paper on the windows we couldn't see in so I pulled on the door. It opened."

Joyce nodded. The officer continued. "We didn't know what to expect. Could have been an unsecured business, employees could have been in here, or it could have been a burglary. We called for backup."

"You find him," Joyce pointed to the body, "Right away...? after backup arrived...? What happened?"

"When we heard backup was rolling, we continued to enter. Saw that almost right away. It seemed obvious the first place to look was behind the counter."

"Where's the caller?"

"Never found um. The place was deserted when we pulled up. No disturbance, no people anywhere...to be honest, pulling on the door was almost an afterthought."

"Show me around."

The two slowly strolled to the back of the store. They passed through a doorway and into what was probably called a store-room. If that was the purpose, the business had little stock that was not on display. Joyce sniffed wondering if he might get a whiff of smoke. Nothing. His eyes passed over the rear exit. His instinct was to open the door but knew better. Let the crime scene techs dust it first. There were two other doors, one to a cluttered utility closet, the other to a bathroom that had not been cleaned in a very long time.

"We got anybody out back?" Joyce nodded to the door as he spoke.

"Not sure."

Joyce pointed to the portable microphone attached to the officer's shirt.

The officer tipped his head and spoke into the radio. Joyce heard the response. No one was in the back. An officer responded saying he would check it out. Joyce nodded.

"This your district?" Joyce was talking.

"Yeah."

"What do you know about this place?"

"First time I've been here."

"Really." It was not a question.

"Yeah, I knew it was here but that's all I know."

Joyce appeared to be thinking. Then, "You know if any of the men come in here?"

"You mean like, as a customer?"

"Right."

The officer shook his head. "Man, I hope not."

"Might be helpful right now. Could give us some insight into this victim." Joyce nodded his head towards the front of the store and began to walk that way. The officer followed.

The medical examiner's crew had arrived. Joyce saw them bending over the body that until now, had not been touched. The Crime scene techs were also on location and had begun video and still photo work. Joyce recognized the two men from the medical examiner. He did not know their names but had seen them before.

The M.E.'s office does good work. They are meticulous in making certain the body is handled in a manner to preserve any evidence that might help determine the cause of death. Second, was evidence that might prove a suspect guilty. Neither of the men would be involved in the post of the body. A doctor in the medical examiner's office would complete that work.

Unlike CSI on television, the crime scene people do not investigate the crime. They do the hard work, the tedious work of collecting and preserving evidence. Beyond the obvious of such things as lividity and rigor mortis, the crew did little to determine the time or cause of death. In cases of gunshots, they are useful to determine entrance and exit wounds. Exit wounds are important in attempting to locate the bullet.

Joyce made eye contact with one of the men from the M.E.'s office. "Any idea how a man gets burned like this?"

"Fire?" He smiled, waited a long moment then added, "No idea detective." He was shaking his head.

The two-man medical examiner's crew was ready to roll the body. Pictures and videos had been taken showing the body just as it was found which was face down. Now it was time to see what the other side looked like. They slowly rolled the body in the tight quarters behind the counter.

"Oh my..." Joyce stopped speaking. He had been training himself not to speak certain words.

The medical examiner did not hold back and a line of words came out detailing his feelings about what he saw.

A uniformed officer blurted out a cop's favorite word.

Joyce forced himself to look at the victim's face. He saw nothing. There was no face. It was gone. His first thoughts told him it had been burned off. He stared, realizing he could be wrong. The body had been burned. That was obvious, but to see the face or the absence of a face, he was not so sure.

"This is bad." The man from the medical examiner was speaking. "I have never seen this before." He continued to examine the face. He had not touched anything since rolling the body. "Let's get shots of this." He stood up.

A crime scene tech with a 35mm digital camera moved in and shot several frames. He backed away shaking his head. He looked a little green.

The medical man returned to the side of the body. "What's this?" he was pointing towards a hand.

"Get a shot of that." Joyce was in charge.

The cameraman returned and took several frames of the hand and the contents.

"This is a bunch of crap." It was a medical examiner.

"How's that?" asked Joyce.

"It's not burned, I don't see a single mark on it, nothing, it's perfect. The body is burned beyond recognition but this, in his hand, is untouched." He was pointing.

"What is it?" Joyce was standing over the body but the medical examiner was blocking his view.

The medical examiner worked a moment before managing to extract the item from the victim's hand. "Holy..." An expletive slipped out. He handed it over his shoulder toward Joyce.

Joyce took the item in his gloved hand. He was careful to take it by its very edge. "This is some kind of card."

"It's a tarot card." A uniformed officer was talking.

"Fortune teller stuff?"

"Don't know much about it, detective but that's my guess."

"It says 'the devil' on the bottom. This image must be Satan." Joyce looked toward a crime scene tech, "Get me a bag."

The tech handed Joyce what might look like a sandwich bag with a white label where notes and names and dates are entered. Joyce slid the card into the plastic bag and sealed it. He turned to the men standing around and held up the bag. "Any ideas?" Nobody spoke.

Chapter 4

"Tommy." The lieutenant was waving his arm from the far side of the bullpen. It was a cluttered office with little sense of order. Just a room full of desks, each stacked with endless piles of paper.

"What's up?" Joyce spoke the words a few feet from the lieutenant who stood in the doorway of his office.

"Heard you got a full-blown who done it?"

"Right. I'm not even sure who the victim is." Joyce was shaking his head.

"Guess that means you have no idea who did it." The Lieutenant turned and walked behind his desk.

A 'who done it' will generally have a few possible suspects. Ex's, drug dealers, junkies, are some of the usual suspects.

"I need to wait till the post to even know how he died." Joyce paused. He wondered for a moment if the victim was a male. "I don't even know his name. I know who owns the store but I can't say our victim and the owner are the same. I mean... it could be a clerk...you know an employee...or maybe a customer." Joyce exhaled loudly and dropped his heavy frame into a straight back leather chair in front of his boss's desk.

The lieutenant settled into his fancy swivel chair and leaned back. "Need any help?"

Joyce shook his head, "I don't know boss. I have the precinct sergeant going out to the owner's house and see who might be there. See if the vic and the owner are the same. I hope we can at least get a photo, a recent one, just in case we need to find friends, associates, you know."

The lieutenant nodded. "You know you will. Any clue if the guy is married? Maybe a wife at home?"

"Guess I should care but I don't. The guy was a porn dealer. How can anyone be married to a guy like that?"

The lieutenant grinned and offered a thought. "Maybe she's a film star."

Joyce nodded but it was time to change the subject. He pulled his notebook out of his sports coat. The coat was big, even on Joyce. It hung on him like a blanket. "The initial call went to 9-1-1, don't know who it was, maybe they check back when this hits the news."

"Burner phone?"

"Could be but I doubt it. More likely just a cheap prepaid thing. The area is pretty seedy, Not a lot of iPhones in that neighborhood."

"Probably right."

"What do you know about fortune tellers?" Joyce's focus was on the Tarot card.

"We used to think of them as a gypsy."

"The victim had a tarot card in his hand. The card of the devil."

"Okay."

Joyce continued. "It's a head-scratcher boss. How is a body completely burned? I mean really burned up." He paused and reached for his phone. "I have a couple of pictures."

"I'll pass."

"Yeah well, how does a guy get that burnt and still have a card in his hand that was untouched?"

"It was put there after the fire."

"Not this time. It was tight in his fist. The ME guy had to work to get it out without ruining the card."

"Did the ME have any thoughts about how he died?" The lieutenant leaned forward and rested his forearms on his desk.

"Smart money is on the fire thing but who knows. No sign as to where the actual burning took place. Nothing. I guess we have to figure he was dumped there." Joyce shook his head. "You know…. I really didn't need this case."

14

"Yeah, but if not you, who?" The lieutenant knew that Joyce was his best man when it came to solving murders. All the teams were good but Joyce had a little edge.

"Yeah well I need to get my report typed up and maybe by then I'll have a cause of death." Joyce sat quietly for a moment. He had been looking at his shoes. He lifted his head and gazed at the lieutenant. "I don't have the slightest idea where to start on this." He shook his head.

"Yes you do, you've already started."

"How's that?"

"You're bouncing stuff off me. That means your brain's engaged. That's where you start."

"I saw one of those CSI shows once where the body did a spontaneous combustion thing." Joyce shrugged. "I don't think that happened here. There is absolutely no evidence of fire at the scene, beyond the body. I can't think of how a body could be a literal torch and not burn anything around it."

"Do you have any ideas about the devil card?"

"Naw." He shook his head. "I don't have squat."

The lieutenant seemed sympathetic. "This one's got you bummed?"

"No, that's not it. I just don't like the feel of it."

"Like what?"

Joyce ran his fingers through his short hair. It wasn't a Marine Corp cut but it was short enough that he did not need a brush when he stepped out of the shower. "Like the guy is running a porno shop, maybe into all sorts of sick stuff. He dies from fire but nothing else is burned and to top it off, a card from Satan is in his hand." Joyce stood up. "You remember Paladin? He had a card, 'Have Gun Will Travel'."

"Yeah..when was that?"

"Late night reruns...Well, maybe the devil left his calling card with our victim."

"I doubt it. Let's see what the medical examiner has to say."

Chapter 5

When the medical examiner finally called, Tommy Joyce was not certain what would be good news and what might be bad news.

He had a tentative ID that came from the store owner. The uniformed sergeant questioned the owner. At the moment it appeared that he had no information as to why his clerk would have been the victim of such a crime. Beyond providing the name of the clerk he had little to offer.

"Tell me what you found." Detective Joyce needed something to hang a case on. The medical examiner would be a good place to start.

"This is not a normal death detective."

"Tell me something," said Joyce.

"The heart. It is intact. No fire, burning, nothing. Intact."

"Is that possible….to be burned as he was but the heart survived the fire?"

"Like I said, this is not normal."

"Okay, so what killed him?"

"Nothing definite yet detective. We're doing toxicology, that'll take a while."

"Right," said Joyce. "But what about trauma. Gunshot, stabbing, cracked skull. How did he die?" Joyce paused, "Could he die from the fire and have his heart intact?"

The medical examiner knew Joyce. He also knew his reputation. Blunt, to the point. Don't give him the idea he was being jerked around. "I don't know detective. I'm working on it. I would say..maybe..probably."

"Working on what?" It was rhetorical. Joyce continued. "What is there to work on? We know he did not die of natural causes, this is a homicide…" Joyce paused, "It is a homicide… isn't it?"

"Actually, I am not prepared to make that call yet."

"What?" Joyce couldn't believe his ears.

"Look, I don't know what killed him. It could be the fire. Probably is the fire but…I don't know." The medical examiner checked himself. "What if your victim, if he died of say, a heart attack? Then a family member, friend, spiritual leader, someone close to him, burned the body as a ritual. Like a funeral."

"You're the medical examiner, did he die of a heart attack?" Joyce did not hold back. It could have been said he was yelling.

"No. Well…actually, I don't think so."

"What?"

"The heart is the only thing not burned. It looks healthy."

"Then what is all this theory stuff?"

"What I am trying to tell you is, I have no idea how this man got burned up." The ME gestured towards the body resting on his stainless steel table. Joyce of course, did not see the move because they were talking on the telephone.

"I need a cause of death, whether it's a homicide, suicide, or natural causes. Let me know when you figure it out." Joyce hung up. He leaned back in his swivel desk chair, interlocked his huge fingers and rested his hands on the crown of his head. He began to think.

Homicide is an imposing idea. He had recently heard a statistic that in the United States a murder occurs every thirty minutes. The sound of it congers up all sorts of notions. But homicide does not mean murder. The words are not synonymous. Homicide merely means the hand of another caused the death of a human. It generally means the death was a crime, but that crime may not be murder. All murders are homicides while not all homicides are murders.

Tommy Joyce could be upset, even mad with the doctor from the medical examiner's office but he knew better. The doctor was only trying to be helpful. Theory, ideas, what-ifs were not uncommon in a bizarre case like this. Joyce was ready to cut him slack. His mind however came right back to the case. How did this man die? Why was his body burned as it was? Where did the burning take place? Where was the victim when he died? What was the thing with the tarot card? And finally, how does the heart escape the fire?"

Joyce had a thought. He dialed the ME back. "Doc, Joyce, one more thing. Any sign of an accelerant?"

"Can't say absolutely, but what I believe now before the lab looks at the clothes, I would say no."

"Okay, can you tell me how deep the burning went? Did he have burned organs, you already mentioned the heart?"

"Great question Joyce. The body showed extensive burning on the extremities, legs, arms, all the way to the bone. The torso showed burning through the skin and into the muscles and fat, everything except, and you know the heart."

"How about the face?"

The M.E. was quiet for a moment. He thought it an unusual question. Finally, "Now that you ask, yes the face was burned all the way to the skull. Nose, lips, even the tongue were gone."

"One more thing."

"Shoot."

"Your guys removed a tarot card from the victim's hand."

"Yes, they discussed it with me."

"Well doc, do you have an opinion as to when the card was placed into his hand?"

"When? No. I can however state with some certainly that it was not placed there post mortem."

"Thanks, talk to you later." Joyce hung up.

Chapter 6

The business was located just outside the main downtown business district. The area might be considered one step above blighted. The building was old brick construction that was prime when built nearly a hundred years earlier.

Joyce descended six steps below the sidewalk to the business's only entrance. The 'Readings' neon sign was conspicuous in the single window to the right of the door.

A small bell tinkled when the big detective opened the door and entered. He paused just inside. His eyes moving, taking in anything if not everything. As stereotypes go, this business was meeting everything Tommy Joyce had considered.

The air was scented by something. Joyce considered it more than just a candle. His eyes finally rested on an odd-shaped ashtray of an aqua green color. The remnants of small cone-shaped incense cluttered the bottom.

It was a small place. He judged it to be no bigger than an average living room and attached dining area. He guessed there would be living quarters further back but he couldn't see it.

Odd pictures in all types of frames hung everywhere. They were drawings and paintings rather than photos. Absent were the Dali's and Monet's.

Near the rear on the right was a round wooden table. It reminded him of an old kitchen table in a sketch of Jackie Gleason's *The Honeymooners* Joyce sees each time he visits his doctor. Three chairs surrounded it.

A matronly woman appeared from behind a hanging room divider. Her hair was teased dating her to circa the nineteen sixties. Not her age but her coming of age generation. Joyce guessed she fit.

"How can I help you?"

Joyce wanted to be cute and ask why she didn't know. It would have been a joke on the fortune-teller thing. He resisted.

"What can you tell me about Tarot cards?" He did not mention who he was.

"What exactly are you looking for?"

Joyce produced a photograph of the card removed from his victim's hand. "What does this card mean?"

"Oh, the Devil. Yes, I have seen it many times. Did that come to you in a reading?"

"No, I just need to get an understanding of where it came from…what it means."

"Probably not what you think. Where did you get it?" She pointed to Joyce's hand. She watched him. His size was nearly overpowering but yet she felt no threat. He seemed calm. His features were as dramatic as his size. Deep cracks rather than lines crossed his forehead. His ears were large. His jowls were heavy with deep creases. His hair was grey and short. He had to be close to her age.

"If it's not what I think, tell me what I should think." He ignored her question.

"Most believe the devil is in everything that goes bad. When they see that," she again pointed to the photo in Joyce's hand. "They think that the devil is at work in them."

"Is he?"

"Usually not, usually a negative part of them, their personality is at work. If they believe it's the devil at work it usually gets worse. If they come to understand that changing the negatives, the influence of the devil will go away."

"Did I hear that once on Dr. Phil?"

"What?"

"Never mind," Joyce waved one of his big arms. "So this does not mean that someone is possessed, nothing like that?"

"If you think someone needs an exorcism you're in the wrong place."

"I am not thinking about anything. I'm trying to find out what to think…. if this card was found in the hand of a dead man."

"Deadman?"

Joyce nodded.

"You a cop or something?"

Joyce nodded again.

"I can't help you." She turned and moved towards the back of the room.

"You believe in the devil?" Joyce raised his voice. More so she would hear him as she walked away.

"Of course I do." She turned back to face Joyce. "When I see that card in a reading I believe it shows there is a force, from the devil, that is present."

"Here?" Joyce pointed to the floor.

"No, not here, in the life of the one I'm reading for."

"What do you tell them?"

"If they think darkness is winning, if they feel beaten, then they are. The opposite is also true."

"Is that a positive thinking thing?"

"No, officer, it's a force for good or evil thing."

"Detective, call me detective."

"You might want a reading."

Joyce shook his head, "No thanks."

"You have hang-ups…detective."

Joyce laughed. "Tell me."

"I call you officer. Most would accept it as a compliment. You correct me with an ego thing….detective." She walked back towards Joyce.

"Okay, you got me," Joyce smiled. "I apologize."

"A dead guy, really?" She asked.

"Not pretty. Had this in his hand." Joyce held up the photo.

"I would not be too quick to think he got it from the devil."

"Where then?" Asked Joyce.

"A reading maybe." She shrugged her shoulders.

Joyce made eye contact and held it. Maybe longer than what was comfortable for her. Finally, "Where are you on opinions of the bizarre?"

"How bizarre?"

Joyce needed to think what he was about to do. This was his first visit to a fortune-teller. He did not know if she was credible, off the grid, or a scam artist. The Lieutenant called these people gypsies. He knew the case would be in the news soon enough. This was not a secret to be protected. "My guy was burned to a crisp."

"That's bizarre?"

"The card was in his hand. The medical examiner said it was there when he died."

"So?"

"It was not so much as singed." Joyce again showed her the photo of the actual card.

She nodded, shrugged, and casually walked toward her table. "Okay, that's bizarre." She sat down.

"Got a take on it?"

She motioned towards a chair. "Tell me your theory."

"I don't have one." Joyce dropped into a straight back wooden chair with a needlepoint seat that was too small for a man his size. "Where do I begin to look?"

"You're the detective."

"Officer." Joyce laughed, she smiled. "There isn't much I haven't seen. This is one of them. By every theory, the guy died right where we found him. The problem with the theory is nothing else was burned. No collateral damage. Not so much as a sniff of smoke." It was Joyce's turn to shrug.

"I'm not telling you how to investigate things like this, but I'll tell you I don't know any readers who would even consider the theory that the devil did this to your victim."

Chapter 7

The park stays open until eleven pm. This time of year, with daylight savings time, that was two hours after sunset.

It was nearly ten when the runner came out of the woods and into the parking lot. He was not just a jogger. He was training to run a marathon and his seriousness had him checking his times almost continually. The endorphins had kicked in. He thought it would be good to pass his car, run to the far end and return. A quarter-mile down and a quarter of a mile back. Just a little extra.

The presence was real but the runner had no knowledge of such things. What he did know was a weight. A pressure maybe, something suddenly slowing him down. Something was causing him to stop.

He looked again at his watch on his left wrist. The time was good. He should not be tired. Fatigue was not the reason for him to stop.

As it was, once stopped he simply walked to his car and began his cool down. The idea to stop his training for the night suddenly seemed like a good idea. It, the thought to stop, just popped into his head.

At the far end of the parking lot, the place the runner had intended to turn around, things were heating up. It was a second force. Not unlike the presence that had stopped the runner yet completely different.

The woman in the only car parked at the end of the lot knew all too well about the force. She had actually invited the power to be with her. She had conjured them from her very private dealings with her *Ouija* board.

Now the car was surrounded with no less than three special creatures that she had wished to join in the power they held. It was not an absolute power, but she may not have known that.

In the beginning, it seemed fun. It seemed like an adventure. It seemed a worthy thing to do. Now she was not so sure. In fact, she was coming to grips with the fact she had been wrong. Really wrong.

The creatures from another realm were done with her. She had served her purpose. Now they were ready to exact their privilege. The privilege was something she did not understand. There are others, many others who know. Many that understood that the woman had wandered into a realm she would not like. A dominion she was ill-equipped to confront. She was in a place from which there was no retreat. She was lost.

As the three surrounded her car, she saw at least two more at a distance. Near where she had seen a runner come out of the woods and into the lighted parking lot. The two were majestic when compared with the three that surrounded her car. She checked the locks again. She looked at the windows to be sure all were up, closed.

It began with a flushed feeling. A sense of being hot. She thought about the air conditioning and turned the ignition key. The car started. She adjusted the a/c. She turned the fan on high. It made no difference. Then there was nausea. She hoped she wouldn't vomit inside the car. If it got bad she would open the door. The idea, the thought of being this close to the creatures was not good.

As the thought passed through her head one of the creatures was suddenly sitting in the seat beside her. He consumed it all. His strange neck and ugly head had to slump to fit. He smelled. A horrible smell that she could not identify. Not dirt or body odor or alcohol or cigarettes. He just stunk.

Next, her chest began to hurt. A form of heartburn but worse. Her head started to spin. Then nothing. She slumped over in the seat where the creature had been seconds earlier, the car running, the air conditioner pouring cold air across her dead body

Chapter 8

"Something is going on. I felt it in my spirit while we were praying." The pastor made the comment as he and one of the church deacons walked into the small church office.

The two men had been praying in the sanctuary where the pastor met several times a week with various members of the staff for that very purpose.

"Tell me." The deacon made the comment as he poured a cup of coffee.

"Can't put my finger on it."

"Good or Bad?" The deacon was a big man. Tall, wide, strong. A sort of football player size. His visits to the midweek prayer meeting were infrequent. A construction worker, his work required him to be on the job from daylight to dark most week-days. Only severe weather would allow a day off. Heavy rain the previous evening had delayed today's start so he joined the pastor in prayer.

The pastor had taken a seat in a small desk chair on rollers and leaned back. He was as small as his deacon was big. In his forties, he was clearly ten years older than this morning's prayer partner. "Can't say really, I just feel something."

The deacon had a litany of questions but knew that most would not be proper. He knew the pastor was privy to many private dealings of church members and the sense he had during prayer could very well be a part of it. He quietly began to pray for his pastor. He prayed that wisdom and knowledge would be given the pastor in the matter that was on his heart.

The pastor watched his young construction worker – church leader and realized he was in prayer. He closed his eyes and privately agreed with the deacon. His cell phone rang. Literally. It was programmed to sound like a desk phone of the mid-1900s.

"Pastor, did I disturb you?" The caller had urgency in his voice.

"Not at all. We've just finished up with our morning prayer meeting."

"That's why I am calling. I just felt the need. I have been pray-ing…for you…and the church….and I just…well…I suddenly needed to call you."

"Did the Lord give you something?" The pastor smiled as he said it. The question was genuine. He had long ago come to know that a frequent and faithful relationship with God in prayer would from time to time, provide such a thing.

"I think so, pastor." There was a long pause and the pastor allowed the time for his member to collect his thoughts. The pastor did not speak. Finally, "I believe the Lord has told me that…", he stammered, not completely comfortable yet faithful enough to make the call as he had felt led.

He continued. "The Lord has shown me. I think, that we are going to be fighting something that is not flesh and blood. That a spiritual battle is coming and we need to prepare."

The pastor sat upright in the swivel chair. He had been listening to every word. When his member had finished he asked, "How did you come to this, I realize you were in prayer."

"I saw something."

"In the spirit?"

"Yes, I think so."

"What did you see?"

"I saw…what I believe to be an Angel of the Lord in battle with a demon."

"Anything else?"

"I heard, not out loud but in my spirit, 'you will not be fighting flesh and blood.'"

"Ephesians 6?"

"I think so."

Chapter 9

The police were standing in the construction trailer when the young church deacon arrived at work. A construction trailer is simply a portable office. A mobile home is set up for business rather than living. It is the place where contractors check-in. It is where plans, drawings, and other papers are kept. The stuff needed to complete the project to specifications. This office had a telephone, copy machine, and computers connected to the Internet. It included a time clock type computer screen for the hourly workers.

When the church deacon/construction worker entered the trailer it got suddenly small. His size has such an effect in small spaces. His eyes made contact with two uniform police officers. Saying nothing, he listened to the conversation. It soon became obvious that the police were there in connection with the office secretary.

The police asked about her next of kin. The project manager and boss pressed them for information. Why were they asking? Finally, they were told she was dead. With that, the boss slammed an open hand into the desktop next to where he was standing. "How?" He's a loud man but right now it was obvious that he was upset.

"We don't know for certain. Her body was found in her car. It was parked in the lot of the park preserve. Do you know if she might be a drug user?"

Everybody shook their heads.

"Not that I know of." It was the boss.

"Do you know of anything that might cause her death? Diabetic, cancer, anything like that?" The officer was blunt yet sensitive.

The boss shook his head. "She wasn't murdered was she?"

"Why would you ask that?"

"You're cops asking about my dead secretary who, as far as I know, was perfectly healthy." He sank into his desk chair and sighed. "I mean, she wasn't killed was she...you know in a crash or something?"

"No," said the officer. "In fact, there was no evidence that anything happened. No trauma, nothing. She was alone in her car slumped across the front seat. The motor was running."

"That's it?" The boss seemed to have quieted.

"All we know right now is she's dead. We checked her apartment building. The manager told us she works here. We're trying to locate a next of kin."

Chapter 10

"Joyce!" The lieutenant was waving to his detective. His arm motion meant come here. He stepped back into his office and waited. The action was familiar. Not just for Joyce, but for all that worked homicide.

"What's up?"

"How you coming on the burned guy?"

Joyce slumped into a chair. He sighed and rubbed his face with his giant hands. "I'm not."

"You got anything?"

"Come on boss, I don't even have a cause of death."

"What's your gut? You think it's a killing?"

"Gotta be, nobody can burn themselves like that and not leave a clue. Oh yeah, it's a murder all right. Just haven't heard those words from the M.E."

"So…where are you with suspects?"

"Same place I was at the crime scene. Nowhere."

"You thinking the store's the crime scene?"

Joyce looked down at his shoes for a long moment. He shook his head as he lifted it to gaze at his supervisor. "Gotta be, don't you think?"

"I wasn't there."

"You read the reports, saw the pictures." Joyce waited a second and then smiled. "You did look at the pictures? Right?"

"Why should I?"

"You're getting soft."

"Seeing the pictures will not make me a better citizen." He smiled to keep anger from slipping into his voice.

"Might make you a better boss." Joyce laughed an almost forced laugh so that no disrespect would be inferred.

"Where are you on the tarot card?"

"Nothing." Joyce scratched his head. "I stopped by one of those fortune teller places. Talked to a nice lady…nothing to hang anything on."

"She say if any of her customers might travel in satanic circles?"

Joyce looked surprised. "You telling me you think this is satanic?"

The lieutenant shook his head. "No…I think it's something you need to consider."

"Right, let me get the sketch artist up here to do a composite on Satan."

"You know what I mean Tommy, you need to head somewhere."

"Yeah, question is, where…what direction I mean. What angle do I need to check out first?"

"Okay, maybe this will help. Not that the plate isn't full enough right now." The lieutenant picked up a copy of a police offense report. "Check this out…" he handed the report to Joyce.

Joyce took a quick look. "This is a DOA."

"I know."

"So…" Joyce was not at all sure what was intended. He looked at the report for a second time, not reading anything but the letters DOA and the location. A parking lot at the park preserve. "You need a homicide detective to check out an everyday DOA?"

"It's not so every day anymore."

"Oh?"

"Right, M.E. called. They did a post and found that the victim's heart was burned to a crisp."

"Oh…" Joyce cursed, turned his head and stood up. He resisted slamming his hand on the lieutenant's desk. He walked to the door and turned back to his boss. "Come on boss, you can't be serious. I mean…come on."

"I'm serious Tommy."

"Give it to somebody else."

"I can't."

"Why?"

"You're the best I have Joyce…but you know that. These young guns are okay with everyday stuff…you know what to do on this weird crap."

"I quit." Joyce began to leave.

"Take this with you." The lieutenant held out a very thin case file. "I'm calling it a companion case."

Joyce stood in the doorway to the point it was uncomfortable for his boss. He finally stepped back towards the desk to take the file.

As he released his grip the lieutenant said, "I really think you need to check out the satanic angle."

"You're serious aren't you?"

"Very…." He thought for a moment, making sure his words were the right ones. "I go to church. No Bible thumper but I go. I believe in Jesus. I've heard about this stuff. Never seen it… but I think it exists." He paused again. He held eye contact with his detective. "I think you need to look into it."

Chapter 11

Tommy Joyce sat at his desk for a long time doing absolutely nothing. Had there been a window he would have stared outside. As it was he leaned back in the small swivel chair on casters and gazed across the room. It was quiet with few members of the homicide squad in the office. Some were off duty, some were working the night shift but most were out doing fieldwork. Fieldwork could include anything from surveillance, interviewing witnesses, checking alibis, or shopping at the local mall.

Finally, he sat up straight and rolled up to his desk. He hit a few keys on the computer and then did a Google search on 'satanic'. He was amazed at the hits. He had a choice of nineteen million pages. The first was a full-blown web page that would lead anyone to believe Satanism was a real and prospering proposition.

The search included such things as satanic temples, a satanic Facebook page, satanic presence at a couple of state capitals, and more. Joyce shook his head, more disgusted than angry, and clicked out of Google. He sat back and wondered where he might find an expert in the things of the devil. There was something dirty about reading the web pages he had just found. Satan was evil. He had little if any knowledge on the subject but it remained in his head as something to avoid. Like a disease. Ebola came to mind. You know it's bad so it's best to just stay away.

Finally, he went back to work. He straightened up in the chair and picked up the file on the DOA. DOA's are called that because the person was dead when the police arrived. Dead on arrival.

The file was thin. In just a few minutes he had learned what the entire police department had been able to gather regarding the death of the young woman. Joyce determined that the best place to start was with the victim.

He had her name and the address as listed on her driver's license. All had been determined by the uniform guys when they found her car along with her dead body. Everything was in the car. It all looked natural.

What did she do, who did she do it with and where did she do it? The answers to these questions were needed. Joyce was the guy to find them.

The uniform guys were following up on notifications. Death notifications were a part of normal police work.

Her apartment would be the best place to begin. The police report indicated she lived alone. Spending quality time in her space might tell the veteran detective just what might have gotten the girl killed.

Tommy Joyce pushed away from the desk and again leaned back. His mind was working. He considered that a good thing. It was when he was thinking that he got his ideas. Kind of a natural thing but it was true. How he thought of cases, the process is what would bring him to a theory and maybe a solution.

His mind moved over to his only possible suspect in the two cases. Satan. He had heard that the biggest lie Satan had ever told was that he, Satan, did not exist. Joyce didn't know. He was not a religious man. He guessed that if God existed, then certainly Satan did. They were, in his idea of such things, adversaries. He wasn't sure of either. Who would know? The answer to that question might find him a solution.

Chapter 12

Joyce had seen this apartment before. Not this very apartment but one just like it and a hundred more spread across his city. An entry door off an exterior staircase that scared every woman to ever climb them in the dark. A burnt-out light bulb on a moonless night was flat scary to most women living alone.

The entry included a small closet just inside the door. It gave way to the living room, which opened to the combination kitchen eating space. The living room had carpet while the kitchen and dining had vinyl flooring. A short hallway gave access to the bedroom. The bath was in the hallway before the bedroom. Joyce simply stood looking over whatever his eyes would see. He wanted a first impression. Joyce wanted to get an immediate sense of the woman that used to live here. Everything he saw said something about his victim. He took his time.

The furniture seemed too neat. Too matching. He wondered if this was a Rooms-to-Go room. The coffee table had nothing on it. No books, no magazines, no newspapers, not even an ashtray or candle. The television remote was resting on an end table to the left of the sofa.

Eventually, he opened the closet door. He noted a red sweater, navy blue hoodie from *Old Navy*, and a tan windbreaker jacket. All on plastic hangers. He also noted three empty hangers and a vacuum cleaner parked on the floor of the closet.

After several minutes he realized there were no pets. A dog would have been obvious and a cat nearly as much. There were however neither fish nor birds. Joyce was thinking, 'Don't all single women have some kind of pet?'

The bathroom was of little help. All the obvious items of a female seemed present. He did not find any prescriptions. The tub was typical with several plastic bottles of shampoo, conditioner, and body wash lining the ledges of the tub. A plastic rack hung from the shower head and contained all the things a normal woman would want in the shower.

The bedroom was the mother lode.

He stood at the threshold for several minutes taking it all in. Joyce concluded that everything before the bedroom was to make an impression. The bedroom however was the real deal.

The walls were purple. The bed, which was made, was all black. Comforter, pillow covers, all of it black. From the door, Joyce guessed it might be satin. He chuckled out loud at the idea of black satin for Satan.

The dresser was covered with dozens of candles. He would count them later but for now, he just looked. All colors were represented. There were tall ones and short ones. Some thick and others were thin. The colors were the full rainbow and more. All were represented. None were lit but had been at one time or another. Joyce sniffed to see if there was incense in the air. Nothing.

When he looked to the left he saw the reversed pentagram on the bedroom wall. It was placed so that when his victim was in bed she would easily see it. It was on the wall where Joyce would have put his television. He noted the TV was absent.

As he studied the symbol of Satan he realized all the possibilities of how such a thing might be done. It was not painted onto the purple wall or an ornament made from wood or iron. This was instead a framed photograph. Perhaps the medium allowed for a more fancy symbol. This one, in the photo, was obviously iron, like that used to make fences. It included artistic twists and curls. Great effort had been made to produce the symbol representing the very essence of evil.

He picked his phone from his coat pocket and called the office. He requested a crime scene crew be dispatched to the apartment. He then used the video setting on his phone to make a quick video. He moved his phone slowly capturing what he could see standing in the doorway. He snapped a quick shot of the pentagram on the wall.

With the phone still in his hand, Tommy Joyce started to move through the doorway. He had taken in what needed to be observed. Now it was time to look through things like drawers, closets, and under the bed.

He had hardly begun to move when something stopped him. Joyce looked behind him. Nothing. The thought to stop had not been a conscious thing. He had not thought to stop. It was not a force. Nothing had grabbed him or tapped his shoulder or held out an arm. But he was, in fact, stopped.

He looked over his shoulder one more time and again started to move through the door.

"Don't."

Joyce stopped. He was uncertain of what to do. He knew he heard something. He knew he had been told no. He stood motionless at the threshold. He wanted to say something. His sense was to be quiet. After several long moments, he opted to enter the room. It made no sense not to go in.

"Stop right there detective." The words were crystal clear. Someone was talking to Tommy Joyce.

Joyce did stop. He turned around this time. He saw no one. He did not want to speak. He was not going to have a conversation with something that wasn't there.

Go see her employer.

Joyce did not think he actually heard the words. He had the idea that it was a thought that just went through his mind. He thought about it. There was a report in the file. Two uniform guys had stopped by a construction site where she worked. They learned nothing. He took one more long look into the bedroom. He had an idea to take another picture of the pentagram over the bed. Then called to cancel the tech van

Chapter 13

Joyce did not knock. He simply opened the door of the mobile office and stepped in. There was just one man inside. At least in the area Joyce could see.

The big man turned in his desk chair and smiled at Joyce. It wasn't every day that Joyce would find himself in the presence of someone bigger than him.

"How can I help you?"

He pulled the door shut. "Police," Joyce flashed his badge. No formalities. Joyce was blunt, maybe curt. "You know this woman?" He held out a driver's license photo of the dead woman found in her car in the park.

"Yes, she used to work here. A couple of policemen came by." The big man stood shaking his head.

"You know her very well?"

"As well as anyone knows the people he works with." The big man paused for a moment. "What happened to her." He considered his next question. Then, "She wasn't killed was she?"

Joyce pointed to a chair. He wanted to sit down. The big man nodded. Joyce sat, as did the construction worker. "Do you know of anyone who might want her dead?"

"You're kidding, right?"

"Actually, I don't know. Just how well did you know her? I mean… what did she do when not at work? What was she like here? How did she dress? Who were her friends? Stuff like that."

"Wow detective, I didn't see this coming." He seemed to consider some thoughts then continued. "She works well here. Not real driven, usually gets her work done but not much more. Easy to get along with." He paused, thinking. "I don't know any of her friends." He paused again. "I don't even know if she has friends."

"How does she dress?"

"We're pretty informal around here." He pointed to himself. He was wearing jeans and a long-sleeved shirt that no one would wear except at work. "She stayed in the office. We," he pointed outside, "Need to wear steel-toed boots and a hard hat when we're out there."

Joyce, looking casual, was listening to every word. "Okay, how about her clothes. Was she…say…clean, well-groomed?"

"Yeah, I'd say so."

"She wasn't trashy then?"

"I never got that."

"Tattoo's?" Joyce knew the answer because he had the report from the medical examiner that performed the autopsy.

"If she did you couldn't see them."

"Was she a….religious person?" Joyce wasn't sure his term was correct.

The construction worker became concerned about the direction of the questions. "What do you mean?"

"Was she a church goer?"

"That's a conversation we never had."

"That's a no, as far as you know?"

The big man didn't answer right away. He turned in his desk chair and pretended he was looking out the window. He wanted to be accurate. He also wanted to be fair to his dead office help. He turned back to Joyce. "I am what you might call a religious person. She was not like me. I tried a couple of times to ask her about her faith but it was, in my opinion, far from being a welcome subject."

"You're religious?"

"I don't generally use that term, but yes I am."

"What term would you use? To describe yourself?" Joyce pointed to the big man.

He didn't say anything right away. He made eye contact with Joyce and held it. Then, "I think of myself as a man of faith."

Joyce wasted no time. "Faith in what?"

"Jesus…God, the creator of all things." He was still holding eye contact. "You don't know Him do you?"

"Who?"

"God."

Joyce shook his head. "Did she?" He held up the drivers license photo again.

The big man shook his head. "Like I said, I don't think so."

Joyce reached into a pocket of his sport coat. The same one he wore nearly every day. He was not fashion conscious. He knew how he looked. How he dressed was not going to change that. The fact that the coat was as much a blanket as a coat meant nothing. Big and tall shops were the only ones who carried what Joyce needed. He made a point of needing little.

He pulled his phone from a pocket and tapped at the screen. When he had the photo from the victim's bedroom he held it out to the big man. "Do you know what this is?"

The big man rolled his chair closer to get a good look. "Where did that come from?"

"You know what it is, right?"

"Yeah, so do you."

Joyce nodded and put the phone back in his pocket. As he did so he held eye contact. Finally, "Tell me."

"Tell you what?"

"Tell me what you know about this." He patted his coat pocket. "You're a man of faith, what does the symbol tell you?"

"Where did that come from?" The big man pointed to Joyce's pocket.

For Joyce, this was part of his routine. He was the detective. He wanted others to know that he knew more than they did. That's the way police work is. Joyce remembered reading about some unknown policeman who described why he was a cop.

'When I was a kid, a crowd always gathered around police activity. Everybody was asking the question, 'what's going on?' I knew that the ones who could answer that question were the police. I decided to become a cop because I wanted to be one of them. I wanted to know what's going on.'

"I took that picture at her apartment this morning. That thing was hanging over her bed."

The big man sat for a while thinking about it. He shook his head and finally made eye contact with the detective. "I guess she got what she wanted." He paused. "That's really sad."

"Tell me what I need to know to get my brain wrapped around this thing."

"I can't tell you about her. I can guess that she decided it might be…..an adventure to follow Satan. In my opinion, from what I know, she was wrong. She's dead so now she knows too." He then added, "I guess you can say she was dead wrong."

Joyce raised his eyebrows at the comment. He considered it might be a cheap shot. In a way, it sounded judgmental. He wasn't sure he liked that.

"That didn't come out right," said the big guy. "I know she was wrong, but the dead wrong part was not the right thing to say….I'm sorry ."

Joyce only nodded, then, "So tell me, is Satan real?"

"He is very real. He is as real as God. As a matter of fact, he wants to *be* god. He never will be, but he thinks of himself as divine."

"She found something about Satan to like, right?" Asked Joyce.

"I guess she did. I don't know how that works. If I was to guess I would think she really didn't believe in anything but was looking for something to be excited about. Like I said, an adventure… so to speak."

Joyce ran the ideas round in his head. "So, this stuff about Satan, it's all real?"

The big man nodded.

"I talked about this a little bit with my boss. He called it demonic," said Joyce.

"Absolutely it is."

Joyce gazed out the window for a moment. He turned in his swivel chair back to the big man. "What does that mean?"

"This is all new to you isn't it?"

"What have I missed?"

The construction worker held eye contact with the detective. "The short answer would be there is good and evil in this world. I am not talking about good and bad. I am talking about spiritual things. I'm speaking of the things of God, good, and the things of Satan, evil."

"Isn't god really an idea? A concept that has brought about a sort of moral code?"

The big man shook his head. "Not at all. God is as real as you are."

"I have missed something."

"You've missed a lot. Tell you what. Here's the number to my pastor. Call him. I'll tell him to expect your call."

"What can he do?"

"He'll have answers that I don't. He also will have the time. To be honest, I need to get back to work."

"Right." Joyce took the paper with the name and number and stood up.

"How did she die?"

"It was her heart."

"She had a heart attack?"

"Not exactly. We're still trying to figure it out."

"There's more, isn't there?"

Joyce opened the door and then turned back to the big man. "We can't explain it, but her heart was burned to a crisp."

"She burned up?"

"Just her heart."

Chapter 14

Tommy Joyce was headed back to the office when his phone rang. "Joyce."

"I need you to swing by the porno book store." Caller ID told Joyce who was calling, but he recognized his boss's voice.

"What gives?"

"Uniform car called and asked that the case detective come by."

Joyce exhaled loudly. The lieutenant took it as a sign of exasperation. "Any idea what they want...need?"

"A guy is giving them a hard time about the crime scene tape."

"I'll take a look." Joyce hit the end button on his phone.

When he pulled up in front of the adult bookstore it was obvious that the uniformed officers were, as they say, holding court with somebody. The citizen was up against the trunk of the patrol car facing the officer. The officer was using a finger to make a point. He repeatedly tapped the guy's chest.

"Hello, detective." The patrolman did not know Joyce by name but recognized him as a detective.

"What gives?"

"This guy thinks he can pull off the tape and enter the store."

"Why do you need me?"

The patrolman shook his head. "I guess I figured it better for you to talk to this knucklehead then for me to arrest him for being stupid."

Joyce looked over at the party in question. "That right? You being stupid?"

"No that's not right." He answered Joyce with a voice that was both loud and sarcastic.

"Talk to me then."

"I just want to go in my store."

Joyce raised his eyebrows. He was truly astonished. "This your store?"

"Yes, it is." Sarcasm was still present.

"So who was in your store two nights ago?"

"How should I know?"

"You don't know who was in your store?" It was Joyce's turn to be sarcastic.

"I hope a lot of people were in there. And I hope they spent a lot of money."

Joyce shook his head. He wondered to himself if this is what all porno dealers were like. "Let's try it this way. When was the last time you talked to your employees?"

"Couple of days ago."

"That's normal?"

"Yeah."

Joyce acted like a detective. He didn't want to argue. "You know your clerk died in there," he pointed to the store.

"Right."

"Did the sergeant tell you what happened when they came to see you?"

"No, not really. Something about a fire."

"Can you imagine what this yellow tape is here for?" Joyce was not sarcastic. "Can you make a wild guess why we have that sign on the door?" There was a bright orange sign with black letters warning all that read it that it would be a crime to cross the barrier made of yellow tape with the continuous words, 'Police Only. Do Not Cross.'

"No, I don't, but it's my store. I have a business to run."

"A man died in there."

"How does me being closed change that?"

Joyce shook his head. "Well...unlike you..we actually want to find out how your employee died. If he was killed in your store, we want to know who killed him." He paused for a moment. "Who knows, maybe you killed him. Do you have video security cameras?"

He shook his head. "No, people won't shop here if they think we're taking their picture."

"Can't imagine." Joyce shook his head yet again.

Joyce turned to the uniform guys and thanked them for their work. "I'll take it from here." He then pointed to his unmarked Dodge Charger. "Take a seat."

Joyce took about two minutes to bring the businessman up to speed on the case. He told him most of the gruesome details. He held back on the autopsy report, but did give him a hint as to what the clerk might have been involved with.

"So you think my guy was a Satanist?"

"Might be a reasonable answer to how and why he died. Especially how he died."

"I don't know, I just don't see that."

"What are you talking about?" Joyce wasn't going to let this man get away with anything other than what it was. A seedy business dealing with seedy people. "This is a porno store. Who exactly do you expect would want to work here?"

"I've worked at this store for years."

"Exactly my point."

The owner was mad. "I won't sit here and be insulted by you."

Joyce hit the door locks. "Yeah, where do you think you're going?"

"I'm not sitting here and listening to this."

Joyce smiled as he held eye contact. "Well right now my friend, you are going to do exactly what I tell you. As far as I'm concerned, you're my best suspect in a murder."

"You're crazy."

"Maybe, but right now I'm in charge."

"Why would I kill my own store clerk?"

Joyce broke out an even bigger smile. "Ever hear of sacrifices?"

The owner shook his head. "What are you talking about?"

"Right now I think you may have killed the clerk. You were… are… involved in this demonic stuff and you sacrificed him to make things better with…whoever…Satan or…" Joyce was winging it. He knew that all this might put the store owner on his heels. It could prove easier to get real information…good information on the clerk

Chapter 15

"This is Detective Joyce, Homicide." Joyce was at his desk.

"Hello detective, I was told to expect a call." The pastor was at the church but the call had come to his cell phone.

"You up to speed on why I'm calling?" Joyce did not believe in small talk. There was nothing small about the death of a human. Especially when it's a homicide. After the talk with the store owner, Joyce was leaning towards the idea of a sacrifice. At first, the thought was just a guess. Something to give him leverage with the porno dealer. Now that he had time to think about it, the idea was gaining momentum in his very short list of theories.

"Yes…I think I am. I talked to one of my deacons. I believe he is the one who gave you my number."

Joyce was a little surprised to hear that the big man was in fact a church deacon. He did not know for sure what role a deacon plays in the church hierarchy, but the big man had called himself a man of faith. "So what do you make of this Satan talk?"

"I am short on details, but based on what I'm hearing and what I know from Scripture, I'd say we have a full-blown spiritual battle going on."

"Really?" Joyce wanted to ask what a spiritual battle was, but didn't.

"I do, and so do some of those here in this church."

"Have you been talking about this case with church members?"

"Oh, heavens no, detective. But I have been talking to members about other things that point to something spiritual rising up around here."

Joyce wasn't sure what to ask. He was talking to a church pastor about spiritual things that he knew nothing about. Until he first showed up at the adult bookstore and came face to face with the tarot card, the thought of Satan being real had hardly crossed his mind.

The mind moves a whole lot faster than a conversation. As Joyce considered just what he wanted to discuss with the pastor, his thinking went from Satan to ideas of God. He realized that he had few. He had seen *The Ten Commandments* motion picture that cast Charlton Heston as Moses. It was one of the old movies he found on late-night television. Beyond that, he had a lifetime of not knowing anything about God, any god.

Just who is God was a question that rose up in the mind of the homicide detective. He had no answer.

As a policeman, he had seen all kinds of violence committed by one person on another. He had seen senseless accidents that had killed people. Over the years Joyce had wondered more than a few times why people got killed. How did the selection process work as to who got killed and who didn't?

War movies were popular when Joyce was a kid. He saw most of them. He always went away with the question, why did some guys get shot and other guys didn't? He had concluded, maybe by the preponderance of the evidence that it boiled down to a matter of luck. For some good luck, for others bad.

Joyce asked, "Is there a god that controls all this?"

The pastor had a heads up as to where Joyce was as far as spiritual things go. "Yes detective, there is." He waited.

"I have little if any knowledge in this area. I am really good at catching killers, but I don't know much about your line of work."

"No offense detective, but I don't think you'll catch this killer."

The conversation was being carried out on the phone. Had they been together the pastor would have seen a winch in the demeanor of Tommy Joyce. "What is that supposed to mean?"

"Just that things like this don't have a finality to them, like taking a killer to jail." The pastor paused, then said, "Look detective, I mean no offense. But if Satan and his minions are at work, it is not a case for the police."

"You must have some advice for me then?" Joyce was asking for help.

"I do, why don't you stop by and we can come up with a plan."

"A plan?"

"Yeah, there is a battle raging. We can't go into battle without a battle plan, can we?

Chapter 16

He was struggling with the idea he had not seen the signs. That someone he knew had gone so far to the dark side and he had not noticed. He questioned himself. Certainly he had missed something, There had to be flags he should have seen.

They were not close. Yet maybe they were. Wasn't she a part of his mission field? They spent hours, every day...all week. How could he not know her? Had he tried just a little harder maybe...maybe he would have seen, heard, sensed something.

A comment she may have made. They could have, would have warned him that she needed help. That she was in trouble.

What bothered him the most however, was the idea that maybe he didn't really care. Was it possible? Was there a chance that he was not truly interested in the sufferings of others? He beat himself up thinking perhaps he was not worthy of being a deacon. Maybe he was a fake.

Maybe he was just a man wanting, wishing, hoping he was a follower of Christ but in truth, he was just like everybody else. Someone wanting to be a part of something. To have a group of friends, people to talk to, spend time with, and share life with. A member of a club. Was he simply going through the motions of life expecting everything to work out. Work out how?

He was on the verge of tears when he dropped his head on the tabletop and began to plead his case. His hands were shaking and his lip was quivering. He wanted to know why. He wanted to know what. He wanted to be forgiven. It was the one thing, the only thing he knew God and only God could do. Because there is a God...and that God loved him.

"O God, Be merciful to me" he whispered. "Because of your constant love. Because of your great mercy, please O God, forgive my sin. Wash away all the evil in me and make me clean from my sin! I know my faults.

"I pray O God that I am always conscious of you and do not forsake what you have called me to do. Strengthen me Lord, that I am able to stand. Help me that I do not sin against you.... and I do what you have called me to do. If I have forsaken what you have called me to for...forgive me I pray. I have seen evil and I stood by. I did not heed your call, I failed. Have mercy on me O Lord, forgive me, my God."

He sat there with his head on the table for a long time. His thoughts continued with his plea for forgiveness. As he waited, listening to hear from God, he sensed his heart was softened and he quietly began to understand his true beliefs.

He loved the Lord. He knew the power of prayer and was ready to hear from God.

"Show me Lord, show me what I must do. Lead me, guide me. Let Thy will be done. I am ready. I don't care how difficult the task. I only ask that you make it clear what you want me to do. Use me O God."

He waited. The time made no difference. He did not know if it had been ten minutes or sixty. He waited. As he did he began to recall his time with the pastor when they all had the sense that a battle was building. That a real spiritual war was on the horizon.

He waited. Again his thoughts turned to spiritual things. Then without real conscious thought, he prayed.

"Create a pure heart in me, O God, and put a new and loyal spirit in me. Give me again the joy that comes from your salvation, and make me willing to obey you."

The words of the Lord caused him to smile.

He waited. Again, after some time he prayed.

"Build up my strength in union with you Lord and by means of your mighty power. Help me Lord put on all the armor that you...my Lord and God have given me... so that I will be able to stand up against the Devil's evil tricks. For I am not fighting against human beings but against the wicked spiritual forces in the heavenly world, the rulers, authorities, and powers of this dark age. It is that power O Lord that is at work here, now. Strengthen me, I pray, in Jesus' Name."

He waited. And he waited...Then..he heard the words. They were audible, real. A voice, strong yet gentle. He heard it with his ears. Clear and unmistakable. But he was alone and no one else heard it. Only him.

"Stand ready, with truth as a belt tight around your waist, with righteousness as your breastplate, and as your shoes the readiness to announce the Good News of peace. At all times carry faith as a shield for with it you will be able to put out all the burning arrows shot by the Evil One. Accept salvation as a helmet, and the word of God as your sword which the Spirit gives you. Do all this in prayer, asking for God's help. Pray on every occasion, as the Spirit leads. For this reason, keep alert and never give up; pray always for all God's people. Pray also, that God will give you a message, so that you may speak boldly and make known the gospel's secret. Thus says the Lord."

Chapter 17

Seated at his desk, the lieutenant casually watched Joyce as he settled his big frame into the straight back leather chair. When Joyce seemed comfortable the lieutenant spoke. "Guess we know more about the victim at the bookstore?"

"Yeah, finally. His boss is a real dirtbag. Guess that's not surprising, but I was thinking, what if this is a sacrifice? The boss used his clerk to please Satan?"

"You think?"

"Thinking out loud."

"What's next?"

Joyce shook his head. "This whole thing is giving me a headache."

"Yeah?"

"I'm going to head over to the victim's apartment later. I just got off the phone with a preacher. He told me we had a spiritual battle going on. I'll probably never catch the killer."

"Really." The lieutenant made it sound like a surprise rather than a question.

"Yeah" He looked around the office at nothing. When his eyes settled back on the lieutenant he continued. "I don't think I'm the right guy for this."

"Suck it up Tommy. You're my guy and you get to keep this case."

"Yeah, well I didn't like *Rosemary's Baby* and I don't like this case."

The lieutenant laughed. "Is that what you think you have?"

"Here is what I'm thinking. I have two dead... one burnt to a crisp except the heart. One healthy in every respect except her heart, the heart was burnt to a crisp. You think there is a reason for any of it? "

"That got you scared?"

Now Joyce chuckled. "I know, I've heard it before. If you're scared, say you're scared."

"Well..."

"I'm not scared as much as lost. I just have no feel for this case and people....like you... are telling me it's demonic." Joyce pointed to the lieutenant. He had been the first to use the term.

"And then I have the religious types telling me all kinds of stuff about spiritual things. I just can't get my head around it."

"What did the pastor tell you?"

"Not much really." Joyce shook his head. "He has people over at his church telling him there is a war going on." Joyce stood up. Not that he was leaving, but because he was agitated. "For crying out loud boss. These guys think there are demons out there killing people."

"He said that?"

"No, not those words, but that's what I think he was trying to say."

"Think that's fair?"

"What?" Joyce raised his voice. "Of course it's fair. That's how I do every investigation. When I talk to a witness, friend of the victim, friend of the suspect, the suspect...it doesn't matter. When I talk to people during a case I want to know what they aren't telling me. What they don't say is...at times, more important than what they do say."

"You're talking about a pastor here?"

Joyce raised both arms in the air like signaling a touchdown. "So...how do I know he's not another Jim Jones?"

The lieutenant smiled. "Tell you what. Treat the pastor as a technical source. Like someone from the crime lab. Trust him. Act like he is trying to give you direction based on the evidence." He paused for a moment to gauge his detective. "If you think something's not right, run it by me."

"And you'll have the straight scoop?" A hint of sarcasm hung in the air.

"I think I mentioned this, but I have some knowledge about the things of God. I may be like the deacon you ran into."

"You're a deacon?" Joyce still did not know just what that was.

"No, but I'm a believer."

"A believer?" More sarcasm. "In what?"

"I believe in God. I believe in Christ. In case you don't know it, that's actually a good thing."

Tommy Joyce was frustrated. As a facts guy, he had great success in solving murders. Some he would admit were not much work. Husbands killing wives and then standing around with a gun in their hand waiting for the police to arrive. Others were no harder than trying to follow an elephant with a bloody nose in a snowstorm.

There were however the really hard cases. The worst might be the serial types. A rapist that kills his victim and then dumps the body where it might be months before she is found. Tough cases that require discipline, tenacity, and the gut of experience.

This time it was neither. According to his boss and according to the pastor this was a whole new type of killing. Usual suspects need not be investigated.

"I'm going to check out the victim's apartment. I don't know why. If our killer is a demon or Satan or something like that I doubt we'll get an indictment."

Chapter 18

The place was a dump. Joyce had been here many times as a patrolman. Drunks, fights, domestic arguments, and burglaries were all a part of the daily routine.

The building was quickly approaching the one hundred year mark since new. Back then it was the place to live. 'High class' where a celebrity was as common in the three-story brick building as a doorman. It has been decades since either has been seen.

Joyce stopped by the building manager's office to secure a key. A simple flip of his badge and the manager was willing to oblige.

The first floor was half a story below street level. The staircase to the lower level was five steps down. That's where the manager stayed. The stairs to the second floor were five steps up. The main entrance was just off the sidewalk. The entry foyer was large enough to be considered a room of its own. At one time there had been a doorman posted just inside the tall and wide double doors. Now the panes of beveled glass had been replaced with pieces of painted plywood. Graffiti was the only source of design. The days of both doors being operable had long since passed.

Joyce needed to make his way to the third floor. As he did he wondered, like so many others before him, cops, paramedics, firemen, and furniture movers, why is it always on the third floor? Doesn't anybody live on the first floor?

Joyce was certain the carpet on the steps and hallway was the same from nearly twenty years ago when he tramped through the building in uniform. Faded red with some kind of floral pattern weaved through the material. Now thinner perhaps, more worn, but the same carpet to be sure.

If the building was a dump, there were no words left to describe the victim's apartment. Joyce wanted to strike a match and walk away. As he stood at the door he pulled on a pair of blue rubber gloves that were actually latex. He then fished a set of crime scene booties from one of his big coat pockets and slipped them over his shoes. Subconsciously he looked down at the cuffs of his pants. He didn't have cuffs. That was a good thing. In a place like this, there was no telling what organism might ride out of the room in the cuffs of your pants.

As is his custom, Joyce stood in the open doorway for several minutes trying to take in everything his eyes could see. He thought to take his phone out and made a short video of the room before him. The why escaped him. The former tenant was dead. Evidence? Maybe, so he took a few seconds of video. Finally, he was ready to delve into the disaster some called an apartment.

"Don't go in." Joyce stopped. He looked down the hallway in both directions. He had expected to see the building manager.

No one was in the hallway. He turned back to the room and began to step through the doorway.

"Don't go in". The words were as clear as if he had a partner with him and they were discussing the case. He again looked in both directions up and down the hallway. Nobody.

Joyce stood at the threshold staring into the room. Who would be talking to him? Who was telling him not to go in? The case was over the top. It had him hearing voices when nobody was around. The incident created one of those times when he was ready to call it quits. He privately wondered what the lieutenant would say. He shook his head as the thoughts boiled in his head.

It was time to do his job. He was a cop. He was big, and he was not afraid. He took a step into the room.

Even big men get startled. In a flash. Quicker than a flash. In less time it takes to form a thought, Joyce stood face to face with a man he had never seen.

The stranger was standing just inches inside the apartment and just inches from Joyce. "Don't go in."

Joyce now had a face to put with the words. If he were to be honest he would say it was frightening. Startling. Confusing. For reasons Joyce would wonder about, he did not have a reflex reaction. He didn't grab the man, put up his fists, or take a defensive posture or move.

How did a man slip past him unseen and appear in the doorway? It took a moment but he was eventually able to speak. "Who are you?"

As he said the words he was shocked that he did not have the instinct to reach for his gun. It had been hanging there on his right hip, under the big coat. It had been that way for years.

It would have been a task to recall the last time he had pulled it on the job. Others might take out their guns more often, but they were not the same size as Tommy Joyce. As he gazed at the man before him, he realized they were nearly the same size. The stranger might be the bigger one.

"Don't go in."

"I got it," said Joyce. "Now tell me who you are... why...."

"This room is not safe for you detective. You will be in danger if you cross this threshold."

"Why?"

"The evil here will destroy you."

He took a couple of steps back. His next thought was to throw in the towel and retire. But it was not his style. He had a case...he would finish it.

Joyce would close the case one way or another. "I'm hearing a lot of that kind of talk. I have a job to do so step back". He stepped ahead and raised his hand. Another half step and he reached out to push the stranger out of the way. It wasn't an overt move but rather a polite way of showing the man the need to move.

When Joyce laid his hand on the stranger he experienced a feeling he could not fully describe. The stranger was fit, like a weightlifter, solid, A rock that would be hard to move. But it was more than that. Words like gentle, sweet, joy all came to mind. None of them did justice to his experience. It lasted only a nanosecond. He stepped back and looked at the stranger. Joyce looked at his hand. He thought that it should tingle but it didn't.

Several long moments passed before he spoke. "I don't know about things like this." The detective knew this had everything to do with the things the pastor had talked about.

"Leave here. Have nothing to do with this room."

"Who are you?"

There was a long pause before the stranger spoke. "Don't go in, stay away."

Before Joyce could say another word the stranger was gone. Gone just as quickly as he had arrived.

Chapter 19

Detective Tommy Joyce found himself sitting in a place he had never dreamed of visiting. The church pastor sat behind his desk. The meeting was casual but Joyce would not have used that word.

"Can you tell me more about what happened... when you tried to move this man...the one you met?" The pastor was almost mesmerized by the idea of Joyce coming in contact with a spiritual being.

Joyce was uncomfortable. He was used to being the one asking the questions. "It was all....like a flash. It was over as fast as it started." He was thinking. Trying to recall a detail he may have skipped over when telling the pastor about the experience at the victim's apartment. "He was a big man, he was a man. At least as big as me." He thought for another moment. "I can't remember anything about him...nothing else. I can't even tell you what he was wearing."

"You mentioned you touched him. You said there was a feeling when you did."

"I did touch him. Only for a second...probably not even that long. I don't have the words to say what it was like....it was...different...just different."

The pastor pressed. "Okay, but was it a good feeling or a bad one?"

Joyce shook his head. "It wasn't bad at all."

"Do you have any idea what happened?"

" None." The idea of being questioned was troublesome. Asking questions was his role. Right now however, he wanted to know what happened. What really happened. No guesses. No theories. He shook his head again. "No idea."

The pastor appeared to be thinking. After a long moment, he spoke. "I think you came face to face with a spiritual being."

"You're going to have to explain what that is."

"There is detective, another realm that you have never heard about. At least as far as I can see." The pastor paused while holding eye contact with Joyce. He continued. "There is what is known as the spiritual realm. It is a dimension that is almost occupying the same space as us, but not exactly. From time to time, some get a view into that realm." He paused again.

Joyce did not speak. "I think you got a glimpse of a spiritual be-ing. You got a look into his realm."

"And who do you think I saw? Who stopped me from going into that apartment?"

The pastor's mind was racing, hoping to find just the right words to explain a not so easy concept to grasp. He considered it to be like explaining Star Wars as if it were a true story.

"Well," began the pastor, "You have no reference point. You're an unbeliever with no knowledge of the things of God." The big detective had already told him he was not even sure that God was real.

The pastor continued, "I believe you saw...talked to...even touched an angel."

Joyce stood up abruptly. "Thanks for your time." He turned and headed for the door.

"You don't believe me?"

Joyce kept walking. He did not so much as look back over his shoulder.

Chapter 20

Joyce returned to his office. What is not seen in the one-hour television cop shows is the paperwork. A real time burner in the life of a real detective. Three hours at a crime scene may mean at least that much time, or more organizing information and completing the reports that permanently record the activi-ties, observations, and interviews of the detective. Joyce was behind in that effort and was busy trying to catch up.

The lieutenant quietly slipped up to Joyce's desk and pulled up a chair. "How you coming?"

Joyce looked up from the computer. There was a time when the typing was completed by dictation to a steno doing the typing and the detective doing the dictating. Those days were

gone. Replaced by Microsoft Word. "Almost done with my res-
ignation. You'll have it in a minute."

"You went by the victim's apartment, right?"

"Which one?" Joyce knew he was talking about the porn
guy but details are important in homicides.

He ignored the question. "I think I have some bad news."

Joyce turned in his swivel chair to face his boss. "I told you
I'm doing my retirement papers. Take the bad news to the JV
squad." He held eye contact with the lieutenant.
"Got another dead body."

The natural reaction would be to cuss. Joyce didn't. He
turned in his chair and resumed typing. "Who you going to put
on this case?"

"I already got my best man on it."

"You didn't get the memo? He quit."

"Would it help if I rode over there with you?"

"Why would you do that?"

"Support, fresh eyes, different perspective." He shrugged.

Joyce didn't see it. He was pretending to be writing a report.
Finally, he hit save, knowing the gibberish of the last few sen-
tences would need to be corrected.
"When?"
"Just now, they just called me."
"You still carry a gun?"
"Riding with you I guess I'd better."

A fire truck, two uniform SUVs plus the sergeant's car were
parked in front of the building. All were at the curb but the fire
truck. It sat squarely in the middle of the street creating an unwelcome traffic problem.

Both men noted a fire hose running from the fire truck to
the building. It would be a simple task to follow the hose to the
scene.

Joyce found a place to park that wasn't supposed to be a
parking place and recorded the time in his notebook. He had
little information. Other than there was a fire and one man was

dead, he knew nothing. The lieutenant had read Joyce's reports. Not this one. The report of the events occurring at this very building was not finished. Now a second chapter was about to be written.

"This is a spooky place." Joyce spoke as the two men climbed the stairway to the third floor. They were careful of the fire hose. Not only was it a trip hazard, likely to move at any minute as water moves through it, it was also dirty.

"Really?"

"Some weird stuff happened here yesterday." As he finished saying it, they arrived at the top of the landing. The hallway was full of people. Four firefighters in full firefighting gear, four uniformed patrolmen, and one uniformed sergeant. Some type of exhaust fan with a large yellow vent tube ran to the window at the end of the hall. The fan was sitting near the same apartment door he had visited.

Joyce stood at the end of the hall and made notes. Pointing a finger, he counted the three people who he assumed were building tenants. The stink of smoke filled the air. Smoke rises and he understood that was the reason he did not smell it while climbing the stairs.

"What have we got?" Joyce was speaking to the sergeant. He noticed the two detectives and walked halfway down the corridor to meet them.

"Had a fire in that apartment." He thumbed over his shoulder as he spoke. "Got one body in the place. Looks like there was one whale of a fight."

"Who's dead?" Joyce tried to sound as if this was just another crime scene. Right now, no one knew he had been here before.

"Guess it's the building manager. That's not confirmed."

"So, any idea what happened?"

"I know this, when the fire department got here, the first guy through the door came out faster than he went in." The sergeant paused and looked back to the cluster of first responders. His eyes returned to the detectives. "Nobody wants to talk about

58

it, but something, someone, I don't know who…or what…but the firefighter is in the hospital."

"Woo. Slow down. Say all that again."

"Look, I don't know what happened. We weren't here yet."

"Yeah good, tell me what the smoke eaters told you."

"They arrived and a guy told him the fire was in that apartment." He pointed to the open door with the fan. "The first guy in got almost to the body. He could see the guy on the floor. The guy had been burnt. Then…all of a sudden he was thrown out the door. Something, someone, no one knows who, picked him up and tossed him out."

"What else?" Joyce tried to sound like a detective.

"What else? Is that what you asked? What else?"

Joyce knew he had said the wrong thing. He probably knew more than anyone what might have been in the apartment. "Yeah, that all?"

The sergeant gave a slight shake of the head and then continued. "This wasn't a big blazing fire. The fire captain told me they thought it might be food on the stove." Again he paused and looked back to the group outside the apartment. "It wasn't. The guy that went in got a look at the body. Before he could do anything else, he was ejected from the apartment like a rag doll. He hit the wall over there." The sergeant pointed to the damage left from the impact. "I think he broke something. An ambulance took him away."

"Got a theory?"

"You're the detective."

"What about the fight?"

"I peeked through the door. No way I'm going in there. Looks like a fight. Everything is upside down,"

"What about the fire…It's out?"

"Yeah, they dragged that hose up here," he pointed to the hose. "I guess they sprayed some water, doesn't look like much. They didn't go in either. I think the hose was kind of a safety measure. Didn't want the whole place to go up."

Joyce nodded, looking around. "You call the mobile crime truck?"

"Yeah."

"M.E.?"

"Not yet."

"Okay, gives us a minute."

Joyce walked back towards the stairs. He motioned for the lieutenant to follow. "I was here yesterday."

"This what I'm beginning to think it is?"

"I don't know boss. I don't like it. Not one bit."

"Tell me what you know."

Joyce spent three minutes bringing the lieutenant up to speed. He did not go as far as the meeting with the pastor.

"You have a plan?" It was the lieutenant.

"You're the...believer..." Joyce held up both hands making the air quote with his fingers. It looked awkward because he had a notepad in one hand and a pen in the other. The boss got it.

"You didn't go in last time, why would you go in now?"

Joyce didn't answer. He pulled his phone out of his coat, scrolled through some numbers and hit call. "Hi, Joyce. I need to ask you a couple of questions."

"Sure detective." The pastor sounded surprised.

"Look, I'm over here at the apartment again. I've got a dead guy in there. Something's going on, but I need to go in there. You know, in the apartment."

"Have you thought any more about the guy who stopped you last time?"

"I don't have time to go over this stuff. My lieutenant is with me." Joyce paused as he looked at the lieutenant. "He's a believer like you. What are our risks...if your battle thing is real?"

"You need a covering detective." The pastor paused.

Joyce started talking before the pastor could continue. "I don't have time for explanations, theories, or theology. I need to know how to proceed."

The pastor knew it was time for action. "Give me ten minutes before you go in. I'll get my prayer team on this now. You'll have a covering detective. For the record, that's a good thing."

Joyce put the phone back in his pocket. He looked back down the hallway towards the apartment. His mind was spinning. Finally he turned back to his boss. "The pastor told us to wait ten minutes. He will get us a cover. He is calling his prayer team.

"Yeah, good, I think it's a covering."

Joyce had not wanted to ask the pastor questions. He wanted answers but nothing technical. He had no idea what a cover was but would not admit that to the pastor. "Okay, covering...what is that?"

What I think the pastor is telling us...you," he pointed to Joyce. "This is a spiritual battle. The apartment has evil living in there. What he and his team will do is pray for you, asking God to protect you. The prayers of the believers will have the effect of putting a spiritual cover over you. The enemy will not be effective."

"The enemy?"

"Right, don't battles involve an enemy?"

"You guys are serious about this battle thing."

Chapter 21

The detectives decided to wait past the allotted ten minutes.

The lieutenant appeared to Joyce to be doing his own praying. It was subtle but Joyce recognized it.

Joyce used the time to talk with the firemen. He wanted eyewitness explanations as to how the firefighter was hurt. When the information was gathered he knew no more than what the sergeant had reported.

The crime scene crew arrived. They were each lugging what looked like big aluminum briefcases. They quickly set up in the hallway. The first order of business was to collect the names of anyone present. The clipboard would be maintained by one of the uniform officers that had been first on the scene.

Joyce pulled a pair of footies over his shoes. He slipped on the all to familiar blue latex gloves. The first to enter were the techs with cameras. Finally, it was time for Joyce and the lieutenant to join in on the fun. As he crossed the threshold Joyce paused for a brief moment, remembering the big man he met face to face for a few brief seconds just a day ago. He continued into the room and over near the body.

Joyce immediately recognized the manager that had given him the key. He shook his head. He knew, even with his limited knowledge, the manager had no chance in the room. If what the pastor was saying is close to being accurate, the dangers of the apartment would be fatal to any unsuspecting soul. The big detective stood and took in all the signs of the struggle reported by the sergeant. Tables and lamps were overturned. The sofa had been moved several feet from where it had been. The Place was a mess when Joyce first looked from the threshold on his first visit. Now it was a disaster.

He kneeled next to the body being careful not to touch a thing. He was wondering just how badly burned this body was. In his opinion it's bad. Not as bad as the adult bookstore, but bad. He was able to recognize the manager.

As he was kneeling he caught a glimpse of something. He lifted his head slightly. His heart raced and an emotion he was not familiar with swelled within him. He sensed a presence but saw nothing. The big man from yesterday was not there.

The detective stood up and looked around the room. Everything seemed normal. He moved through the room, just getting a feel. A lot of the property was burned. Not completely destroyed, but burned. There was one item. It was on the floor near an interior wall. He looked closer. A Bible. It was a surprise to see a Bible knowing whose apartment this was. The bigger point was the Bible was untouched by fire.

"Make sure to get a shot of this." Joyce pointed to the Bible.

The evidence techs were collecting evidence. The photographer was taking pictures. She nodded.

The medical examiner's crew was at the doorway signing the clipboard controlled by the uniformed police officer. The lieutenant was looking at Joyce with a look that said, 'what are you doing?' When the eyes of the two detectives met, Joyce simply shrugged. The lieutenant nodded his head like he wanted Joyce to follow out to the hallway.

Chapter 22

The pastor did not know the woman. She looked familiar but her name, her circumstances were unknown.

"I need your help....I just don't know what to do. I've never seen anything like this." She paused. It was obvious she had more to say. Then, "It has me really scared."

"Tell me." The pastor gestured to a chair in his small but neat office.

"Thank you." As she moved to take a seat she dug deep into her oversized purse. By the time she was settled in the chair she had managed to find her cell phone and remove it from the purse. She tapped a couple of buttons and handed the phone to the pastor. "Look at this." Her voice was excited. Not excited happy, but excited nervous.

"What in the world am I looking at?" The words followed a brief study of the picture displayed on her cell phone.

"I thought you would know."

The pastor gave the woman a long stare. He would intermittently look back at the image on the screen.

"There's more. Just scroll. There are three of them." She was talking about the number of photos but the pastor took it to mean there were three creatures in the photos.

"Where did this come from?" He now was holding the phone up, almost pointing it at the woman.

She gave him a strange look. "My daughter gave it to me for Christmas."

"No, no not the phone, the pictures? Where did they come from?"

"I took them when I was waiting for the bus."

"Do you have any idea of what this is?"

"No, that's why I came over here to show you. I'm thinking it's the devil, but I don't know." She looked like she wanted to cry. Tears were building but had not yet released.

The pastor became gentle. He had several thoughts run through his head. The first was the growing concern over a building spiritual battle. "You took these at a bus stop?"

"Yes, I was waiting for the bus when they were suddenly there in a shopping center across the street."

"Tell me what happened."

"Nothing really. I was sitting just looking around when suddenly one appeared. Then another and then another. They weren't doing much but sort of moving around in front of one of the stores. It was closed and I didn't see any people....you know...real people."

"That's it?" The pastor sounded sensitive.

"Well yes. Pastor," she paused. Tears were now flowing. "It was scary. I didn't know if they saw me, if they would come after me. I just didn't know."

The pastor handed her a tissue. He waited, showing a gentle smile.

In a moment she was able to continue. "I took the pictures because I wanted people to believe me."

"Have you ever seen this type of thing before?"

She didn't answer. She dropped her gaze to her lap where she was twisting the tissue she had used to wipe her tears.

The pastor studied her while she appeared to be thinking. She was a small woman, and most likely a grandmother. Her hair was dark with more than a hint of grey. She wore it just off her shoulders. She was well-groomed but appeared to spend little on makeup or hair styling. A close look at her hands revealed a gold band on her left hand. It seemed pretty clear that whatever work she did, she used her hands a lot. Her clothing was clean and simple. She gave the general appearance of being frugal and hardworking.

When she raised her eyes she smiled. "There were others."

The pastor nodded, coaxing her to continue.

"Angels were on the roof...above where the devils were standing."

"Angles? You actually saw angels?" It was a question. He did not leave the impression that he did not believe her.

"It was such a relief to see them there. It was then that I suddenly felt safe."

"Anything else?"

"No, the bus came and I got on. I tried to look out the window but they were gone."

"When did this happen?"

"A couple of nights ago. I was going home from work. It was late. I always catch the last bus."

"Have you talked about this with anyone else?" The pastor continued in his gentle manner.

She shook her head. "No, I almost told my daughter but I didn't want to frighten her. I need my job...you know. I need the work and she doesn't like me out that late. She thinks it is dangerous."

"Is it...dangerous, I mean?"

She shook her head again. "Not any more so than anyplace else."

"Why did you come here? Why have you shared this with me?"

"I had to tell somebody. I come to your church every week. I just thought you would believe me."

He smiled. "Oh, I believe you alright." He considered what he should say. "I am glad you told me. We have been getting reports of what I am inclined to call Spiritual Warfare going on. What you saw helps me, us," he waved his hands to indicate the whole church. "We need to get ready."

She wasn't sure what he meant so she said nothing. She appeared ready to just listen.

"Can I ask you if you have ever seen anything like this before?"

"You mean the devil?"

The pastor nodded.

"No, I've never seen them before." She was shaking her head.

It appeared she had more to say. He waited. Finally he asked. "How about the angels?"

She acted surprised. She sort of cocked her head as if the question was not a serious one. She got no response from the pastor so she answered. "Well of course I've seen them before...doesn't everybody here?"

"What do you mean?"

"Come on pastor. I'm serious about this. I took the pictures as proof."

The pastor sounded pleading. "I know, I know..." he paused, "Actually I am surprised you would capture them with a camera...but what do you mean ....? Doesn't everybody?"

"That's what I mean. Doesn't everybody see them here?"

"See them where?"

"Here," she waved her arms indicating the church.

"You see angels here? In the church?" He was astonished.

"Every week."

Chapter 23

Joyce was glad to leave the apartment. The fact that his boss was motioning for him to do exactly that was a plus. He pulled off the booties and dropped them in a paper bag outside the door. He did the same with the blue gloves. Without any conversation with those in the hallway, he made his way towards the stairs.

"What happened there?" The lieutenant said the words softly.

Joyce dug his phone out of his coat and thumbed through his numbers. He hit one and lifted the phone to his ear.

"Detective?" The pastor had answered in two rings. "Are you alright?"

"Yes.. I...we are. Everything is good here. Thanks for your work."

"What happened?" There seemed to be a sense of excitement in the voice of the preacher.

"Nothing really. We waited the ten minutes and then went in. Everything was cool."

"Did you see anything?"

"I think I know what you're asking, but no. I can imagine they were there because of what happened to the fireman, but no, I didn't see anyone...anything."

"Well, that sounds great." The pastor paused for a moment. Then, "I heard from someone that helps us a lot. I have some photos. I'm texting them to you now. I can't get into the details, but these will give you an idea of what you're up against." The pastor paused, long enough to think the signal had been lost. Finally, "You need to understand that they are very real, not a trick, and were taken outside the store where this all started."

"What?"

"Look at the pictures detective, you need to know how real this is."

"Okay," Joyce had no idea what the pastor had. He couldn't even guess. "I'll have a look."

"May I suggest that you stop by...maybe Sunday for services and we can talk?"

Joyce didn't answer right away. He and the lieutenant were making their way down the stairs. He looked to his partner for the day as he held the phone to his ear. "Let me work on that. I have a lot on my plate right now but I'll try."

"Okay detective, but I want to encourage you to not tackle this alone."

"I understand. Oh thanks for the cover, I guess that stuff works."

"Any time, stay in touch." He sounded frustrated as he said goodbye.

Chapter 24

Joyce and his lieutenant sat quietly for a few minutes. Joyce was the driver and had started the Dodge Charger to take advantage of the air conditioning. His gaze took in the city equipment that was still on the scene. It included everything that had been there when they arrived with the addition of the crime scene truck and the medical examiner's van.

His phone beeped. He expected it to be the text message the pastor was sending him. He fished the phone from his coat and thumbed to the message. "What the...."

The lieutenant's full attention went to Joyce. "What?"

Joyce didn't answer. He was staring at his phone. He scrolled. "Where....? Where did this...." he didn't finish. His mind was whirling. He looked for several more long moments completely ignoring the lieutenant. Finally he turned to his right. The shock on his face, his entire countenance displayed the sense of fear, unbelief, and surprise all rolled into one. He slowly handed the phone to his boss.

"Mother of God." The lieutenant stared at the first photo. He then thumbed to the others. He stammered, "What....where is this? Where did it come from?"

Joyce was anxious to get going. He looked over his shoulder trying to figure out the best way to snake his way through all the emergency vehicles blocking the street.

The street was essentially shut down. Nobody was directing traffic so the blind, that is, those who drove all the way to the blockade before seeing that the street was closed, needed to back out. These were not high society citizens. Most of the traffic, which was actually light, were older cars in varying degrees of disrepair. Loud mufflers, dramatically cracked windshields and donut spare tires with no hope of being changed were a good sampling.

It was obvious to Joyce that he was not getting out without some help. There were two offenders. The M.E.'s van or a marked police SUV needed to be moved. He continued to look out the window as if he did not care. Finally, he edged over the curb and snaked his way down the sidewalk and back out to the street.

Once free and rolling, Joyce held out his hand for his phone. The lieutenant laid it on his palm. Joyce quickly scrolled to the last call and dialed. He put the phone on speaker.

"Detective."

"Where did these come from?" Joyce was loud and blunt. "I've got you on speaker, my boss is with me."

"A lady came in earlier. She took those pictures...she was waiting for a bus and saw...whatever you want to call them...in the shopping plaza."

"Do you know this lady?" It was the lieutenant.

"Not well, but yes, I know her. She is a member."

"So this is real...as far as you're concerned?"

"I have no reason to believe otherwise."

Joyce turned to his phone as if he would be able to see the pastor. "This changes everything. Don't let those pictures get out....please." He turned back to traffic. "We're going to need some help on this. Do you think this lady," he pointed to the phone as if they all were looking at the pictures, "Do you think she will be willing to talk to us...help us?"

"I'll work on it." He paused. "But yes I think you can expect help." He paused again. "You can certainly count on us here to help in any way we can."

"Thanks pastor," it came almost in unison from the two detectives.

"I'll call you," said Joyce and he pushed the end button.

"Talk to me." The lieutenant was also gazing blindly out the window.

Joyce was driving, he looked to have tunnel vision. It would be a good bet that if a mugging were to occur right there in front of them, both cops would miss it.

Joyce turned to his right. "What do you mean?"

"The pictures move the needle, right?"

"Guess we have an idea who did the porno clerk."

"Does this change your thinking of spiritual things?"

Joyce was quiet, purposely driving someplace but his boss didn't know where. Finally, "I...I'm not sure I believe it, the pictures and all, I want to talk to the lady who took them...but the truth is, it's going to be hard NOT to accept this 'enemy' I'm hearing about...and seeing...I guess." He gestured to his phone still sitting in a dash cup holder.

The lieutenant nodded as he gazed out the side window. He knew where they were. He knew the city as well as anyone. He had been working these streets for nearly thirty years. He was waiting for Joyce to tell him what they were going to do. Where they were going.

"Got any new opinions on this whole thing?" The lieutenant's voice was low, soft.

"What do you mean?"

"Pretty simple isn't it? Do you believe in God...now?"

Joyce shook his head. He turned back to the windshield. "I'm not sure."

"You're not sure?" His voice was non-threatening. Casual.

"Right." Joyce's answer was soft, uncertain. There was little conviction.

" Tell me," The lieutenant looked left towards Joyce and waited for Joyce to make eye contact. Then, "If you had not been stopped from going into that apartment yesterday and you ended up like the building manager, would you have gone to Heaven?"

"What's that got to do with anything?"

"Just everything."

Joyce looked back to the windshield and then to the left. "Yeah, I hope so."

"You're going to bet your eternal soul on, 'I hope so'?"

Joyce wanted to snap back to his boss but resisted. He simply said, "Please, this is not the time...okay?"

"All these years and no one has taken the time to tell you about Jesus?" The lieutenant shook his head. "I'm ashamed of myself Tommy. Please forgive me."

"For what?"

"For never telling you why....for never telling you about Christ. About salvation. About eternal life."

"I know about Jesus."

"Tell me."

Joyce shook his head ever so slightly. "I don't know." He was quiet for a long moment before continuing. "I know about Christmas. Being born in a manger, the wise men, you know?"

"And?" It was the lieutenant.

"Easter. The cross. The Romans killed him."

"Do you know why?"

"Why? Why what?"

"Why they killed him."

Joyce interrupted. "Not now boss. I have three dead. I need my head clear. We'll talk about this another time."

"With this new information Tommy, you need your head exactly where I am trying to steer it."

Chapter 25

Joyce pulled to the curb in front of an aging building. The neon 'Readings' sign that hung in the window was unlit. The business was a few steps below street level. There was once a popular practice of buildings having the basement level accessible to sidewalk traffic. Perhaps it was a simple way to build taller buildings that still allowed for effective fire fighting. A second theory had to do with elevators.

"What's this?"

Joyce slipped the car into park and turned off the key. "We're going to see a lady."

"You mean gypsy?"

"She's not so bad. I think you might even like her."

Joyce entered first. The familiar tinkle of a bell announced his entry. The business was empty.

"Nobody home?" It was the lieutenant.

"I'm here." The voice was that of a woman and Joyce recognized it. Seconds later she emerged from behind the curtain. "Detective...or is it, detectives?"

Joyce smiled a weak smile. Something the deep crevasses of his face were not used to. "I have a request." Joyce was angry having seen the photos. He tried hard not to let his anger show. His thoughts on how she might help was a wish more than a hard detective strategy.

"You couldn't come alone?" She showed a rye smile. The lieutenant raised his eyebrows.

"This is my boss...he's got me on a short lease."

"How can I help you?" She was suddenly all business.

"I would like to see your Tarot cards."

She moved towards her table gesturing for the two policemen to have a seat. "Do you have time for a reading?"

"I doubt I could afford it."

She located a tall stack of large thick cards. She set them on the table and took a seat. "Anything special?"

"Let's just look at them all and we'll see if I find anything familiar."

"Familiar?" She leaned back in her chair while raising her eyebrows.

Joyce shook his head. A way to say 'let's just do this'. "Just show the cards…I've got a murder to solve."

She turned to the lieutenant. "Tell your detective that if his killer is in this deck he's not going to solve the case."

"See how big this man is?" The lieutenant rested a hand on Joyce's shoulder.

She nodded.

"We don't tell him what to do."

She showed a weak smile. "And you men think the killer is in this?" She pointed to the stack of cards.

"I know the killer." Joyce's voice was low, quiet. "I have nothing left to solve. I need to make it stop."

"You know the killer?"

"Show me your cards…please."

She began laying them out on the table. Joyce watched. He had a feeling that he was not going to find what he was looking for. The first several cards were nearly the same…or at least similar.

"These are regular cards. Ace through king…Swords. Think of it as a suit…like hearts." She did not look up.

Joyce thought it odd, maybe telling, that she would reference hearts. The heart was central in his case. He said nothing as he watched each card as it was played.

She seemed to be taking her time. Certainly in no hurry. Both cops stayed quiet. Her instinct seemed to talk. Small talk - idle chatter. At the moment she was saying nothing. More than twenty cards were showing. She had moved past 'swords' into another strange collection of images. Joyce had begun to think he was on the wrong track.

"You know, Tarot cards don't kill people." She was looking at Joyce.

"Neither do guns."

She stopped dealing. "How can you say that?" Her voice showed a passion Joyce had not seen before.

He waved his hand in a circular motion telling her to continue dealing. "People kill people." As he said it he realized he could be wrong.

"Then what are you doing here?"

"Please deal." He was annoyed and it was beginning to show. He watched her. There was a long moment of eye contact. He sensed she wanted to say something but hoped she wouldn't. She looked away as if looking out the window. She gave an ever so slight shake of the head and turned another card.

"There it is." Joyce was matter of fact. "That's the one."

"What?"

"That's the card I'm looking for. What is it?"

"The devil, but what do you mean that's the one you're looking for?" There was genuine surprise in her voice.

"Tommy?"

Joyce looked at his boss. "Later."

She had no idea what the cops were talking about.

"Little different?" Joyce pointed to the card. "Can that guy dress differently? Is this just an artist's guess what the guy might look like?"

She shook her head. "What are you talking about?"

Joyce was in police mode. He was talking facts. No excitement. No emotion. "This guy," he pointed to the card. "Can he look a little different? Maybe a red robe, horns more like a bull. Bigger nose, like the bull thing?"

She stared at Joyce. This was actually a police thing. The big detective was here for the second time just to see the Tarot cards. "Yeah…sure…I guess."

"You deal in this stuff every day?" The lieutenant joined the investigation.

"Yeah, most days…why?"

"You don't believe a word of this stuff do you?"

"What do you mean?" She was shaking her head.

The lieutenant held a long gaze. Not unlike watching a suspect during an interrogation.

"This is legit detective…lieutenant. I help people. They come to me….I help them find what they're looking for."

"Sure you do, but it's fake…it's all fake." He paused. "Isn't it?"

"No, this is a real spiritual experience for my clients."

The lieutenant continued his police gaze. The look that says 'I know more than you think, don't try to con me'. "Be honest. If not with yourself then with us." He gestured to Joyce. "What you do here may be spiritual but you're not helping anyone. You are in fact hurting them."

"That's not true, I am not hurting anyone."

"Oh but you are. You're contacting spiritual beings. You don't think they're real but what you do…what you're really doing is bilking people for more and more money…all the while the only spirits listening to you are the evil ones."

"You think that," she pointed to the card with the image that said devil. "Is the devil?"

"Actually I don't." The lieutenant was smug. "What I think is, that image represents all that is evil. That," he was pointing to the card, "Is an image of a demon right from the pit of hell."

"That's not true!" She jumped from her chair and headed for the room behind the curtain.

"It's all a scam and you know it…..what I am afraid of is what you don't know," The lieutenant was almost shouting now.

She paused. "What you don't know is these creatures exist. They're real." He had softened his tone. She made eye contact and he held it. "Tell her Tommy."

"He's right, let me show you something." Joyce reached into his pocket for his phone.

"Tommy."

"We need a break, she may have something, anything. She may not even know it."

The lieutenant shrugged and then nodded.

When she got back to the table Joyce opened his photos and held up one of the pictures sent to him by the pastor. "What do you see?"

She moved in close, too close to be comfortable so she took the phone from Joyce. She looked surprised. She looked up to Joyce but said nothing. Then she worked the small screen to enlarge the image. She looked at it for several long moments. Then, almost as a reflex, she thumbed to the next photo. When she did she gasped. Again she enlarged the image. She looked at Joyce, Shock, fear, bewilderment. All could have described her look. "Where...where is this...how?"

"Looks familiar doesn't it?"

"Like I said, you have no idea what you're doing here." The lieutenant motioned to the room they were all in.

"It's not real." She held up Joyce's phone. "This is a joke....right?"

"Sit down." Joyce motioned to a chair at the table.

"You travel in this....what? Genre?" The lieutenant was getting what Joyce was looking for. An ally in the effort to find where the demons were coming from. They had to have a 'base' of sorts. A home, a church, someplace where they congregate. And they had to have a leader.

"What do you mean?"

"You do see the likeness of this," Joyce pointed to the Tarot card. "And this?" He pointed to the photo of the demon.

She gave the feeling that her shock was only an act. It wasn't. It was real. She was shocked to see the photo and to see the likeness of the card.

"What can I say?"

The lieutenant softened. "You never really believed what you've been selling, right?" He nodded expecting agreement.

She didn't want to answer. It would be hard to recover as a business if she admitted it was fake. The word fraud ran through her mind but she was never going to use it. "I only want to help people find what they're looking for."

"Find something that's not real?"

"It's real."

"Yes, this is real," said Joyce. He again gestured to the phone. "But that's not what you believed...is it?"

She wasn't going to say it. "I give people what they want."

"Okay, but have you had people who seemed to be obsessed with this stuff...Satan, evil, demons?"

She shrugged an indifferent shrug.

Joyce thumbed to another set of photos. The ones he took at the adult store. "How does this look?"

She gasped, pulled her hand to her mouth. Joyce's first response was to expect her to vomit. She didn't.

"Have you ever seen something like that before?"

She almost welcomed the question. It was a distraction. It allowed her to pull away from the picture. "No." Her eyes darted between the two detectives. "Is there more?" Anxiety grew. She wondered if she should be scared. She was. Was it normal?

"You won't become a better citizen if I showed you everything I have on this phone...just from this case."

The lieutenant added, "You will be a better citizen if you give us everything you know about people who are attracted to this stuff." He gestured to the card.

"Most of my readings are people more interested in things like their sign. What's their horoscope telling them. What they should expect. Will they fall in love. That sort of thing."

"You've had others though, right?"

"Once in a while.....but I never considered people would want to be a part of what you're investigating. Your case."

The lieutenant made the sound of a heavy sigh, suggesting disbelief. "I'll be blunt. Who has come in here and given you the idea they worshipped evil?"

It took longer than what Joyce would have expected but she finally answered. "I have probably seen three. If there were more they didn't give me a feeling like that."

"Do you keep a client file, names, anything like that?"

"I'm what I call, cash and carry."

"What do you remember about those three?"

"Not much, except for the young girl. She didn't seem like the type...if you know what I mean."

The lieutenant couldn't resist. "You just told us your people are consulting horoscope stuff but now you say, 'she didn't seem like that type.'"

She didn't respond.

Joyce tried again. "Look, people are dying. Three so far... that we know of. This Satan thing is for real and it's for keeps. If we don't stop it, it will take over the city and maybe more. If you're okay with that then do nothing. If you can help then tell us what you know."

She didn't want to. She was scared. Not of the police but what was out there. If she helped the police and the evil she didn't think was real, was real, and it's been watching her because of the things she says and does to milk more money from customers, then that evil would certainly know if she is helping the police. Finally, "I can't."

Joyce was losing patience. He found another photo on his phone. "Who's this?" He held it up, the move was intimidating.

"That's her. I don't know her name. She may have used one but they rarely use a real one."

"She's dead."

She shook her head. On the verge of tears, she covered her mouth. She said nothing.

"Evil is real." It was the lieutenant.

"I never…." She stopped. She got up and retrieved a box of tissues. Then, "I only know one thing…." She paused and looked around. "They are probably here, aren't they?"

"It's too late to worry about that."

"You're probably right. I remember her talking about a place...I took it she meant a real place. I don't know but I got the feeling she was talking about a church. Not a real church like the one over there." She pointed like the church was someplace up the street.

"What did she call it?"

"Strange you ask like that." She squinted a little like she was thinking. "She called it lion...or something like that. lion's den maybe, I don't remember."

Chapter 26

Tommy Joyce was wearing a blue blazer, white dress shirt, and a burgundy tie. Those that know him would not recognize the blazer. He never wore it to work. As things go, Joyce himself did not recall the last time he wore it. He had to brush the dust off the shoulders when he took it out of the closet.

Wearing the blazer however, was not a first. That distinction belonged to his trip to a church service. While showering and getting ready to leave he remembered the moments that he was actually inside a church. Excluding the current case he was able to recall two funerals of fallen cops. There had been a third but he had remained outside for the service.

Some fifteen years earlier he had to spend time inside a church sanctuary because of a stakeout assignment. Homeless were finding their way into the church late at night. The police had gotten a tip that an unhappy churchgoer was going to take the law into their own hands. Joyce was one of the cops there to stop whoever might try to do harm to a hapless homeless person.

Today he had an uncertain feeling. Maybe just a sense of anticipation of what might take place in the church service. Joyce understood that the pastor of this church was in full battle mode. It was certainly a good bet that whatever he said, it would somehow include the events of his case.

Joyce wondered if there would be a 'calling all cars' sort of event. A call to arms. More than just a speech, but an announcement of what was happening. The pastor may make a dramatic call to join in and fight this evil that was descending on the city. Evil had killed three for certain with unknown losses yet to be discovered.

The big detective wondered just how many have died from the evil. If he understood the possibilities, an auto fatality could very well be a casualty of the battle. The thought of making that determination was a case he would not relish.

Finally, he hoped that the pastor would not call him out. For reasons unknown, the pastor would point out the seriousness of the case by naming him as the lead detective, joining forces with the church to fight evil.

When Joyce pulled into the parking lot his first observation was the number of cars already there. He was not early where he might expect fewer cars, nor was he late when expecting a full lot would be reasonable. Instead he was arriving at a time when most everybody else should be vying for a parking spot. Not the case. Many, it appeared, had already found parking spots and made their way to the building. Finding a spot was not a concern. There were attendants directing traffic.

He guided his fifteen-year-old Suburban into a spot much farther away than he wished. He slipped the transmission into park while getting angry with himself for the thought. He muttered the word lazy.

He checked the time and figured there was no hurry. He sat for a moment wondering again about what he might find in the service. He hoped the pastor would not mention him by name or point him out to the congregation. He wondered if he would see the big man the pastor called a deacon.

Joyce suddenly realized a steady flow of cars were entering the lot and many more people were making their way to the front entrance. He climbed out of the old Chevy and headed to the building. As he walked he concluded that the blazer and tie were not required. Many of the men were dressed in golf shirts and slacks. A few were wearing shorts. Who would have known.

Not knowing what to expect Joyce simply tried to blend in. There were several men and women greeting visitors at the door. Many seemed to be friends.

Kindness was everywhere. In Joyce's world it didn't seem genuine. The crowd was heaviest near the door and the movement slowed. When it was his turn to be greeted he forced a smile and let his arms hang at his side. No one made an attempt to shake hands. He figured it was a size thing. He understood better than most, that his size and appearance were not normally greeted with a smile and handshake.

When he walked into the sanctuary he was awed. Music was playing and a small group of younger people were on the stage. Joyce figured they did not call it that but had no idea what word they might use. He did not recognize the song.

He could not decide if it was bigger than expected. He was a detective and observations were a part of him. The number of cars in the parking lot told him the sanctuary was too small. He opted to sit as far back as possible. He found a seat in the very back center. His back was against the wall.

Chapter 27

An early morning run seemed like a good idea. He had parked his car in the lot like so many others. Today however, he was nearly alone. He guessed that others would show up a little later. Sleeping in on a summer Sunday was a choice for many.

After going through his stretching routine he headed into the park reserve. The path was a combination of finished asphalt and hard-packed dirt and gravel. Vegetation varied as well. At times one almost had the feeling of running through a tunnel because of the high trees and shrubs that lined the path. At other points the scene was wide open. It included a view of a quiet swamp area that gave way to a large lake that was out of sight. Birds of all types could be seen by those taking the time to look. This morning he was not one of those.

His only focus was the timer watch he wore on his left wrist. A similar device, one that measured heart rate was strapped to his left bicep.

As he ran he would allow his thinking to range to nearly anything. No real focus on a single subject. From time to time he would be aware of the sound of his hundred-dollar sneakers crunching on the dirt path.

The plan was to take the trail approximately two and a half miles into the reserve. He monitored his distance from his time. He knew his miles per minute and did the math. It was academic. He had made this run several times, maybe dozens. He knew where he turned around.

It began with a foul smell. An odor he had never experienced. He stopped…completely. No running in place. Bending over with his hands on his knees, he resisted the impulse to vomit. He retched but held back any volume. His attempt to identify the smell was weak at best. He simply did not know. He wondered, only a fleeting thought, if it might be the smell of a decaying body but dismissed it. As he tried to regain himself he turned in a three-hundred-sixty degree circle, mostly looking at the ground.

Finally he raised his head thinking of heading back to his car. That's when he saw him.....it. The source of the stink. The visual part, what he was looking at had the effect of stopping his heart. It didn't. Not a first at least. He was scared. Every attempt to not vomit failed. He bent over at the waist. It was fast, the vomiting. Using his arm he attempted to wipe his mouth as he straightened. Nothing had changed. The creature was there. Huge, horrible looking. He was human but then again not human. He had big scales of some sort on his shoulders. His head was bald with ears like Spook. The worst was the sword. Big, with a jagged edge. That was all he saw. It ended.

Chapter 28

Today was no different than any other Sunday. She was standing, worshipping, singing just like most everyone else. The praise singers were as good if not better than normal. She had been singing, swaying, raising her arms, all with her eyes closed.

Then she opened them. There they were. Three. Seated on a crossbeam above the modern sanctuary. She smiled and closed her eyes. *Thank you Lord.* Her lips moved but she would not have known. It was a deep yet conscious thought.

When the music stopped she and everyone else sat down. She glanced up to the large white overhead beam that appeared to be bisected by the giant brown cross illuminated by crossing beams of light. Everything was behind the altar area and would not be seen by the singers, pastor or orchestra. They would need to turn their back on those seated in the sanctuary to see what she did.

She knew better than most what was happening in the city. She had seen it. The knowledge was upsetting. Her son was out there. She did not know where. She didn't know what he was doing or if he was safe. She prayed for him. Quietly, sitting in the pew, detached for a moment from the order of service.

As she prayed she wondered if she was fair to her daughter. Her heart was with them both, equally, but she knew she prayed for him more than her. She knew she loved them equally, but the love for each was different.

Her daughter was with her. They talked daily, a lot. They saw one another numerous times a week. Her daughter helped with needs. Her cell phone was only one example.

Her son was another matter. He was a good son. She loved him. She remembered the many wonderful moments of his childhood. She also had memories of those times when all was not well. Injuries, sickness, misbehavior. She cherished them all. She was his mother.

When she heard the story of the 'prodigal son' she often wondered if he might be just that. She of course did not send him off with a large inheritance. She in fact didn't send him at all. He left. He left with nothing. It saddened her to think about it, but he was good, strong, honest. She hoped, prayed each day, several times a day that he was safe. Then she prayed.

"Oh Lord. Protect my son. Give your angels charge over him." She opened her eyes for just a moment to look up to the cross. They were not there. "He has been raised up in the way he should go. Let him not depart from You. Protect him at this time. Oh God, I lift him up. I pray for your protection around him. I pray he does not see destruction. I pray he has Your protectors around him."

She paused for a long moment to again look at the huge cross hanging behind the altar. This time she was not looking for the angels she knew were there. She closed her eyes and whispered. Only she…and God would hear her plea. "Oh God, you know what it's like to lose a son. You, oh God, gave Your Son for me. I know that. I love You for that. But God please send my son back to me. Protect him now and change his heart to return home. To return to You."

She kept her head bowed for several more long moments. Then she smiled and lifted her eyes. Again they were drawn to the cross and the long wide white beam that extended left and right across the full width of the church. They were there. A calm came into her heart. She silently thanked God for the blessing of seeing His angels. She knew that most did not. It was a gift of God and she cherished it in her heart.

Chapter 29

When the singing stopped the pastor came across the stage from Joyce's left. He had not noticed the small man previously. To Joyce, the pastor merely arrived as if on a cue from the singers. He stopped in the center where a small lectern or podium was positioned. He was empty-handed.

"The apostle Paul wrote an epistle to the church in Ephesus. He said, 'Grace to you and peace from God our Father and the Lord Jesus Christ. Blessed be the God and Father of our Lord Jesus Christ, who has blessed us with every spiritual blessing in the heavenly places in Christ.'

"I send you this day that same blessing. Today we find that the blessings of God our Father will be the very strength we will need in the time of this present trouble.

"Remember saints, 'In Him we have redemption through His blood, the forgiveness of sins, according to the riches of His grace.'

"'In Him you also trusted after you heard the word of truth, the gospel of your salvation; in whom also, having believed you were sealed with the Holy Spirit of promise.'"

Joyce had not expected this eloquence from the pastor. After several calls and meetings in person, Joyce had not seen what he was seeing now.

There was a long moment of pause as the pastor simply looked over the church. Joyce thought for just a second that maybe the pastor was looking for him. As quickly as he thought it he dismissed the idea as stupid.

Then, "'God created all things through Jesus Christ: to the intent that now the manifold wisdom of God might be made known by the church to the principalities and powers in the heavenly places, according to the eternal purpose which He accomplished in Christ Jesus our Lord, in whom we have boldness and access with confidence through faith in Him.'"

The pastor paused again. He gave the impression that he was surveying the crowd before him. He was not. He, if asked, would acknowledge that he was not even 'seeing' those before him. He was waiting on God.

"Dear saints," He began again. "I tell you these things to remind you who we are in Christ Jesus. Today, perhaps more than any other day we must know, we must remember who we are." He paused again as he walked away from the podium. His delivery so far was strong, yet measured. His pace of speech had allowed Joyce to follow the words he had never heard before.

"Today," he said in a raised voice. "We are under a spiritual attack. It is not us only… but everywhere." He waved his arms to emphasize the extent of the attack. He continued, "I am not speaking of Satan trying to get you to sin…. Yes that's important but it is not the message today. There is an attack on this city, and people have died at the hands of evil…an evil that comes straight from the pit of hell."

She sat up a little straighter in the pew. Maybe the pastor was about to reveal what she had heard in the rumor mill. She waited.

"I tell you today…. each of us resting in the faith must stand. We must stand against the powers and the principalities and the rulers of the darkness of this world. We must stand on the solid ground of Christ to withstand the attacks of the enemy….attacks that have already begun."

Joyce was tuned in. He wondered just how much the pastor would say about the deaths. Would he get specific? Would he name names? Would he talk about the victims and how they actually courted their own demise?

"Now... today..." His eyes scanned the sanctuary. He paced the full length of the platform and then began again. "'All things that are exposed are made manifest by the light, for whatever makes manifest is light. Therefore He says: 'Awake, you who sleep......Arise from the dead....And Christ will give you light.'"

He paced again back across the stage. His eyes scanned the crowd seated before him. He came to the very edge of the platform to Joyce's left.

"'See then that you walk circumspectly, not as fools but as wise, redeeming the time....because the days are evil. Therefore do not be unwise but understand what the will of the Lord is.....'" He moved along the edge to the far right and continued.

"'And do not be drunk with wine, in which is debauchery; but be filled with the Spirit.'" He stood for a long moment and then moved back to the podium.

"Brothers and sisters....I tell you that a great presence...an evil presence has come upon our city. I know of no less than three deaths attributed to this evil." He stepped out from behind the small podium. "I have reports, I have talked to some who have direct knowledge of the presence of evil. Spiritual beings here." He raised his voice and pointed to the floor as he said 'here'.

She smiled. There was a story. While being a believer, she was an infrequent visitor to church. She was here today hoping for a scoop. She was certain she now had it.

"There is however good news. The reports, those that have been in or have seen the battle before us also report the angels of the Lord being in the fight.....We are not alone, praise God."

Joyce was surprised that there would be applause in a church service. It was strong, long, and hearty.

"This is the time when each of us needs to submit ourselves to prayer. We are needed in the battle against the powers of the devil. God is faithful and He is just.....The fervent prayers of the faithful will bring much from the Father of truth."

He was back to walking the full length of the stage as he spoke. His voice was rising and falling with an emphasis that was not contrived. Even Joyce, no expert on sermon deliveries knew that something special was going on.

"Hear again the words of Paul, 'Finally, my brethren, be strong in the Lord and in the power of His might....put on the whole armor of God, that you may be able to stand against the wiles of the devil.'"

He was still moving. He walked the entire length of the stage, first to the left, and then back to the right. At the far right extent of the platform. He gazed down as if making eye contact with someone. Joyce could not see who.

"'For we do not wrestle against flesh and blood.'" The pastor broke eye contact and raised his gaze to the auditorium. He began to move to the left as he spoke. His voice raised several decibels. "'But against the principalities, against the powers, against the rulers of the darkness of this age,'"

He had arrived at the far left. He looked down and now seemed to make eye contact with someone else. Again Joyce could not see from the very rear of the building.

"'Against spiritual hosts of wickedness in the heavenly places.'" He moved back to the middle

"'Therefore take up the whole armor of God, that you may be able to withstand in the evil day, and having done all, to stand.'" He paused, longer than what was comfortable for some. Joyce had no idea. He figured the pastor was forming his thoughts. It was obvious he was not working from notes. There were no Teleprompters.

"'Stand therefore, having girded your waist with truth, having put on the breastplate of righteousness, and having shod your feet with the preparation of the gospel of peace.'"

Standing at the very center of the platform, right up against the edge, the pastor looked down. Once again it appeared as though he was making eye contact with someone. Then, slowly, he raised his eyes to the full house before him. His head turned slowly left andright. There was little chance that those present would miss what he had to say. His action secured all of their interest.

"'Above all, taking the shield of faith with which you will be able to quench all the fiery darts of the wicked one.'" Another pause without moving. Then a gentle, soft voice, he said, "'And take the helmet of salvation, and the sword of the Spirit, which is the word of God. Praying always with all prayer, in the spirit, being watchful to the end.'"

He now raised both arms high in a motion of welcome. "Let us pray." The benediction was beautiful. Joyce had never heard such words. The sermon moved him, in his heart, but the benediction even more so.

He finished. "'Peace to the brethren, and love with faith, from God the Father and the Lord Jesus Christ. Grace be with all those who love our Lord Jesus Christ in sincerity. Amen.'"

Chapter 30

Tommy Joyce had come to talk to the pastor. He wanted to speak with him about his case. It was the only reason he was in church.

He stepped into the aisle and found himself being moved along with the stream of people filing towards the door.

He felt the vibration deep in the inside pocket of his coat. The phone was on vibrate. Something he and everybody else had been asked to do.

He slipped out of line and answered. "Joyce."

"Where are you?" It was the lieutenant. Not a good thing for a Sunday.

"I went to church."

The lieutenant didn't know if it meant he was in church, going to church or done with church. "How long before you're free?"

"Not long," said Joyce. His head was turning left and right hoping to get a glimpse of the pastor. "What's going on?"

"Uniform guys are calling for detectives on a DOA." He paused, waiting for Joyce to comment.

"What? Can't you send them one....?" He paused, thinking it through. His desire to locate the pastor had him distracted. There was no logical reason for his supervisor to be making this call, especially on a Sunday. "We don't have another one, do we?" Joyce knew better. It would be the only reason he was getting this call.

"Maybe...I'm not sure but I got the call. Uniform guys are at the park reserve."

Joyce interrupted. "Same place they found the girl?"

"Yes... they say they have a body....but no head."

Joyce dropped his arm holding the phone. He took a deep breath and then exhaled. Finally, he raised the phone and put it to his ear. "Okay, I'll head out there. I'm not going to come by and pick up a car. I'll take mine." Joyce thought for a moment. "Crime scene guys there?" He may need supplies, but nothing the crime scene van wouldn't have.

"I don't know if they're there yet but I'm certain they've been called." He in fact did not know that but would check after finishing with Joyce.

"Who's in charge right now?"

"Not sure," said the lieutenant. "There is a sergeant on scene."

"Good, I don't have a radio. Call and make sure the entire park is closed. No one in, no one out. Unless the body is in the parking lot, use that as a muster area. I need ten minutes here and then I'm rolling." Joyce paused trying to think if the lieutenant would understand what he meant. "You know what I mean? Everybody musters. Tell the men on scene to muster....stay away from the body!"

By the time Joyce was off the phone the front area of the church was nearly empty. He walked to the large entry doors. To his relief, the pastor was standing just outside.

"Detective," the pastor took a step towards Joyce extending his hand. Joyce took it and they shook. The pastor then placed his other hand on top of Joyce's large hand. Joyce saw a warm smile. "I cannot tell you how wonderful it is to see you here."

"I enjoyed it. I think …. what's going on?"

"Well….we have a lot of work to do detective. There are some people you need to meet, I'll arrange that. You are in danger so we need to pray…a lot… for God to protect you."

"Okay….I guess." Joyce was not comfortable.

"Be sure you ask God to protect you. Ask Him to keep you from the enemy, to have His angels be with you." He looked the big man in the eye. "It's not complicated. Just believe Him – in Him, you'll be good."

"Yeah, well maybe you can do that." He paused looking up to the clear sky. A few clouds were scattered about but he did not see them. After a long moment he returned his gaze to the pastor. "I might have another case. I'm going out to the scene right now. It's in the park reserve where the woman was found… now…we have someone else." Joyce paused, it was obvious there was more. Then, "We have men out there. I hope it's not like the apartment and the firemen."

The pastor looked around. Joyce had no idea what he was looking for. Then, "Come inside, this won't take but a minute." He headed back into the church expecting the detective to follow. He did.

As soon as they had entered the sanctuary the pastor saw who he was looking for. So did Joyce. In seconds they were standing next to the big deacon.

"Join us…we need to pray." The pastor was gentle while being firm.

The deacon and the pastor each laid a hand on one of Joyce's giant shoulders and the pastor began to pray.

Joyce did not know what to do or say. He just stood, uncomfortable to be sure, while the two men prayed for his protection. Had he been asked, he would have said the experience had given him a calming sensation.

Chapter 31

She was thinking of what might be going on, but not looking for anything. Not here while still in church. She felt she had enough to start digging but had no thoughts of finding anything while in church. Like most, she was casually leaving a church service while ideas were running through her head.

Others might have been thinking about what buffet to go to. Her ideas were going towards the first step, or the next step in finding information about the battle the pastor was talking about. Were there crimes? Has anyone been hurt?

It was a lucky break. That's how she would think of it. Just a lucky break. The big man could not be missed. She knew him. She had actually met with him in the past. A serious man that was hard to look at and harder to talk to. But he was a detective, a homicide detective. He certainly should remember her. Wouldn't he?

The pastor and another man were with the detective. They had to be praying. Why else would they have a hand on him with all heads bowed?

This was the beginning of what had to be an important story. She was going to follow it wherever it led. Scoops were hard to come by. This was a chance.

When Joyce was finished with the pastor and his deacon he thanked them and headed for the door. He checked the time on his phone. Not bad. He had promised ten minutes, he would be on time.

She approached him at the main church doors. "Detective?"

He slowed but did not stop. She looked a little familiar but he couldn't place it. He was certain he had no friends that attended this church. "Yes."

She introduced herself. For Joyce it did not register. "You know, from the Tribune?"

He wanted to ask if that rag was still in business but resisted. "Oh, yeah. How are you?" He kept walking but at a slower gait.

"Fine..thanks...I would like to ask you about this battle." She had to walk faster just to keep up. Joyce had stepped up the pace when he found she was a reporter. He didn't like the press. He liked talking to them even less.

"Yeah, what's it about?"

"You know, the spiritual warfare....the things the pastor was talking about."

Joyce stopped. She nearly ran into him as he turned to face her. "Seems to me that's something to take up with the pastor. He's the one talking about it."

"Yes, but you're the police."

"Right, and he's the pastor." He nodded his head back towards the church. "Go talk to him." He turned and walked away, headed for his aging red Suburban.

Once seated in the car he leaned his head back and closed his eyes and whispered, *How in the world did that happen? How can it be that a reporter would find me at my very first church service?*

He unlocked the glove box and pulled out his gun and holster and slipped them on his belt. He also retrieved an extra notebook. The one he was using on these cases was still in the pocket of his other coat. He found his cell phone and checked the time of the lieutenant's call and recorded it in the notebook along with his location and the current time.

He started the car and slipped the lever to drive and headed to the park reserve. As he drove he thought about the final words of the pastor and his deacon.

Chapter 32

"Pastor, pastor...could I have a moment?" It was unlikely the pastor would know her. She was a newspaper reporter. Her picture shows up nowhere.

The pastor paused, turning to greet the voice. "Yes?"

Walking quickly she closed the distance before talking. A few steps away she began. "Pastor, I enjoyed your sermon. I was wondering...is that detective," she pointed towards the main doors. She did not recall his name but the pastor would know who she was talking about. "Is he part of the battle that's building? He's on the front line isn't he?" She was improvising but the pastor was more than a pastor in all this.

The pastor smiled. "I don't believe we've met."

She introduced herself but did not mention the newspaper.

"You know Detective Joyce?"

"We've met but to say I know him would be a stretch." She showed that she was honest. "Is he somehow involved in the spiritual warfare you preached about?"

He was still smiling. "I think we're all on the front line...don't you?"

She stuttered for just a moment. "I guess pastor, but...I think I need to be honest. I really have never thought of this stuff as real. Today...maybe you made it more real to me."

"Oh trust me young lady, it's real. Not to believe doesn't change anything except to make you vulnerable." He raised his eyebrows and nodded.

She again waved her hand towards the front door. "Does the detective believe that?"

"Trust me on this one, he believes."

She acted hesitant before asking, "Were you praying with him earlier?"

The pastor appeared not to like the question. He did not speak for a moment. It was not uncommon for people to approach the altar for prayer. It is commonplace when an invitation is given for unbelievers to come forward to accept the gift of salvation. "We were praying, yes."

She formed one final question. "People are dying aren't they?"

"I'm afraid so."

"That's where detective Joyce is going?

Chapter 33

Detective Tommy Joyce found himself in the midst of a small group. Most were uniformed police officers. One uniformed lieutenant, someone Joyce had not expected to see, one uniformed sergeant and four patrolmen. As he sized up the crowd he noted four more people, all dressed in various forms of clothing suitable for jogging, walking, stretching, or doing other forms of exercise. He had a passing thought wondering why people would willingly exert themselves with running and walking in a place like this.

Joyce recorded his observations in his notebook just below his time log. "Lieutenant?" He was just a few paces from the senior officer. "Brief me."

It took about two minutes for the senior uniformed officer to tell Joyce what was known. It wasn't much beyond the knowledge that a man had been decapitated. The body had been found by a second runner. That party was waiting with the other civilians. He was not happy being held at the scene. He was visibly upset. The uniformed officers had his personal information plus a very short oral statement as to what had occurred. When the lieutenant had finished Joyce thanked him and went to see the witness.

"I'm detective Joyce." His voice was soft – sympathetic. "I'm told you were the one to find the body?"

The witness nodded his head and offered a weak, "Yes."

"I understand how hard this is…I don't like these things either…but, I need to ask you just a few questions. Sorry if I am repeating what the other officers have already asked."

The witness nodded, "I understand."

"Were you running or walking?"

"I was running, I'm a runner."

"Were you headed out, or returning?"

"I was going that way." He pointed indicating he was running away from the parking lot.

"Do you recall seeing the victim here," Joyce pointed to show he meant the parking lot. "Before you headed out?"

He shook his head. "No I don't think he was here, I didn't see him."

Joyce noted the comments in his small book. "What time did you head out?" He recorded the answer. "What time did you find him?" He recorded the answer. "How did you contact the police?"

"I carry my cell phone with me. When I saw the guy I turned and ran. I think I was thinking an animal may have attacked him." He paused, shaking his head. It appeared that he might begin to weep. Then he continued in a weak voice. "I stopped for a minute and called 911. I was walking as I talked to the operator."

"Before or after you found him… did you hear anything? A cry, yell, growl, bark, anything?"

"No, but I wear earbuds… I was listening to music."

Still taking notes Joyce asked, "Did you smell anything?"

Joyce got an odd look. Finally, "I don't know what you mean."

"I mean did you notice any unusual smells. Something not normal, maybe something you never smelled before."

96

He stood, his head general turning looking around. He appeared to be thinking. A good guess would tell Joyce the witness did not like any of this. "I think I did smell puke."

Joyce made the appropriate note. "Okay, thanks, you have been very helpful. I may need to call you again." He handed the witness his card.

As the witness was turning to walk towards his car Joyce decided to ask one more question. "Oh," he said, a little louder than normal, "One more thing."

The witness stopped and turned to again face the big detective. "Yes." It was a polite response. It seemed he wanted to help.

"Are you a Christian?"

The question was something he did not expect. Not now, not in a million years. He started to show shock but changed and became more matter-of-fact. "Yes, actually detective, I am a Christian."

"I think that is a very good thing….if you were not, you too may be back there on the trail." Joyce thumbed over his shoulder indicating the direction of the victim.

The witness stood quiet for a long moment. When he finally spoke he stammered his words. "What are you saying?"

"Thank God for protecting you. Evil is at work here and it is not very pretty." Joyce wanted to say a lot more but stopped.

The witness shook his head.

"Talk to your pastor." Joyce nodded his head until the witness nodded his.

Chapter 34

She did not recognize the voice. Perhaps a college intern who agreed to work the weekend so that the paid staff could be home doing what people do who have a life. She identified herself and then said, "I need to know if the police scanner has been busy talking about something bad."

"Anything special?"

A big deal as it pertains to the police is fairly easy to spot on the scanner if you know what you're looking for. The intern probably didn't know it. The scanner is simply a radio type device that scans the police radio frequencies so that anyone listening can hear the police broadcasts.

She asked, "Have you been listening?"

"Yeah, sure, it's on… right here."

"Did you notice radio calls where more than two or three police cars went to the same place?"

"Yeah, I think so," he paused for a moment to check his notes. He had been writing things down. "Yeah, I have this." He pointed to his notes that only he could see. "There are two cars plus a supervisor out at the park reserve."

"Great, anything about detectives?"

"Not that I heard."

"Okay, do you know what time this all happened?" she glanced at her watch as she spoke.

He rechecked his notes. "About two hours ago."

She was already aiming her car towards the exit of the church parking lot. "Have you sent anybody out there?"

"No."

"Great, thanks, I'm going to check it out. Anybody calls you tell them I'm on it." She stepped on the gas.

Chapter 35

"Which one of you has been to the body?" Joyce asked the question as he walked towards the uniformed officers. He had just finished talking to the witness.

"We've seen it." The patrol cars are two-man units. The guy who answered pointed to his partner.

"You walk in, or drive?" Joyce was now standing next to him.

"No... we drove in, but had to back out." He exchanged looks with his partner. "We met the witness out here and he directed us in."

Joyce thought about it for a moment. He had not asked that question of the witness. It made him angry. Such a lapse in thinking, mistakes like that are not good. This lapse could be salvaged. How about the next one?

"Did the witness go back in there with you guys?" Joyce pointed with his left hand, the one holding the notebook.

Again he exchanged a glance with his partner. "No. He refused. He waited here."

"You two went in alone?"

The patrolman looked at his partner.

"What's going on here?" Joyce waved his pen back and forth from one man to the other. "Can't you answer without looking at each other? You got something to say or what?"

Joyce was not mad but his tone showed that anger was not far away.

The patrolman who had been quiet until now spoke up. "No...that's not it at all. I lost my lunch in there. I wasn't sure I would make it out. I sort of panicked."

"That bad?"

The patrolman nodded.

"You ready to go back in?

Joyce got a blank stare. He let it go for a long moment. "I take that's a no."

The first officer answered. "We can go in there but it's not going to go well."

Joyce turned and took a couple of steps towards the trail. He started to talk when he turned back to face them. "Are either of you men a Christian?" It was an unusual question but it needed to be asked. He got a dumbfounded sort of look from both before one of them answered.

"What does that have to do with anything?"

Joyce was in charge. His tone displayed it. "Today," Joyce turned and looked down the narrow path. When he turned again to the officers he spoke. "Maybe everything." The look plus the tone from the biggest man in the parking lot carried some weight.

The younger of the two patrolmen, the one who lost his lunch when viewing the body responded again. "I think of myself as an American, not a Christian. It is something I happen to believe."

Joyce looked to the second officer. "How about you?"

The reply was slow to come but it seemed to have conviction. "Yeah, I am...I believe in Jesus."

Joyce pointed to the unbeliever. "You stay here." He then pointed to the Christian cop. "You and I will go in and get this thing figured out."

"You mean I am staying here because I don't happen to believe in Jesus?" The officer sounded offended.

"Exactly." Joyce then turned to the partner. " Get your car and bring it up here. We'll go in together."

The officer nodded and headed to the car at a quick pace.

Joyce turned to the lieutenant next. "What do we know about other entrances and exits? Is there another lot like this somewhere down the trail?"

The lieutenant looked to his sergeant. He raised his eyebrows but did not repeat the question. The sergeant answered. "Yes, maybe three, four miles up the trail it comes to a second lot. Smaller...not used much.

"Do we have anybody there?"

The sergeant assumed the question was for him. "Not that I know of. I'll take care of it."

Joyce nodded and turned back to the lieutenant. "Have your men get the names and contact information from everybody here. Ask if they saw, heard, smelled, or suspected anything unusual. Then get them all out of here. This place is not safe."

"Not safe?"

"Yes...not safe." As he spoke the words he noted a car enter the lot. "Whoever that is, get her out of here." There was no mistaking the order.

The patrolman pulled up with his car. Joyce took a look and knew it would be a tight fit. The modern police cruiser not only had all kinds of lights on the outside, it also had all kinds of electronics including a laptop computer inside. All placed somewhere in the front seat. He squeezed in.

"Drive to the end of the lot and stop." Joyce was pointing ahead. Once stopped, he turned his head to the patrolman doing the driving. "This can get bad. To be honest, I am not sure I'm ready for this."

He got an odd look from the patrolman but it included a nod of the head.

"If you're a man that prays this would be a good time." He got another odd look. "There is evil out there. If you need some divine protection, I would certainly understand."

The patrolman continued with the odd look. Then he turned to look down the park's path. Joyce thought he saw his lips move if ever so slightly. Then the officer looked back to Joyce.

Joyce nodded. "Let's do this." He pointed down the trail.

Chapter 36

When the police approached her car she quickly stepped out and walked a few steps to meet him. He had held up a hand gesturing for her to stop.

"You can't be here."

"Press," She was almost shouting. "I'm from the Tribune." She didn't know if it would help. Lot's of cops don't like the press. Her success with crime stories usually came from a relationship of trust built up over time. She had a few contacts in the detective bureau but Detective Joyce was not one of them.

"Sorry, you can't stay here." The policeman was firm. His tone was like the one used when asking for a driver's license and proof of insurance.

"Where will I find Detective Joyce?" It was the only card she could play.

"Who is Detective Joyce?" The patrolman left the impression that he didn't care.

"Homicide guy," She knew she was right. It was still a gamble. "Big guy." She paused, made a face. "Not very good looking...he's big, really big." She held her arms out to show size.

He turned towards the trail. "Oh yeah, he went down there to see the body." He half extended an arm.

"Good, I'll just catch up to him there."

"Not today you won't." His official police voice was back.

She sounded in charge. "I'll wait here then."

He shook his head. "Sorry, but you need to leave."

"It's a public park."

"It's closed."

She looked confused. "Why?"

"Not safe. Your homicide guy said to clear this place out." He pointed towards her car in a manner that told her to get in and get going.

"Okay, I understand." She pointed down the trail. "He went down there?"

"Yes."

She moved towards her car. "You said the body is on the trail?"

He nodded as he spoke. "Time to go."

When she was out of sight she stopped and began a search on her phone. She pulled up a map program and pinpointed the park. She found a second parking area on the far side of the park.

Her luck was more than she could have hoped. The police were nowhere to be found when she rolled into the second parking lot. It was small, a fraction of the size at the other end of the trail.

She took only a moment to consider her options. There was only one course of action. She slowly drove her Toyota onto the trail and headed toward the area that the police and the body should be. Once on the scene, it would be difficult to send her away.

The trail was narrow but ample to allow passage for her car. As she was not a runner, she had never been on the trail. The nature setting appeared it might have a certain attraction to bird watchers or other similar groups but again, she did not qualify. While her paper may hold opinions in support of many things and issues such a park might embody, she did not share most of those views.

She continued around several bends in the road. She had not checked her odometer before setting off down the path and did not know how far she had driven. She also did not know how far into the park she would find the police.

Mental notes were a part of her job. She would capture the observations in her written notes later when parked. For now, the foliage, remoteness, and the quality, or lack of quality of the road...path, were on the list.

The theme of the pastor's message returned to her thinking. The urgency of the sermon seemed obvious. It gave her the thought that something beyond everyday temptations was in play. To see a detective receive prayer and then head out to a murder scene was simply frosting on the cake. This was an unfolding story.

What to expect once at the crime scene was still being developed. While she has seen more than one dead body, she was not an old hand at it. She assumed, hoped really, the body would be covered with a sheet or something similar and she would not actually see the body. She had no camera beyond her phone and that was rarely used for jobs like this.

Chapter 37

With Joyce at his side, the patrolman moved the patrol car slowly over the dirt, gravel, and occasionally asphalt path. To call it a road did injustice to the word.

Joyce was not comfortable with things of God, or how to explain them. He wasn't even sure what he believed. He had gained a little knowledge of things from the spirit realm but he was still trying to find himself in all of it.

He chose to simply say what he knew. "This can be really bad."

"So you said." He kept his eyes on the path ahead. He never had anyone suggest he pray, except when his grandmother was dying.

Joyce let the comment pass. He pointed for the officer to watch where he was going.

"Here's my case. I have three dead, this is number four. All are somehow connected to evil... Satan... demons. I can't explain it."

He looked at the officer and waited until he had eye contact. "I had never known about this stuff until this started...I still don't know much...except that it is real and people are dying."

The office soaked it in for a few moments. "What's the plan?"

Joyce chuckled out loud. "You think I have a plan?"

"Do I need to be scared?" He knew something about that. Most cops do. Going into a crack house at night with no lights, not knowing who could be there can get any man a little scared.

Joyce took his time with an answer. He knew he was scared but for some reason he did not have a sense of fear. For him fear was different. With fear you can't function. At least not as you should. Being scared may actually give you an edge. "What I know...think... is we have God on our side. We have people who are praying for us. I mean right now." He looked to the officer to be sure he was getting it. "It worked last time. It'll work now."

Chapter 38

She was moving slow. It would be obvious that she was scared, that she might think of things like pedestrians running with earbuds and being unable to hear. They might run right into an unexpected car. Unexpected? Of course a car would be un-expected.

Then there could be the idea of animals standing on the path as she rounded a tight turn. A deer can do major damage to most any vehicle let alone a small Camry. The other possibility - coming upon the crime scene and being unable to stop in time. Not a good thing to run over Detective Joyce's murder victim lying in the road.

She probably never considered the possibility that the killer of what was believed to be a homicide might still be in the park. If she were to assume anything it would be that such a person was long gone. A killer would want to get as far away from the scene as humanly possible. Right?

But 'humanly possible' would not apply should the killer not be human. That is why she never had a conscious thought of such a thing.

She slammed the brake pedal to the floor. She screamed as she did it. Shrill - loud. No one heard her. She was alone in a place she should not be. She had been warned. Not what the danger was, but that there was a danger.

He was there. In the nanosecond she had she considered him a 'he' but maybe these types are not he or she. Big, ugly, bad. Just plain bad. "Oh God...save me please. Protect me Lord." It was spontaneous, honest, real.

Then the fear set in. More than scared. It was hard not to scream again. To scream might embolden it. Screams would mean fear. It was fear – wasn't it? But she is not *given a spirit of fear.* The tears however could not be stopped. She sobbed un-controllably. She had closed her eyes to hide the awful sight. She muttered to herself as she slammed her fists on the steer-ing wheel.

He was gone. In an instant. Less than that. He was standing in front of her Toyota and then, just as she called out a loud panic call for help, he vanished.

It was now crystal clear. The sermon, the big detective, the pastor, and staff praying, it all was now fully explainable, under-standable, real.

The power of darkness was in fact, present in the city. Evil, that with which the big detective was charged with defeating had done its work in the park reserve. She had not seen the danger. She had scoffed at the warnings. She had come face to face with something not of this world. Now what?

It took several long moments before she was able to retrace the course of events that had just played out on the nar-row path. It had been an ugly creature with an obscenely large bald head, scales like armor on the shoulders, and a giant sword with a jagged blade. She knew what, but did not know why.

He was there and then he was gone. She thought hard before realizing what she had done – said, when she saw him.

She recalled her cry for protection. A prayer. When the words came to her she closed her eyes and prayed again. "Thank you God for what You have done to chase away the presence of evil." Then she asked that He would continue to place around her His hedge of protection.

Chapter 39

"Are we close?" asked Joyce.

"I didn't actually clock it. We backed out. A lot faster than was probably safe."

"And where was he?"

"Right in the middle." He nodded his head indicating the road in front of them.

A few short moments passed and then Joyce thought he saw it. A lump. Something about the size of a body. Another moment and he knew. "Yeah, that's it. Don't get too close." He strained forward in the tight car attempting to get a better view. "Where did you guys stop?"

"Not sure really. About here I'd guess."

Joyce didn't like guesses at his crime scene. He thought about it for a moment and decided to let it go. "Okay, park right here." He wanted room to work. He wanted to check for tracks, footprints, blood trails. He checked the time on his cell phone, made a note and stepped out of the cramped quarters of the police cruiser.

Next, he took a picture of the body with his phone camera. A couple of shots and then nothing. He simply stood by the car, the door still open, and began to look around. Slowly he made a full 360-degree turn. His eyes moved up and down.

The uniformed patrolman watched the detective. He wasn't at all certain about what a detective actually did at a crime scene. Uniform guys generally get little exposure to a scene like this. Or any other homicide for that matter. The odds of getting a call to a killing were slim. Perhaps, in a city like this, no more than once a year. It was probable that some never, in a career, were dispatched to a murder scene.

"What do you want me to do?" He was talking to Joyce but looking around as if he expected trouble. Trouble was something a patrolman understands. Calls to bars, parties, or domestic disturbances all carry the risk of being assaulted. Occasionally two men fighting seize the opportunity to join forces and fight the cop there to break up the fight. Generally, it would not end well for the combatants. There are those times however that a policeman gets hurt.

"Just look around. See if there is anything out of place. Look for the unusual." Joyce was doing exactly that.

"Got a hint as to what might be unusual?"

Joyce looked across the top of the car and smiled. Not a big glad-to-see-you smile, but a grin. "Watch where you walk. Take the time to see what might be on the ground. Stuff like blood, tracks, drag marks."

He nodded and then asked, "What are you looking for in the trees?"

"It's possible that our killer can fly. I'm looking for anything." He glanced at the patrolman. The detective wanted to see if the officer was really listening. He was. Joyce had considered the idea of the presence of angels. He said nothing.

"Maybe we'll see a piece of clothing or broken limbs." Joyce shrugged.

He switched his phone camera to video and started to make a quick video of the crime scene. He slowly approached the body holding the camera out in front of him. When he got close enough for a good shot of the headless body he stopped.

Slipping his phone into his coat pocket he knelt down to get an idea of what type of weapon may have been used to decapitate the body. To his eye, it seemed a clean cut. He stood up and took another look around.

The hard-packed dirt and gravel path was covered in blood. He noted a couple of lines that were most certainly from blood squirting from the body as the head was severed. He shook his head.

"Where do you think we'll find the head?" The patrolman had no clue as to how to find it. The idea of using a K-9 was considered but he didn't know if a dog would be the right choice.

"I'm thinking we won't." He paused and scanned the treetops. "At least not around here." Joyce pulled out his phone and called for the M.E. and crime scene techs. He advised dispatch that both could drive into the park. He would meet them at the scene.

As he returned the phone to his inside coat pocket he heard the unmistakable sound of tires crunching on dirt and gravel. He spun in the direction of the sound. No one should be driving in from that direction.

"Stop that car." Joyce was shouting. He had not yet worked the section of road where the Toyota was driving. It was on the far side of the body. Opposite of where the police car was parked.

The patrolman had seen the car. As Joyce shouted his order, the patrolman raised both arms and started yelling. He waved his arms telling the driver to stop. She did.

"Find out who that is." Joyce was agitated. He thought he knew.

She was out of the car before the patrolman could reach her.

"Detective." She waved as she said it. It may have been a greeting or a question.

Joyce considered it to be the former. His thoughts processed quickly. She knew who he was. She knew what was going on. She was not a cub reporter and had put things together back at the church. She probably called her city desk to find out where the police activity was. Now she was here in the middle of his crime scene.

"What are you doing here?" Police have a tone to express authority. When used there is little doubt as to who is in charge. The patrolman used just such a voice.

"Detective." She tried again.

"Did you not hear me?"

She fumbled for her press ID. "I'm with the paper." She held it out for the patrolman to see.

"I'm with the police. Get back in the car and leave…Now!" He had raised his voice.

Joyce had made his way towards the newspaper lady. There was no mistaking her. She was the one who stopped him at church. He wanted to show some respect for her. Not for her job but because she was a church-goer. A Christian.

"Didn't my men tell you you couldn't be here? That the park is closed? That this area is restricted and not safe?" Joyce's voice was loud and authoritative.

Her impulse was to say no. The big detective would find out that it wasn't true. Never lie to the police. "Yes but…"

"Arrest her," Joyce shouted the words and then turned his back to walk away.

"I saw him." She was shouting. The words sounded like a plea.

Joyce stopped and turned around. He saw the patrolman had his handcuffs out.

"You saw who?" He too was yelling.

By now she was standing still. Her demeanor was changing. She tried to answer but words did not come out. She bowed her head, looking at the ground with her eyes closed. She steadied herself and raised her head.

"I saw him." The words were now faint - weak. They had barely crossed her lips when the shaking started. She wanted to sit down but there was nothing handy. Her car was several feet behind her.

Joyce realized she was in trouble. Her complexion paled, her eyes filled with tears and she was shaking uncontrollably. Then he saw her crumple…from the knees, and settle quickly onto the roadway.

When he reached her side she was sobbing, a seemingly deep, grieving sob. He tried to be sensitive. It was a police thing.

Most policemen have one thing in common. They generally meet and deal with people on their worst days. Be it a victim, a

110

witness, or a suspect. If they need the police, it's a bad day. How to be sensitive is learned. Most were good at it. Joyce was better than most.

When it appeared she was catching her breath, Joyce asked her again. "You saw my killer?"

She did not answer. She did not yet trust her voice. Closing her eyes she nodded.

He considered the next question for a long moment before asking. "How do you know he was my killer?" He thought he knew the answer. He did not expect the words he heard.

She looked up at the now kneeling detective. She was amazed at how big he was. It was a conscious thought. She knew he was big. She had talked to him earlier. Now, sitting in the dirt with him kneeling down, she got a whole new sense of his size. The thought, only a blink of the eye in time, left her. "He was holding the head."

"The head?" Joyce hated dumb questions. He knew he had just asked one.

She only nodded. The detective stood and looked around. He wondered if the killer was lurking nearby. *We need your protection God. Be here with us.* He didn't speak the words but wondered if he should have. Prayer was unfamiliar to him.

He offered a hand for the newspaper reporter. He figured she had regained her strength to stand.

Chapter 40

Unlike popular crime shows on television, real-life detectives spend a lot of time at a crime scene. Especially homicides. The case of the missing head was no different. Joyce finally cleared the scene, being the last one to leave the park nearly five hours after he had arrived.

Now he sat at his desk with the unwelcome prospect of another five hours documenting what had occurred, what he had seen, and the directions he had given to others assisting in the investigation.

His cell phone rang. He looked at the screen to see the lieutenant's name. "Hey boss."

"How's it going?"

"If I said great would you believe me?"

A chuckle, "Probably not. Where are you?"

"Just got back to the office. Got a ton of work to do."

"Got a minute to brief me?"

Joyce leaned back in the swivel chair and nodded. "Yeah sure, you're the boss." There was no sarcasm in his voice.

The boss knew what Joyce meant. "Need some help?"

Joyce rubbed an eye with his free hand. He thought about the question for a moment wondering if it was small talk or if the lieutenant really meant it. Finally, "You serious?"

"Yeah I'm serious. Your plate is getting full Tommy, you need help, say the word."

"Who do you have in mind?"

The lieutenant took a deep breath. One that his detective would not hear. "Who do you want?"

"Based on what we know, I think I need you."

"Okay," His answer was quick like he expected it. "You eat yet?"

"You gotta be kidding."

"No, I'm not. I'm on the way. I'll get a pizza."

"Thanks boss. I have a couple of uniforms here. Make it enough for four. I'm good for it."

Anybody can go to Pizza Hut. Cops however know where to get really good pizza. Those that have a great sauce and just the right crust. The lieutenant showed up with two large.

Joyce and his boss sat alone, away from the two patrolmen who were each busy on separate computers filling out their reports.

They did not even mention the case until each had consumed two slices each.

"Now that you have something in your stomach let me show you something." Joyce picked his phone off the desk and punched some buttons. He held it out for his lieutenant to see. "Our victim."

The boss simply shook his head. He thumbed through the other stills Joyce had taken when he first got out of the car. He then handed the phone back to Joyce.

"There's more." He selected the video he had taken and slid the phone across the desk.

"Wow, this is not fun." He shook his head as he watched the short video. "I'm not sure what to say." He pushed the phone across the desk back to Joyce. "Got any thoughts?"

"I'm wondering where the head is…. I'm afraid that it's going to show up someplace and really cause us some heartburn."

"Can't worry about stuff we can't control."

Joyce looked to his boss as if there was something he wanted to say. He was leaning back in the swivel desk chair with his hands behind his head. Several long moments passed before he leaned forward and grabbed a slice of pizza.

He took a bite and started talking. "I don't get this whole case boss. I mean, why, all of a sudden, does this evil, this presence, decide it's time to wreak havoc on this city? Why now? Why here? What is the reason?"

"Okay."

"No, really. What is…was… the catalyst? What happened or is now happening to cause all of this?" He took another bite and watched his boss as he chewed.

The lieutenant didn't answer. He pulled a paper towel off a roll setting on the desk, laid a slice of pizza on it, and carried it to the microwave on the far side of the office.

Joyce watched him every step of the way. He watched as he punched the buttons and then waited for the pizza to be reheated. He watched as he made his way back to his chair next to

Joyce's desk. He watched as the lieutenant tested the pizza's temperature and then began consuming it. Several long minutes had passed. Joyce waited for his answer.

The lieutenant was wiping his hands on the paper towel when he finally spoke. "What?"

"What happened to cause all this? There has to be a why."

The lieutenant shook his head but offered no reason.

"You've been at this church stuff a while. How does stuff like this start?"

"This is not 'church' stuff...this is spiritual warfare."

"Yeah, I know...but you know what I mean." He paused for a long moment. He glanced at the pizza considering if he wanted more. He did but he was telling himself that he didn't need any more. He began again.

"I'm all in on this stuff. I've seen it. What I need to know, not for me as a person but for this crazy job. I need to know why." He paused again making eye contact with his boss. "People are dying and we need to know why....we need to know how to stop it."

The lieutenant leaned forward in the chair and rested his forearms on his knees. He had to look up to see Joyce. "Okay, so let's brainstorm a little. What is the one idea you have as to why this is happening?"

Joyce nodded. "You pray about this stuff right?"

The boss nodded.

"So maybe those on the other side are doing the same thing. Maybe there are Satan people out there asking for Satan to wage war on us. Maybe they do it because they don't like us."

The boss shrugged. "I don't know."

"Well we need to know. We need to find out....before it blows up in our face."

"How would that happen?"

Joyce shook his head, exhaled loudly, and leaned back in the chair. "Had a visitor at the park today. Lady reporter."

114

"Oh, that's just great." He too leaned back in his chair. "What else?"

"She knows what we're up against, that's for sure."

"How?"

"She saw the guy."

"When? Where? How?"

"At the park. I had just taken that video you saw when she drove right up to us."

The lieutenant started to laugh but did not think it funny. "You're serious aren't you?"

"Like a heart attack."

The lieutenant turned in the chair. First he looked at the pizza box and then out the window. The office was a story off the sidewalk. "What did you tell her?"

"Nothing, I told that guy," he pointed to one of the patrolmen typing reports on a computer, "to arrest her."

"Did he?"

"No."

"Why not?"

"She's a witness boss."

"A witness?"

"We have an echo in here?"

"Okay then, what did she witness?"

"She saw the killer."

The boss closed his eyes as he shook his head. He didn't speak for several moments. Finally, he opened his eyes and made contact with those of his favorite if not his best detective.

"She didn't see a man did she?"

"No, she saw something new, not like the tarot card, different. I suppose we can call him a new player."

"And he is the killer?" asked the lieutenant.

"He was holding the head."

Chapter 41

"I need you to come in. We need to talk about this. My lieutenant is here and wants to go over what happened."

"What can I possibly tell you that I haven't already said?"

"You know how this works, you're a reporter, people need to talk about this stuff to make sure they get it all out."

"When did you want me to come in?"

"Now would be nice." Joyce looked at his boss for moral support. Both men knew this was a form of conspiracy. Joyce would come up with new questions, something that would sound like a deep detective sort of probe but they both really wanted to tell her to keep a lid on the story.

"You do know about the first amendment?"

"What does that mean?" Joyce did his best to sound incredulous.

"I mean... you don't think you're going to quash the story."

"Why, are you afraid of printing something?"

"Of course not."

"Why did you bring it up?"

Her answer was quick. "Because you might think you can control the press."

Joyce smiled at the lieutenant. He loved this stuff. "I don't want to control the press, I want to solve a murder. Right now you're the only one who has seen my killer. I think that's more important than a by-line... don't you?"

"I'm not a witness." Her voice had changed. She was no longer the confident writer of crime stories of a minute ago.

"Yeah, well, as I think you know, I've been at this awhile. You're the first one I ever met that saw a man holding a head in one hand and a sword in the other."

As soon as she arrived at the homicide office Joyce had her sit down with his sketch kit tech to make a composite drawing of the killer. Joyce had briefed her regarding the nature of the suspect. She was cautioned as to the sensitivity of the information.

"That's creepy." was all she said.

When the sketch was finished both Joyce and the lieutenant were amazed. First with the seemingly human features, but even more so with the ugly, ghoulish look. His size could not be determined but the reporter thought he might be as tall as ten feet.

Joyce had offered coffee, water, and a soda. The reporter had turned everything down.

Questions started. "Where does a guy like this come from?" Joyce placed his big hand on the computer-generated sketch that had been printed.

She gave the impression that the topic was something she would rather not talk about. During the session with the sketch tech, she had gotten into the effort trying to get it right…as she remembered it. It wore her out and no longer was she a willing witness. "The pit of hell would be my guess."

"Any thoughts as to why?"

She pursed her lips and shook her head.

"You know this is not the only murder." It was not meant to be a question.

"I thought as much."

"This is number four…that is, that we know of."

She only nodded.

"You approached me in church this morning. What was that about?"

"I was just trying to connect the dots."

"Where do you think the dots end?"

"I don't know." Her voice was soft.

Joyce thought back to the moment in the park when she slumped to the ground. "Is this a story you're ready to run?"

"Why not?"

Joyce leaned back in his chair. His eyes passed to his lieutenant who had only been observing. He nodded.

"Panic is something we don't need right now," said the lieutenant. "There are any number of reasons to keep this quiet but the best is so we don't get a bunch of copycat murders."

"You mean people killing hoping to get away with it because of this?" She pointed to the image.

"Exactly." The lieutenant nodded to Joyce.

"How easy would it be to say the devil did it?" Joyce's voice showed that he was trying to lighten things up a bit.

She nodded.

"Tell me, you're a perceptive woman. Where can this stuff be coming from? What's behind it? I mean...we haven't seen this here before. Why now?"

"I have no idea, a new cult in town maybe. Something like that."

Joyce considered it, then, "You were in church today, is that something you normally do, or was there something that drew you there?"

She gazed away for a moment. It was apparent she was thinking. She brought her eyes back to Joyce. There was a quick glance at the lieutenant but then her eyes fixed on the detective. "I'm a member. I don't do much, as far as activities and such, but I go. Not every Sunday but maybe most."

She paused a long moment, then added, "More or less... As a member, they have my email address. I have gotten some prayer requests, you know, prayer chain stuff. Recently it's been about some attacks from the enemy."

"The enemy?" Joyce interrupted.

"That's church speak for Satanic attacks," said the lieutenant.

Joyce nodded.

"Right," she continued. "I thought this would be a good day to be in church, if for no other reason than to see what was going on. At first, I wasn't there as a reporter, but when I saw a story in it I naturally had to follow up."

"And now you're in the middle."

"I guess."

The lieutenant leaned in a little. "We really need this under wraps for a while."

She didn't say anything. A reporter's instinct would be to object. In the end, she only nodded in agreement and asked, "Do you know who the victim is?"

"Not yet," offered Joyce. Without a head or ID, there was little to go on. Forensics would fingerprint him at the autopsy but that would be a day or so. The only unclaimed car in the lot was registered to a leasing company. Nothing on that would be available until tomorrow, Monday morning.

That prompted a question from the lieutenant. "Did you not find the car keys?"

"Nope." Joyce shook his head.

"Strange."

"Yes.. it is all very strange."

Chapter 42

Tommy Joyce couldn't sleep. He had the sense there was an anchor. Not so much on him, but on the case. He used the time to think. Between ideas he would doze off. Ten minutes, maybe fifteen. Then he was awake. New thoughts. New ideas. Nothing made sense.

He and the lieutenant agreed, sort of, that an arrest in the headless case was not going to happen. The next move would be to find a common thread. Something the three victims shared. The apartment manager was collateral damage.

Monday morning should give him the name of the last victim. He was edgy about it. About all of it. He would have to wait. He turned on some music in hopes to be lulled asleep.

"You're early." The lieutenant was at the coffee pot.

"Couldn't sleep."

"Visions of sugar plums?"

"Right, what kind of Monday are you in for?" Joyce walked up to the coffee pot.

"Not bad, night shift got things cleaned up. But the guys will have work today.

Tommy Joyce filled a coffee cup. "Guess you would have told me if we got another one, right?"

"You're good." He walked away. At his office door, he turned. "For now." He laughed and closed his door.

Detective work takes a lot of thinking. Television makes it look like fast action. One gunfight to the next. Doors are always being kicked in and a confession is almost guaranteed after some shrewd questioning and pounding on desks.

Joyce was in the thinking mode. It had lasted nearly all night. His phone had a 'do' list. It was personal. Not a 'to do', not a 'honeydew' not any of those things. It was simply a way to re-member. Using his phone made it erasable. The question was once asked, "Why didn't you do that?" The answer can always be, "I didn't think of it." Notebooks are permanent. Lawyers can see them. Not so with notes on the phone. At least that's the theory.

"Sylvia's mother says Sylvia's busy, too busy to come to the phone, Sylvia's mother says Sylvia's tryin' to start a new life of her own.

Sylvia's mother says Sylvia's happy so why don't you leave her alone? And the operator says forty cents more for the next three minutes."

"What's that?" The lieutenant pointed to Joyce's phone.

"Pandora." Joyce was staring at his computer, his hand mov-ing the mouse.

"I know that, who's singing?"

Joyce stopped and looked up. His look said, 'really?'

"Yeah," said the lieutenant.

Joyce laughed. "Dr. Hook," He went back to his computer. "And his medicine show."

The lieutenant sat down. "What's on our plate today?" Roll call was over and the lieutenant had divided up the work from the weekend. The biggest part of his job was deciding what detectives got what cases.

"It's full."

"Good, where do I start?"

Joyce rolled away from his desk. "We need to toss three places. The sooner the better. Shouldn't need a warrant, not for dead people but we'll need one of your covers. Three actually."

"You want me to call your friend the pastor?"

"No, I'll do it, but we still need to go to all three places. I think you need to be part of the cover when the work begins."

"Covering Tommy, covering."

"Right, but I also want you with me. To be there."

"Any ID from yesterday?" The lieutenant knew the answer. He asked to move the conversation along.

"You can do that for me." Joyce handed him the information on the leasing company. Joyce was certain the car left in the parking lot yesterday belonged to the runner.

"On it."

Chapter 43

Joyce called the DA. He got a friendly sounding lawyer. "I need to get full financial records on three individuals." He paused. She didn't say anything. "I need bank records, ATM usage, and credit card information. Stuff like when and where they were used."

"And you have probable cause?" She was polite.

"No, I don't need it. They are not under arrest, nothing like that. Can you help me?"

"There's a thing called privacy detective. I know you know all that, so tell me why you're calling."

"These people are all dead, killed, at least two were. I need to find the killer."

"I see, any family?"

Joyce shook his head, "None, at least that we know of. I'm sure they have a family, somewhere, but no, no one we need to worry about. You know, on the privacy thing."

"Let me see what I can do."

"We're in a hurry over here."

"I understand. Email me what you have. I'll need socials for sure."

"Got it. I'll give you what I have now and get the rest for you." He paused. "We're still trying to ID the third victim. It just happened yesterday."

Joyce hung up. He called the M.E. "What's the deal on our headless horseman?"

"You getting all these cases?"

"Yeah, with this luck I should be playing the lottery." It sounded funny but Joyce was anxious.

"Pretty savage detective. Looks like a single cut. The blade had to be big. I'm guessing a machete or a sword."

"I'll tell you about that sometime Doc. But is there anything else? Anything weird?"

"Weird like how?"

Joyce couldn't tell him everything. Not yet. "Weird like a cult thing. You know, Manson, Jim Jones. Weird cultish stuff."

"You mean Charles Manson? Tattoos on the forehead sort of stuff?

"Doc, we can't talk about foreheads. The killer took it with him."

The M.E. didn't go there. "Nothing like you're talking about detective. This guy is a real runner. He's fit. He might even look

122

skinny but he's not. He's the real deal for a runner. At least we know who he is, sent you an email with his name."

"That's something, thanks." Joyce changed the subject. "How about the burned guy, we need to confirm who he is...his boss told us who was working that shift. His apartment seems to confirm he's our victim."

"Good to hear that. We'll have to wait on the DNA results. At least for my end."

"Thanks Doc."

The lieutenant dropped a paper on Joyce's desk. "Anything new at the morgue?" He didn't wait for an answer. "Info on the park victim, second park victim." It included a DMV photo. The lieutenant didn't have to ask anyone for the photo. With the name in the email, he simply entered it into the computer, and there it was.

"He," Joyce pointed to the photo. "That's him? Medical examiner said he had that head removed with a machete or sword." Joyce studied it for a moment. "That's not the same name."

"How's that?"

Joyce pointed to the DMV photocopy. "That is not the name we have for the lease car."

The lieutenant nodded. "You're right, now you get to check out two places."

"We."

"Right, we, Oh yeah, got a call from the sergeant that was at your scene yesterday. Seems like a patrolman's got his pants in a wad."

"What?" Joyce acted surprised.

"Says you wouldn't let him go to the body 'cause he's not a Christian."

Joyce sat for a moment. "You saw him you know? He ate your pizza."

The lieutenant gestured towards the computers the patrolman had used.

"Yup, where's the sergeant now?"

"At the precinct I imagine."

"Call him. You're the boss here. Tell him you want that wimp up here now." Joyce laughed, "And use Tom Selleck's line. Tell him to get up here 'forthwith'."

"You still watching *Blue Blood*?"

"Doesn't everybody?"

Chapter 44

"Good morning, pastor."

"Oh, good morning detective. How we coming?"

Joyce didn't want small talk. The pastor was a good guy but he didn't need to waste time right now. "I'm good. Just got the ID on yesterday's victim."

"I guess that's good... progress anyway."

"Right, but that's not why I called. We're planning to enter the home, apartment, whatever, of our victims. Can I ask that you and your team give me, us, the cover you do so well?"

"Absolutely detective. I want to assure you that the prayer is now non-stop. Twenty four hours a day."

"Aren't you sleeping?"

"Oh it's not me alone. We're working shifts. We have developed a schedule and every hour is covered by someone, usually several people."

"Okay, then," said Joyce. "I don't know how anyone can pray for an hour or more without stopping but that's your business. Thanks for the help."

"We're glad to do it." The pastor paused. "The battle is against us detective. Satan is against the church. He wants to get in here and cause things to derail. Wreak havoc. Cause strife and all kinds of trouble. Your work is for us, the church. We understand that. We'll do our part."

Once off the phone, Joyce thought about the pastor's words. The victims, to his knowledge, had nothing to do with the church. The first one was a porno dealer. Hardly a vocation for members of a church. The second was a self-proclaimed Satan follower. Not proclaiming to everyone he knew of, but she certainly lived it. Her bedroom told that story.

When it came to the third Joyce didn't know. The case was too new. They had only this morning learned who he was.

The lieutenant dropped a single sheet of paper onto Joyce's desk. "Got an email, printed it for you."

Joyce read the first couple of lines, 'Plat book, parcel deed number.' "What am I looking at?"

"It's the deed record of the place you call the lion's den. You know, the place your fortune teller mentioned."

"She's not my fortune teller." He pointed. "What's this telling us?"

"It looks to me...all we know is it looks like the place is owned by a guy named Lion, Walter Lion Tax records show he has a non-profit company."

Joyce looked up. "It's a church? A Satanic church?"

"I believe they call them temples, but that's what it could be." The lieutenant pulled up a chair.

"I saw some of this crap on the internet." said Joyce, "Saw a website that was all black. Said absolutely nothing but it was all black with a red pentagram and a demon inside it."

"These folks are real Tommy. Satan is real. As real as God."

"So how are we going to stop something like this?"

"I don't see that we are." answered the lieutenant.

"So it goes on forever?"

"I think it's up to God. He can stop it."

"Yeah? I want to know why he let it start." Joyce leaned back and stared at nothing. Finally, "I get God, I mean... I'm sure there is one. I don't get all this other stuff."

"It may seem complicated but with a certain level of trust, I call it faith, and an understanding of what He has told us in His word, well... it gets easier to believe."

"His word?"

"Yeah, that's what we believers call the Bible. It's the Word of God."

"So what does His word say about demons cutting heads off of runners on Sunday morning?" Joyce pointed to the sketch of the demon.

"Job."

"Job, what's a job?"

"A part of the Bible, Old Testament. God allowed Satan to test a man named Job."

"Did he cut Job's head off?"

"No."

"So why did he allow your guy....Job...to be tested?"

"To show Satan that there are people of God who will remain God's people even when the going gets tough. They belong to God."

"Why?"

"One answer is that it would glorify God."

"So how does this case of mine fit in?" Joyce slid back into his desk. "Is God glorified?"

"Not yet."

Joyce shook his head. He stared at his desktop. "Well, from what I see, our victims are not Job. They don't...um, *did* not, belong to God." He raised his eyes to the lieutenant. "A porno dealer and a Satanist?"

Chapter 45

"Officer, thanks for coming up. You remember me?"

"Sure detective, I remember."

"You were here all afternoon yesterday?" Joyce watched the patrolman.

"Yeah, I was."

"The lieutenant fed you...you had pizza."

"Yeah."

"If you had something to say why didn't you say it then when I was right here?" Joyce pointed to the floor emphasizing *here*.

"Say what?" The patrolman sounded confused.

"According to your sergeant, you're upset that I didn't let you go back into the crime scene yesterday morning." It wasn't a question. "You shot your mouth off about it."

"I didn't think it was right."

"So why didn't you say it to me?"

"I don't know."

"You're a cop, you're *supposed* to know."

"How am I supposed to know what you're thinking?" He still showed confusion.

"Same way all cops find out. You ask questions. How hard would it have been to simply say, 'Why'?"

The patrolman nodded but didn't say anything.

"Would you like to ask me now?"

He nodded, "Okay."

Joyce stood waiting.

Finally, the patrolman got it. "Why didn't you want me at the crime scene yesterday?"

"It was too dangerous. I didn't want you killed."

"Killed?"

Joyce picked the sketch drawing of his killer and handed it to the patrolman. "This is what my witness says the killer looked like."

"What the…" He cursed.

"Tell me what you would have done if you met him?" Joyce smiled. "Besides mess your pants."

The question was rhetorical. The officer did not answer.

"Your partner with you?" asked Joyce.

"Yeah, he's waiting downstairs."

"Get him, we have work to do."

"You mean...?" The patrolman paused.

"Yeah, I mean bring him up here, we're gonna go get this guy." Joyce pointed to the sketch.

Chapter 46

The scene was chaotic when Joyce and the lieutenant rolled into the dilapidated trailer park on the wrong side of the tracks. Following them in a marked police cruiser were the two uniformed officers.

"What's going on here?" asked Joyce, not expecting an answer.

Several fire trucks were parked around and near a cluster of mobile homes. The term was a generous one. The smoldering remains of what was most likely a trailer could be seen through the mass of equipment and a crowd of onlookers. It's a hard call to know which was a bigger draw. A good fire or a police crime scene. Flashing lights, be red or blue, were certain to bring out the curious.

"What are the odds that place belongs to your victim?" asked the lieutenant.

Joyce laughed. Not because it was funny but because the thought was satirical. As they got closer, watching the numbers, those they could see, the idea became more believable. "You might be right."

Joyce parked and approached a fireman. "What happened?" He showed his badge.

"You guys got here quick."

"What do you mean?"

"Place just blew up, looks suspicious. I think the captain called for the arson squad." The firefighter was watching the gauges on the side of the fire truck. Hoses were attached and water was obviously being pumped to the fire.

"You got an address?" Joyce pointed to the burnt-out trailer.

It was a match. The fire and the address for the victim were the same. Joyce wondered if the fire thing was normal, a form of punishment used by Satan. Maybe?

"You guys start working the crowd." Joyce was pointing. "Don't say anything about the case. Just find out who knew the guy that lived there." He gestured to the smoking pile of metal. "See if you can find anyone who can tell us anything. I'd like to know when was the last time anyone saw him."

The two uniformed guys nodded and headed into the crowd.

"Hey," Joyce stopped the one who had a problem earlier. "This might have been a break for you."

"How?"

"Maybe you won't get killed now."

"What?" He showed complete confusion.

"You think that fire just happened?" Joyce had a serious look. "Be glad we didn't get here earlier. You would have been inside when the place went up." Joyce held eye contact and then nodded.

"Little hard on the guy." The lieutenant had a slight smile.

"I'm saving his life." Joyce turned back to the car. "I want those two to work. I want them to figure this out. They don't know enough about the case to make guesses. Maybe we'll learn something.

Chapter 47

After wrapping up at the fire, the four stopped for burgers.

"Bring your notes." Joyce shouted it to the patrolmen as he made his way across the parking lot.

"Tell me what you guys learned." The food orders were in and Joyce wasn't going to engage in small talk.

"Not a lot really." He looked at his notes. "Sounds like he was a loner…"

"Sort of a jerk the way I get it," said his partner

"Anyone actually know him?" asked Joyce. They were at a normal table with two chairs on each side. The patrolmen sat side by side. Joyce moved his eyes from one to the other.

"A girl…lady, not sure, said she's talked to him."

"What she say?"

"Not a lot, she looked like a meth head. Skinny, missing teeth. Pretty typical. Said he was weird. 'Kinda spooky' were her words." He was looking at his notes. "Asked her if she ever did meth with him. Believe it or not, she said yeah."

"Anybody ever been in his trailer?"

"I asked a guy that." said the other patrolman. "Told me nobody liked him. Didn't think anyone would go in there. Leastways not with him."

"This isn't adding up."

"How's that?" asked the Lieutenant.

"What is a meth head from a dump like that doing with a leased car and jogging at the park?"

"Wrong guy?"

"It's gotta be. M.E. said the vic was a runner. For real. Training like he was competing. That doesn't sound like a meth head."

One of the patrolmen commented, "Maybe the trailer was a lab and blew?"

"Still doesn't answer the deal with the car." It came from the patrolman with issues.

"Maybe," It was the other officer. "Suppose the victim in the park had the trailer guy on his payroll. Running a lab. Dealing."

Joyce nodded. "Good call, we'll circle back to this later. We have another place to look at. Nicer. I've been there. It'll have its challenges." He glanced at the lieutenant. "When we get to the runner's apartment, we'll have a better idea."

"So where's the guy from the trailer?"

Joyce smiled. "Right now, that's the fire department's problem."

The burgers arrived.

"You always do that?" Joyce was almost whispering.

"Do what?" asked the lieutenant.

"What you just did, say grace."

"I try."

Joyce let it go. The whole church thing bothered him. He knew that God was real. Just like Satan and the demons they had to deal with. The church thing had him frustrated. He liked the pastor. He was grateful for the cover he and the men were getting from the prayers. But the whole church thing had him thinking.

Joyce picked up the check. The lieutenant was not surprised but both patrolmen were wide-eyed about it. For one of the patrolmen, it was confusing. A couple of hours earlier Joyce 'ate his lunch'. Now the big detective was buying his lunch.

Joyce moved the Charger into traffic and checked the mirror. The men were following. He wondered if it was a normal reaction. Habit maybe, or did he really think the two cops would get lost?

"What's bothering you?"

Joyce glanced to his right. "What?"

"Something's bugging you, what is it?"

"Nothing."

"It bothers you that I say grace?" The lieutenant looked straight ahead.

"Everything bothers me right now, especially when I'm continually reminded about other people's views of God."

"Good."

Joyce glanced right again. "Good?"

"Yeah."

"What's that supposed to mean, 'Good'?"

"It means you're thinking." The lieutenant paused. Then looked at Joyce. "You're thinking about God."

Joyce was angry, but not sure why. He had stuff to say but didn't. He remembered something he had read. *Be careful what you spit out. You may have to eat it again.*

Finally, he felt like talking. "Don't jam this Jesus stuff down my throat, Okay?"

"Sorry Tommy, but that's not what I'm doing."

"I think it is. I understand you're my friend and all, but I have my mind made up on this God thing. I believe in God, okay, so keep the rest of the stuff to yourself."

132

"Okay... but tell me... how did you get so jaded about church?"

"I'm not jaded," answered Joyce.

"What do you call it then? From where I sit it looks like you're really mad. Question is, why and at what...who?"

"You ever pay attention to how many churches there are? Look around. They're on every corner, and for what?"

The lieutenant lowered his voice. "This is a big deal isn't it?"

"I hope you're talking about the case."

"I'm talking about you...and yes, the case is part of it."

"Well let's go catch a demon or two, what d'ya say?" He pulled into the apartment complex and parked.

Chapter 48

The four stood in front of the dime a dozen style apartment complex. There were several buildings, all three stories. The individual units had an exterior door. No interior hallways, elevators, or stairways. Everything could be seen and accessed from the outside.

"We've been here." said a patrolman.

Joyce pointed to the third-floor unit belonging to his victim. "There?"

"No, not up there. We were down here." He waved his arm showing the parking lot and front sidewalk.

"What was it? Why were you here?"

"I'm trying to remember, it was a while ago."

"It was a disturbance call," said his partner. "We met a guy here. Said there had been a noisy group hanging out. They were loud. Everyone was gone by the time we arrived."

"Yeah, now I remember. The caller thought there may have been a costume party by the way they were dressed. He saw them from his balcony. Didn't see them up close."

"You have notes on that?" asked Joyce.

"I don't recall making a report but we'll have an interview card at the station."

"Get it for me when we're done." Joyce nodded. "This apartment belonged to one of our victims. The only female victim to date. She died from a burnt heart."

"What's a burnt heart and how do you get it?" asked a patrolman.

"When I find out, I'll let you know. " Joyce headed up the steps. "She lived here. She was into all things Satan. I've been in there. What I've learned since... I wonder why I'm still alive. This could get ugly." He pointed to the non-Christian officer. "Might be a good time to get out your rabbit's foot."

The men climbed the steps. Joyce pulled a set of keys from his pocket. The same set used on his first visit. They had been recovered from the dead girl's car. The ring also had her Honda key, the key to the construction trailer, plus one key Joyce was unsure of.

Joyce thought that the place was as he remembered it. Except there was an odor. He stopped just inside the door. He wanted to get a better sense, a feel maybe of what might be waiting. It wasn't hard to remember the scene at the apartment.

But the odor was new. He remembered no smells the first time. No cat odor, no candles, no incense. This smell was none of those though. It was stink.

"You smell that?" Joyce looked at the lieutenant.

"Might be a good time to pray."

"That's your job...but I agree." He whispered a few words that only he heard. He looked at the Christian patrolman. "You smell that?"

The officer nodded.

"That's the stink of evil. He's in here. Bet on it."

Joyce tapped a quick text to the pastor. He looked at his boss, "You ready?"

"Let's do it."

"The action is going to be in the bedroom. Something stopped me from going in last time." Joyce turned to the patrolmen. "So you know, If there's something, someone in there, your gun is useless."

"Let me go first." The lieutenant was serious and he was in charge.

The four men slowly made their way past the living room, down the short hallway past the bathroom, stopping at the bedroom door.

The lieutenant took a deep breath, raised his hands, palms up, and prayed. "Protect us Lord, we trust in your presence and your protection. Be glorified in what happens here today." He wasn't loud, but the other three policemen heard him.

Joyce and the lieutenant made eye contact. Each nodded and turned their attention to the room's interior. The lieutenant saw the giant reversed pentagram and recognized it from Joyce's video.

Suddenly, before either detective could move into the room there came a great force, a wind of sorts, but it was more than that. It was like thunder. The noise was loud but it was the vibration, the concussion of sorts that was most noticeable. Something, a presence...a sense that something large passed over and around them and...through them, but not pushing them, it moved into the room ahead of them.

The lieutenant saw it, something. A glimpse. An image. Not clear, not complete, but something. White, majestic, huge, wonderful, powerful. A feeling maybe. "Praise God."

"What?" It was from Joyce.

"Thank you Jesus," the Christian patrolman had a similar sense. He actually didn't see it but felt it. He knew it, like he knows oxygen, that something was there. That God had sent his….angel? Maybe...but something.

Then Joyce heard a thunder of sorts. A loud sound. He didn't hear words but still understood they were words. "This fight belongs to the Lord." It penetrated his very being. His soul.

The bedroom quickly filled with smoke. There was a great noise, like that of a battle but the police did not see any of it. The smoke was dense, like the fog of war, shielding the fight. Then it ended. A loud, sharp shriek.

As quickly as it all began, the four cops were pushed from the doorway. The unbelieving officer banged hard off the wall on the opposite side of the hallway. A stink, the same smell they noticed earlier filled the hallway, but only for a moment. Then a rush of wind. Then everything was quiet. In moments, the smoke cleared. There was no sign of those who had engaged in battle.

It was a battle, wasn't it?

Joyce and the lieutenant exchanged looks. Nothing was said for several seconds that seemed like minutes. The lieutenant knew he was on the right side of this case. He was grateful for what God had just shown all of them.

Joyce didn't know it. This was his moment. Some find it in church, kids might find it at a camp, some find it at the edge of a river. Joyce found it at the doorway to Hell. He should have, almost instantly, come to an understanding that everything inside the bedroom door was the dominion of Hell. But God had taken over. His warrior, what Joyce should have known to be an angel of God had taken over. He had not seen him, but he felt him. God had saved the four men from destruction.

Chapter 49

When the four had returned to the homicide office, they began to exchange notes. Each would need to put on paper their own idea of what had happened. There would never be a trial or other public review of the facts and evidence of the case, but paperwork was paperwork, and reports creating a record was part of the job.

It would not be the everyday debrief. The events at the apartment were something none of them would want to talk about.

Before the typing began, it was good to have a soda or coffee and talk about what had just happened.

"Does anyone else realize that evil actually lived in the homes, or… apartments or wherever?" Joyce was personally surprised by that fact. He had three victims of Satan and one death that was collateral damage. He found first hand that evil not only lived in the apartments but saw to it the places were destroyed. They still didn't know what happened at the trailer park.

"It's the nature of evil," said the lieutenant.

"How's that?"

The lieutenant was drinking a can of Arnold Palmer iced tea. He set the can on the desk. "There is a Scripture verse. It's used a lot by preachers as they describe evil, the devil. "It says the thief, or the devil, comes to steal, kill and destroy."

There was a long pause in the conversation. Then Joyce said, "I guess he did all of that, didn't he?"

"What do we call it in our report?" It was one of the patrolmen.

The lieutenant answered. "Whatever you want."

"I'm using the word presence," said the other patrolman.

"I'm going home." Joyce turned off the computer on his desk and stood up.

"You done?"

"For today I am."

"What about your report?"

Joyce grinned and began to walk away. He paused, turned. "You ever know me not to get the paperwork done?"

He got a nod from the boss, with, "See you in the morning?" It was a question.

Joyce waved one of his big arms as he walked out the door.

By the time he got home, it was late. At least it felt late. He was ready for sleep.

He was done. Shot. Finished. He would have welcomed anyone to stick a fork in him just to prove it. He needed sleep. But he was afraid he wouldn't. He sort of felt like Kenny Rogers' *The Gambler*. 'Too tired to sleep'.

He laid down to *Pandora* playing low on his phone. He could only hope that he would find sleep.

The darkness was without words. None could describe just how black things were. There was a complete absence of light. Any light. He lifted his hand to the front of his face and did not see it. It was dark. That's how it was.

Fear is a strange thing. When people don't know there is a danger, even while swallowed up in complete darkness, fear is not part of the equation. Something evil could be lurking out of view, beyond the senses, yet fear doesn't come into play.

With the slightest hint that all is not well however, everything changes.

In this case, it was the smell. There was a sudden wafting of an indiscernible stink that consumed his senses. What...where... who? His memory wanted to remember but couldn't.

So it began. A single unknown, a what, and it started to creep in. The fear. Fear began to have its way. There was more.

Nearly as soon as the smell filled his nostrils, a wind began to blow. A wafting at first, not unlike the smell, then a summer breeze. But it continued. An ever-increasing wind. Ultimately, the wind grew to that of a tempest. Where it came from, the direction wasn't clear. It was whirling, like a tornado. Standing in such a force wouldn't be easy, but he wasn't standing. Was he? As the idea flooded his thoughts, he wondered why. Could the darkness affect his senses? Could it affect him to an extent that even the simplest knowledge of sitting, standing, laying was not perceivable?

138

Fear...is that the emotion? Was he now sensing there was something, a thing, to be afraid of? Evil had been a part of nearly everything in recent days. Could the blackness, the stink, the whirling wind be evil? That evil?

There was more. The wind changed. Not its direction. Still strong, violent, it developed a sound. It was building. A low babbling. It moved quickly to a rumble, and then to a roaring form of thunder. Ear bursting sounds that had the effect of explosions complete with concussions that moved him. Not up, not down. The motion, the movement caused by the building roar was not known...at least not for certain.

The fear was certain, and it continued to grow, it grew at the rate of the growing noise. The only sense that seemed not to be involved was his sight. There was nothing visible in the blackness. Light, any light is not appreciated, no matter how small, until it's gone. What price would be paid to see, to know what was there? To understand, to see what can be seen.

Be careful what you wish for... As quickly as the hope for light entered his mind it was there. The darkness lifted. Ever so slightly, but it lifted. It lifted just enough.

There was no missing the massiveness of the evil. It was that, evil. The giant creature, part bird maybe, part something else. Animal, not exactly sure what, but a cow perhaps...with horns. Maybe not, but the horns, two, were real. What kind of cow...or bull...or beast with wings? But then, suddenly, the creature hovered, turned, then spiraled up in the darkness. Next, it was swooping back, but the wings were gone, and now there were arms. Or legs. In one hand, but not a hand, more of a cloven hoof, was wedged a giant sword. The blade was long, maybe as big as a man. It was a dingy gray steel. The dingy appearance left the impression of old. Ancient. The blade was jagged. Large irregular jags with points. Like that of a spear. Large enough that just one, alone, would cause a fatal puncture.

His mind was racing. His heart pounded. The heavy drumming was going faster and faster. The rate, his heart rate, grew exponentially. If the increasing rate continued, it would certainly explode, maybe even burst into flames. The heart would burn up.

Tommy Joyce bolted straight up in his bed. His eyes scanned quickly, taking in the room. His head spinning like on a swivel, looking for whatever it was that had been there only seconds earlier. He was panting, his lungs screaming for air, his hair matted from sweat. His tattered gray tie shirt, big even for him, was soaked from the collar to the chest. Then slowly, ever so slowly he began to find his bearings. He was returning to reality, to normal. "God help me."

Chapter 50

"Hi honey." Her daughter stopped in several times a week. Usually around the noon hour.

"Hi Mom. I came empty-handed today". It was not uncommon for her to have something, usually groceries. That generally included a call first to see what her mother needed, if anything. Today she didn't call.

"Coffee?" She had retreated to the kitchen after hearing the front door open and close.

"Sure if it's made, I can't stay long." She dropped her purse on the kitchen table. "I've got a bunch of things I want to get done."

"That's fine." Her mother smiled. "Tell me what's new." Their ritual seemed to include small talk, updates about family and maybe a complaint about aches and pains.

When the coffee was poured and both women were seated at the kitchen table she blurted it out. "I have something to show you." She picked up her phone and started pushing buttons.

"What is it Mom?" She knew her mother was anxious. There was nothing normal about the urgency of what her mother was doing.

"You need to see this."

"See what?"

She pushed the phone across the table. "I want you to see these pictures." She said it as she pulled her hand away from the phone.

"Okay". The response was casual but she felt anything but. The tone from her mother told her this was a serious thing. It needed her attention, all of it. "What...what..." She lifted her eyes from the phone and looked at her mother to see a face filled with anguish. "Where...you take these?"

Her mother nodded as she reached for a tissue box sitting on the counter.

"Mom...where were you?" She was afraid for her mother. That she had somehow gotten into something. Something bad, really bad. It was obvious the photos had been taken at night. Instinct told her the late-night bus ride was not safe.

Twisting a tissue she said, "I was waiting for the bus. I saw it...them... across the road in the old shopping center."

Her daughter knew the shopping center. It was old, nearly abandoned, like most buildings in that part of town. Studying the photos, "Mom, do you know what this is?"

"I'm afraid I do."

"They're real...not just kids with..." She didn't finish.

"Oh, they're real. I know that much."

She thumbed through the pictures. "I'm not sure..." she paused. Finally, "Mom, I know this is real to you. You have seen a lot. But...I'm..for me...this has always been." She stopped talking as she studied the pictures.

Her mother gave a look only a mother knows how to do.

"Did they see you?"

"I don't know. I was really quiet. I wanted to scream but I didn't. It really scared me when they just appeared. One second nothing, then they were there."

"What do you mean?" Her voice..tone..made the question important.

She stared at her daughter. "They're spirits, honey, they come and go. I don't know if they really go, just that they disappear." She twisted the tissue.

"Oh Mom, I wish I had been there..." She reached out and took her hand. "It's not right that you were alone. You must have been terrified."

"I was...but you know... I wasn't alone. I'm never alone."

She cocked her head and smiled as she watched her mother share such an amazing, albeit ugly moment. "I know Mom. Jesus is always there...sometimes though, I wonder."

"I know, but I never wonder because I know."

"I hate it that you had to go through it."

"I don't think it was that bad but I was worried. Just not for me. But there is something you can't see because I didn't get a picture."

"What's that?"

She smiled, a sense of radiance came over her. "What's always with me. There were three beautiful angels on the roof just above the ugly demons." She pointed to her phone. "Saw them, not at first, but at about the same time I noticed the demons were starting to move more. One actually left...disappeared."

"Angels... Mom...really." It wasn't a question, but a statement of amazement. "I guess I know you're okay with this... now. You know Jesus is here... and His angels are all around you. You're so strong."

"I don't know, maybe not so strong...but I worry about your brother."

"That's what really has you upset?"

"I pray for him all the time."

"I know you do, so do we." She took hold of her mother's hand again.

"When I saw evil," she pointed to the phone, "I thought of him, I hoped, prayed that he's not involved in something like that."

"He's okay Mom."

"I sometimes have a feeling, like the Holy Spirit reminding me to pray for him, to pray he is protected. Will you pray for his protection? That your brother is not touched by Satan or his evil demons?"

"Why don't we do that right now Mom?"

"Oh thank you."

Chapter 51

The tiny bell over the door tinkled. She heard it from the room behind the drape that functioned as a wall and a door. When she stepped out to greet the customer she found a woman obviously new to the business. She was confident she had not been there before. "Hello, you're new...!"

"Hi, yes I am."

"Nice to see you, how can I be of service?" She quickly began to size up the stranger. She wanted to get a feel about who exactly was looking for her services. If she could get a read, a feel, an idea about a personality type, it would help in what services she would push. What she would sell. Might sell.

"I'm not sure...really...I..." She was looking around. She looked to the proprietor. She took longer than was comfortable. What she saw was a middle-aged woman dressed in a light dress of pastel colors covered with a heavy robe type covering. It was ornate, embroidered, a set of jewels for buttons that ran the full length of the garb. It gave the impression of something royalty might wear. There were no royals in this town.

"I want...I'm not sure...this is new."

"That's fine dear, take your time. Be comfortable." She smiled a friendly smile. Her instinct was to treat the new customer, young girl, lady, as though she were her aunt, or perhaps an older sister. She gauged her age to be early twenties. As she did her work to size up this potential client she was suddenly struck with the likeness there was to the girl Detective Joyce was investigating. The young woman who found an attraction to evil.

"What do you do here?" She waved a hand lightly. After several moments she continued. "I am looking....I would like to find a friend."

"Can you tell me more?"

"I lost a friend." She paused, looked around. Not at anything particular, but rather as a way of thinking.

A silent alarm went off. "Have you ever had a reading?" She needed to get her head around just what was happening. Who this lady was.

"A reading...? I'm...no, I don't think I have. What is a reading?"

"There are a couple of things we can do....Do you engage with your horoscope?"

She was gazing at nothing but finally answered. "Like my sign?"

"Yes."

"No, that's nothing I've found interesting. I don't see how a few words in the paper every day makes a difference."

She motioned her new customer towards the table. "Have a seat, we can talk...I would love to hear more about who it is you're looking for."

The two sat at the old wooden table. It was as much a prop as a workspace. The idea of things being old lends a sort of credibility when dealing in the realm of things not real. At least that was the theory.

"I lost a friend recently."

"If I may, are you telling me your friend passed away?"

She began to wring her hands. Rubbing, massaging her fingertips. She glanced down and focused on her nails. She liked them. She had gotten her money's worth. The nail salon was a place she would use again.

"Yes, she died." She looked again at her fingers. "I miss her...and..how does a person reach out to a friend who has…"

"Died?"

"Yes...do you do that?"

She considered it for a moment. She thought for just a fleeting moment about the big detective's case. "Well, yes...but I may not work in the area you have in mind."

"What do I have in mind?" It was a sharp, unexpected response.

She thought there was a change, ever so slightly, in the voice. It was like someone else was talking. "I don't know, but I was thinking you may want to reach out to the dead." She paused, then, "Am I right?"

"We had some mutual friends." Her voice was now the same as when she arrived. "I have the feeling that those friends may...might be able to help me...Maybe you could help find them?"

"Mutual friends of yours and your late friend?"

"Yeah."

"Do you know where they might be?"

"Almost anywhere..I think." She waved her hands over her head in a circular motion.

The fortune teller was beginning to sense she would need to tread lightly. If this was in fact a friend of Detective Joyce's victim...part of his case...there's no telling where it might lead. She wondered if she was safe. "How much do you know about this...these friends?"

She stood up without a word and began to slowly wander around the small store. She paused momentarily near just about everything that was displayed. Most of the items were props. Like the table. Designed to give the impression of something exotic, supernatural. She paused a long time by a waist-high, wrought iron ashtray pedestal. The incense was burning. Small cone-shaped things that smoldered and burned, slowly, giving off an aroma created to heighten the senses.

"Excuse me a moment."

"Sure," said the new client.

She made her way to the room behind the curtain. Only a moment or two and she was back in the front room. The store, or salon, or reception area. It was hard to find a name for the area where such work is conducted. The new client had hardly moved. "Come sit here and tell me everything."

The two settled back into their chairs. The new client resumed massaging her fingers and inspecting her nails. This time she was not thinking of the nails. She considered who..what she was looking for. "I think the...friends I want to contact are not really friends. They are acquaintances."

She was getting the idea. It was time to take a chance. "Are they human?"

The question took the young woman by surprise. Her initial thought was to answer but changed her mind. "Why would you ask that?"

"Things lately...I know some things. There's been activity that is...how do we say it? Not of this world."

"Like what?" She was interested. Too interested.

"Like.. what you're looking for. Your friends...acquaintances."

She slumped a little in her chair, pushed her head back, and looked at the ceiling. She noticed an ornate pattern of some kind. "I thought they would be here...with you."

"Me?" It sounded like a question but it was not.

"I heard they had a friend here."

"Who…" She was anxious.

"You...that's what I heard."

The fortune-teller stood. She was anxious, mad, scared. "I don't know those...I don't know any of them. I've never seen them. I don't talk to them."

"You call them out all the time."

"I what?"

146

"Every chance you get." She stood and faced the fortune tell-er. "Who do you think you were talking to? Why would you do it if you didn't want them here?"

She stared at her. She was taller than the girl. "Here?" She pointed to the floor. "You think I want them here?"

The girl grinned. It was more than that. There was a sort of sinister look. "Well, you got them whether you know it or not."

It was getting clear. She was one of them. "You're one. Right? Who else is here?"

"She's mine." The voice was new. It came from the girl but the tone, the sound, was different. It was hard to tell. It could have been male.

This was never part of the plan. Her business was to help, entertain. Give people something to be excited about. It was simply a business. A living. It is better than working at the bath shop. "I never..." As she said it she slipped her hand into the large pocket of the red rope.

"She's mine...and so are you." The voice no longer disguised itself as the girl just stopping by. It was a low, vibrating, rasping, ugly sounding evil.

As quickly as the words were spoken, the girl changed. In a matter of seconds, her countenance transformed from a perky co-ed to a ghoulish figure that has no name.

Fear is one thing, terror is worse. The fortune-teller felt the sensation of moving from one to the other. As terror took hold, her hand came from the deep pocket of her robe. She pointed the small revolver at the girl turned evil and pulled the trigger, twice.

Chapter 52

Tommy Joyce rarely gets involved in voice traffic that comes across the police radio. That is to say, he generally does not listen. If he hears his call sign, he'll answer but that is rare. Most of his communications are via cell phone.

Today he heard a radio call. Cars were being dispatched to an address he recognized. He thought he knew what it was, but he needed to confirm. He pulled a notebook from his coat pocket and paged through several pages of notes. There it was. The address was the same. He considered his action for only a moment.

The report of this shooting was significant. Joyce was fully engaged in what may be happening. He headed to the scene. He had not been dispatched. He had not advised dispatch that he was in route. While driving with a purpose, he was not responding as an emergency vehicle. The car was equipped with a siren as well as hidden emergency lights, but Joyce was not using them.

When he arrived the scene appeared hectic. In most crimes that require a homicide detective, the scene is secure by the time the detectives arrive. That wasn't the case when Joyce pulled his car to the curb a few hundred feet from the entrance to the small shop located just below street level.

An ambulance, fire truck, two black and white police SUV cruisers were in front of the address. There was activity, but it appeared that the initial emergency was waning. The ambulance paramedics showed no urgency. His gut instinct was that the shooting victim had not survived.

"Tommy, to what do I owe the pleasure?"

"Hey boss, I'll make this quick. I'm at the fortune-teller's. There's been a shooting. I'm going in. If it's what I think...well...you know."

"Got it...call if you need help."

Joyce punched the red end button of his iPhone, made a note, and slid out of the car. Moving to the trunk, he collected a clipboard, a brown box of crime scene booties, and a box of blue rubber gloves.

He would not be expected. His quick response may give the uniform guys a reason to believe detectives, at least some, actually work.

148

"Joyce, homicide." He spoke the words to a patrolman standing at the top of the steps that led down to the business's door. His voice had authority but was also casual. "What do you know about the victim?"

"DOA, a female."

"Suspects?"

"One, inside." He pointed down the steps.

"Anyone else hurt?"

"No."

"This your call?"

"No, back-up. We were second to arrive."

"Okay, here's the register. Get everyone signed in. They need these if they go inside. You know the drill." Joyce nodded, handing the boots and gloves to the officer.

"Got it."

Joyce pulled a set of paper boots over his docksider style loafers and descended the steps. He gloved up on the way down. Another patrolman stood just inside the door.

Joyce stopped. "Be sure everyone signs in." He pointed up the steps. He handed an extra set of boots to the patrolman. "He's got a box of these." Again gesturing up to the sidewalk.

Joyce looked over the business that had recently become all too familiar. The victim was obvious. She lay uncovered near the round wooden table that he sat at when visiting. She was actually between the chair the lieutenant used and a tall iron ashtray. The victim, the body, was not the fortune teller.

"Detective." The familiar voice came from the back. What was once a curtain, a heavy, embroidered drapery was pulled open. The curtain was held there by a piece of furniture. She attempted to move toward Joyce but a policeman held up a hand to stop her.

"What happened?" Joyce said it as he took the half dozen or so steps to reach the fortune teller. A middle-aged uniformed officer was standing with her.

Before the officer could answer she blurted, "I had to, it was horrible."

Joyce held up a hand telling her to stop, don't say anything. He looked at the officer. "What happened?"

"She shot her." He held up an evidence bag that contained a small revolver. There was a second bag with bullets. "Twice actually, she admitted it as soon as we walked in."

Joyce asked, "Who called it in?"

The officer pointed. "She did, that's what she told us. I haven't confirmed it with 9-1-1 yet, but she said she called."

"I did, I called." She wasn't shouting but she made it clear that she wanted to be heard.

"You read her her rights?" asked Joyce.

"Actually, no. But I haven't asked any questions."

Joyce turned to her and said, "You know you have the right to remain silent, right?"
She nodded.

"You know that if you say anything to me, us...it can be used against you in court, right?"
Again she nodded.

"You know you have the right to have a lawyer?"

"I know."

"You know you have the right to have your lawyer with you when we ask you questions. Right?"
She nodded.

"You are going to come with me...and I'm going to ask you a lot of questions."

"Are you going to arrest me?"

Joyce looked at the officer. "Have you placed her under arrest?"

"Not yet."

"No you're not under arrest...but this," he waved a big arm around the room, "could end with you going to jail."

"I had to shoot her. She would have killed me, I'm sure of it."

"Are you waiving your right to have a lawyer here?" Joyce was official in his tone, but he wanted to come off as gentle. He used what police sometimes called a soft touch.

She nodded that she was.

Joyce looked around. It was the first time he got a look at what was behind the curtain. It looked like a small apartment. He saw an overstuffed chair.

"Have her wait in that chair," he was talking to the officer. "Stay with her."

Joyce turned his attention back into the main room. The crime scene. He resisted going to the body. He turned back to her.

"I need to get a look at what happened." He gestured to where the body was still lying. "I'm going to find someone to get you out of here...take you to my office. The lieutenant is there, you remember him, don't you?"

She nodded. "Thank you."

Chapter 53

Once the shooter had been removed from the building Joyce went to work on the crime scene. The medical examiner had not arrived. Crime scene technicians were now there and doing what they do. That included both video and still photography. When they were done, the case file would include a permanent record of how the scene looked moments after the shooting. Photos would include multiple images of the victim, from every possible angle, both before and after the arrival of the M.E. The body would not get moved without the medical examiner.

Moving the body would mean rolling or turning it to expose not only what was under the body, but how the opposite side looked. In this case, the victim was lying on her back when the police arrived. Wounds or other evidence relating to her back would be important in figuring out what actually happened.

Joyce squatted over the body. It was a position that he would not be able to keep for long. He blamed the discomfort on his ever-aging knees. "This doesn't look right." He was talking to anyone who would listen.

"What's that?" The comment was from a tech with a cumbersome camera hanging around her neck. Most don't realize that even in the digital age, commercial-grade cameras are large.

Joyce glanced her way. "Get a tight shot of this." He pointed to the relatively small hole in the victim's blouse and a circular bloodstain surrounding the hole. It was fairly obvious that it was an entrance wound.

"Sure...what are you thinking?"

"It's too small...the stain...there should be more blood." Joyce said it as he stood to get out of the way.

"How many times was she shot?"

"The shooter said she fired twice. A 38. Looked like an old-style Smith and Wesson five-shot."

The tech got the pictures Joyce wanted and stood up straight. "Any idea where the other round went?"

Joyce backed away from the body. He tried to imagine just where she might have been when the fortune teller fired. He knew that a torso shot like he was seeing would generally knock the victim backward, or away from the direction of the shooter. He was trying to picture the victim and the shooter facing each other.

Joyce had known of a number of body shots like this one where the victim actually did not go down. At least not right away. It would not be uncommon for the victim to double over, perhaps turn one way or the other as they tried to manage the pain of a gunshot.

In several cases, the victim did not die from a single shot. Usually, if it were fatal, the bullet had penetrated the heart or an artery that caused the victim to bleed out fast. A matter of minutes. Certainly quicker than medical help could arrive.

The body Joyce was seeing, with such a small amount of blood was confusing. In a fatal shoot that causes the victim to bleed out, blood should be everywhere. If all, or at least most of the bleeding was internal, there should still be more bleeding at the entry wound area. Joyce would continue to wonder until the M.E. arrived.

Once they would be able to roll the body, they would know if there was dramatic internal bleeding. The pooling of blood due to gravity would show what the medical examiner would call lividity. There would be large bruise type marks on the skin. Actually, under the skin.

"Okay people, we need to be very careful. Watch every step you take. We have a missing bullet. The gun was fired twice but the victim was only hit once. We need to find that bullet." Joyce scanned the room. "We don't know where the shooter was in relation to the vic...at least not precisely. Let's start looking over here." He pointed with his left hand that held his notebook. "It could be in anything. The gun used is a 38 so you can guess how small the hole is going to be."

"At least it wasn't a 22." The comment came from a tech.

"Yeah, too bad...but a 22 may not have killed this girl." Now it was photo tech talking.

Joyce ignored the chatter. It was simply cops doing cop work. The people were good at what they did. He was more anxious to see the backside of his victim. Waiting for the M.E. required patience. Not always a strong suit for the police. Police work is very often spending long periods of time in an almost sedentary state. Then, at seemingly light speed, everything changes. It's all action, breakneck action. Life or death decisions being made in nanoseconds.

When they were finally able to roll the victim, Joyce was not sure if he was disappointed or relieved. The back of the victim revealed no new information. There were no exit wounds, no sign that the bullet had passed through the body and exited out the back. It did prove what most already believed. That the wound in the front was in fact the entry wound.

When Joyce left the scene, the second bullet had not been located. That was not unusual. Sometimes they go over the same area several times before they would find what they were looking for. The crime scene people would figure it out. He needed to get back to the office and talk to his shooter. He didn't know where the case was headed, only that it was one more item on an already full plate.

Chapter 54

Patrol had transported the shooter to the homicide office. Joyce explained to her that he had a lot to do and they would talk when he was done. In the meantime, she should wait for him at his office. He assured her she was not under arrest, but that could change based on what he learned.

Joyce called his boss and briefed him on what was happening. He asked that when their suspect arrived, that they obtain consent to collect a blood sample. He wanted to be certain she was not under the influence of some type of substance. Even if it was legal medication. A confession today does not preclude a rigorous defense tomorrow. Second, he wanted her hands swabbed for gunshot residue. Lastly, he wanted to collect the long red robe she was still wearing when she left the scene. He was disappointed with himself that he had allowed her to leave with the coat. He felt there was likely little evidentiary value, but he wanted it. He wanted to inspect the pocket. He wanted to know if there was any evidence that a gun may have been in the pocket a lot. Like all the time. Did she carry a gun when working?

She was waiting in the interview room. A small space painted an off white. The paint was not new. The walls included small places of graffiti courtesy of suspects left unattended. There were scuffs on the wall, and if a crime tech were looking for trace evidence, there would be other substances. The room furnishing included a Formica topped table and three plastic chairs. The important feature however was the closed-circuit television camera stuck not so inconspicuously in an upper corner of the room. Its function was to record everything that happened in the room including audio. The added benefit was the ability for others not in the room to monitor the interview. Extra eyes for added perspective.

"You okay?" Joyce sounded like he cared how she was doing.

Killing a human being is generally a traumatic event. Even when done in self-defense. The shooter is often traumatized. Joyce needed to know that she was able to sit and discuss what happened. If she was she mentally and physically able to talk about it.

"I'm okay...but even if I wasn't, it's important that you know the truth."

"I need to know if you think you're okay..healthy. That you're not injured, even emotionally." Joyce wanted to sound sincere. He actually felt bad that she was in the middle of a horrible case, but, in the end, he had a job to do.

She sat erect. She fidgeted a bit with her hands, a sort of wringing motion. She was anxious. "I had to do it, detective. You know me, we've talked. I'm not a killer. You know that."

"No…" He didn't want to sound flippant. Sarcastic. "You are a killer. You killed a woman. You shot her." He hoped he sounded compassionate.

"You think I murdered her?"

"I said you killed her...you told me so."

She was shaking her head. It was so confusing. She had killed her. She shot two times. She certainly killed her.

"Why don't you just take your time and tell me exactly what happened?"

And she did. She began when the girl, lady, showed up at the business. She explained everything. She told Joyce all the details.

"Is that everything?" asked Joyce when she was done.

"Yes."

"You left out some details."

"Like what?"

"Where did the gun come from? Is that something you just happened to have just when you got scared, terrified?"

"I keep it in the back. There is a small bureau with two drawers. It's always in the top drawer. When she started acting strange, I went back, got it, put in the pocket of my imperial robe...the red one."

"Imperial?"

"It's something I wear, quite often really. It's part of the ritual."

"And you slipped your 38 in the pocket and shot a customer?"

"No...I told you. She was getting really weird. I had figured out that she was a friend of your murder victim who...you know."

"The creature...you saw it?"

"Not saw, saw...but I heard it...and she was changing."

"To what?" Joyce looked up at the CCTV camera. He knew his boss was watching.

She didn't answer right away. She didn't seem to be thinking. She was just looking. Not at anything, like in a trance. Then, "It's evil. I know it now. It's evil and I was a part of calling it."

"Not much of a living is it?" Joyce regretted the touch of sarcasm.

"You don't believe me...do you?"

He shook his head, made eye contact. "It's hard to know what to believe." His thought slipped away for a moment as he remembered the nightmare. The evil he saw come out of a darkness he didn't know existed.

Joyce sighed. "It's hard to know what's real and what's not."

156

"Do you remember when you were the most scared? Some time in your life that you were so scared you thought your heart would explode, or just burn up?" She turned her head up and looked at the ceiling, her eyes passed over the camera without any thought of why it was there.

A thought flashed through Joyce's thinking. Maybe she can read minds. "Is that how scared you were? The worst time of your life?"

She was thinking. "I can't explain it. The evil in her, and I mean in. That evil is something that can't be explained."

Chapter 55

"Morning pastor."

"Is it raining?" He had a surprised look on his face when he saw the deacon who had quietly slipped into the office.

The big man smiled. "No, I just felt the need to come by and pray with you all this morning." He hesitated for a moment then continued. "I can be a few minutes late...the world won't come to an end if I miss the first hour."

"Well...it's always nice to have you here...rain or shine." He grinned thinking his play on words was clever.

"Can I have a moment?"

The pastor recognized the tone. His deacon had something on his mind. "Sure...tell me."

The big man grabbed a black fabric office chair and rolled it over to the side of the pastor's desk. "I need to talk... share something."

The pastor sat down and nodded.

"I have been struggling with the death of our secretary... at the site. I had a....a huge weight...a sense of guilt. Like I did not do my part."

The pastor nodded, "How's that?"

"She was there all day. If I had been doing what...what we are all called to do, I would have reached out, I would have...at least tried to be a witness."

"So you prayed about it, didn't you?" The tone suggested the answer was obvious. He knew his deacon. He's a prayer warrior.

"I did, you know that...but."

The pastor waited a long moment. He would not need to prod.

"I made a confession...I asked God to forgive me if...and... now I realize that was a very big if, if I had missed it. I wondered, though... if I had forsaken the call that is on my heart to serve the Lord. To be what He has called me to be."

The pastor nodded. He knew the deacon saw him agree.

"You already know all this...don't you?"

"I think we all have times like that. I think that may be a good thing, right?" The pastor half-smiled.

He nodded. "You've been through it too?"

"Every Christian has. How are you doing now?"

"Good I think..but I am concerned...I don't want to say afraid. I know that we are not given the spirit of fear, but I think this stuff that's going on is bigger than we want...think. It needs all our attention."

The pastor already had a Bible open on his desk. He was turning pages like he was looking for something. He looked up and caught the big man's eye.

"He who dwells in the secret place of the Most High shall abide under the shadow of the Almighty. I will say of the Lord, *He is* my refuge and my fortress; My God, in Him I will trust." The pastor paused and lifted his eyes.

The deacon looked at his pastor. He wanted to talk but his thoughts were still forming. Recent events were very likely going to continue, to grow, become bigger, stronger. He sensed. He believed he heard something.

"I think I got a word."

The pastor wanted to hear, but didn't want to rush anything. He wanted to allow a man of God to express what he believed without any influence. A comment now may do exactly that. He simply nodded.

"I really poured my heart out on the guilt thing...and I am sure it was a good thing...God is merciful."

The pastor continued to listen.

"I sensed, after a long time, that God had sort of released me. It wasn't a physical thing, but I just sort of had a feeling that everything was good. It's that feeling of grace being poured out on me." He paused for a long moment. He now had his arms resting on his knees, bent over. He was looking at his boots. He lifted his eyes back to the pastor.

"This battle is real...I mean absolutely real. This is not an episode of the Zombies or anything similar. As I sensed God's grace release me from my guilt, I also sensed there was something I needed to learn...maybe to hear...like God was going to tell me something." He paused again. He was still looking at the pastor. His eyes were wet now. The idea that tears were close would have been correct.

He began again. "It was a voice. I believe it was a voice. But...I'm not sure. But...I don't think it makes any difference. I heard what God wanted me to hear. He was speaking to me....me." He pointed to himself. It was a natural motion. Like a form of animated speech.

"I've gone over this a hundred times...in my mind." He paused again. The story, the information, the event, it was hard to label the experience, but he wanted to be accurate.

"If it wasn't God talking, it was his agent. An angel maybe, I really don't know, but it was a word from the Lord."

When the deacon paused again the pastor nodded and waited. This was significant. God was working.

"He said, and this is verbatim. I have been over it like I said, a hundred times and it's always exactly the same. I can't forget anything. He won't let me. At least that's what I think. Anyway.

"He said, 'Stand ready, with truth as a belt tight around your waist, with righteousness as your breastplate, and as your shoes the readiness to announce the Good News of peace. At all times carry faith as a shield for with it you will be able to put out all the burning arrows shot by the Evil One. Accept salvation as a helmet, and the word of God as your sword which the Spirit gives you. Do all this in prayer, asking for God's help. Pray on every occasion, as the Spirit leads. For this reason, keep alert and never give up; pray always for all God's people. Pray also, that God will give you a message, so that you may speak boldly and make known the Gospel's secret. Thus says the Lord.'"

"You are a blessed man." The pastor was near tears when he said it.

The big man nodded. "It's that last part that makes me think it was an angel speaking. Either way, it was from the Lord."

"We have to redouble our prayer. I'm going to talk to the police again. The devil is doing his work here and we must be ready. Just as the Lord has told you." The pastor smiled. "Thank you...thank you for telling me."

Chapter 56

"You wanna go with me?" Joyce had stuck his head into the lieutenant's office.

"Lunch?"

Joyce looked at his watch and smiled. "Sure, when we're done."

"Where we going?"

"It's time to check out the apartment of the headless guy. Heading over to see what kind of evil is staying at his place." Joyce had stepped into the office.

The lieutenant opened a drawer, retrieved his 9mm and holster. "Ready?"

It was another apartment. Not the proverbial dump the porno victim had, but not as nice as the construction secretary. It certainly was not in a rundown trailer park.

The place was circa 1960. Solid, well-built brick construction. The building had one entrance in the front and a matching door in the back. A flight of stairs was inside each entrance. There were three floors of apartments. Without looking the detectives would know that the first floor numbers would start with 101. The pattern would be repeated on the other two levels. The second floor would begin with 201 and the third with 301.

The victim's apartment number, according to the DMV, was 307.

"Let's go up and have a look. Knock and see if anyone is home."

"Girlfriend maybe?" The lieutenant had a tone of sarcasm.

"Would be a nice change."

Apartment 307 was where they expected it to be. Joyce knocked. It was a police knock. If the resident had been in the shower, they would have heard it. No one answered. He knocked again just for luck.

"Hear that?" It was the lieutenant.

"What?"

"There's music in there." He pointed to apartment 306 just across the hall.

Joyce knocked on 306. A moment of waiting and the door opened. She was past middle age, red hair, glasses and dressed in a housecoat. The housecoat was a dress that mothers wore in the '50s and '60s when doing housework. Something that isn't so popular anymore. Joyce had the idea that she may have been an original tenant in the building.

"Morning ma'am, police." The lieutenant was polite. Maybe an attempt to be charming. He held out his badge.

"Good morning officers. What can I do for you?"

"Well ma'am, we were just looking for the party across the hall. He's not answering the door... and we wondered if you know the man?"

"Well...I've seen him..several times, but I wouldn't say I know him."

Joyce showed her the DMV photo. "Is this the man?"

She took a long moment looking at the photo. Longer than normal if she had seen him. "No...he doesn't look like that. Similar I suppose, but not like that."

"What does he look like, if this is similar?"

"Well... for one, he has a beard. A thick black beard."

Joyce looked to the lieutenant. "I guess that's one thing we wouldn't know."

"Does he live alone?" The lieutenant was asking.

"Oh...I wouldn't know that. I don't think he's married. I never got the feeling he was...you know...I never saw anyone like that."

Joyce asked, "How often do you talk?" He thumbed over his shoulder to indicate the apartment where the victim was supposed to live.

"Never...really. I've said hello a few times but I don't think we ever talked...you know...like neighbors do."

"You ever see him get in or out of a car?" The window at the end of the hallway allowed a view of the rear parking lot. Joyce pointed to it as he asked.

She looked down the hall where Joyce pointed. She shook her head. "No...no, I don't think so."

"Is there anything you can think of about your neighbor that sticks out in your mind?"

She appeared to be thinking. The men from homicide had the sense she wanted to help. She just didn't know much about her neighbor. Finally, "There may be one thing...I'm not sure what it was, garbage maybe. Something burning on the stove...I don't know."

When she stopped Joyce prodded. "What exactly are you saying? What got your attention?"

"Oh," she covered her nose and mouth, "a smell, something awful."

Both detectives nodded. The lieutenant asked. "Do you remember when that was, the smell?"

She leaned a little and looked past the men to the door across the hall. Apartment 307. After a moment she straightened up and answered. "Not exactly, it's been a few days I think."

"Did it happen more than once?"

She made eye contact with Joyce. "Just that time...I don't think it happened more…" Her tone seemed uncertain.

"If there is one thing about your neighbor," again Joyce gestured across the hall, "that stands out...how would you describe him?"

She appeared to be thinking. "I don't like to gossip...you know."

Joyce nodded, "I agree."

She continued, "He has a problem…"

"What kind of problem?"

"Hygiene I think describes it."

"Is that where the smell came from…?"

"No...that was different. That was an awful stinking smell. Worse than old garage."

"Was he unkept?"

She smiled, "I don't want to talk about people, you know...it's not...It's always a bad idea."

Joyce and the lieutenant exchanged a look. Then Joyce asked, "Can we step inside a moment?"

Her reaction was a matter of fact casual. "Sure." She moved to the side and allowed both men to step into her apartment. She followed, closing the door as she did.

The apartment was what the detectives might expect. It was neat, with no evidence of odors. No dog, no cat, no air freshener. The furniture was new decades ago but appeared clean and functional. A couple of pictures on the wall may have come from an art sale at the Holiday Inn. A spattering of family photos largely from a time long ago. The television was from an era between console and flat-screen.

Joyce gestured to the sofa for permission to sit.

She nodded, "Please."

Both men sat on the couch while she settled into a less comfortable chair across from them. The lieutenant moved a pillow to make room for himself.

"We have some information...It's not pleasant but in light of what you know, it's important that you know why we're here." Joyce nodded to see if she was listening.

She nodded back.

"This man," Joyce held up the DMV photo. "He is supposed to live in that apartment." Joyce pointed towards the door. "This man," still holding up the photo, "was killed in the park reserve. We are trying to track down anyone who may know him to help find the killer."

She had gasped, putting her hands over her mouth. She seemed genuinely shocked. After a few moments, "He was killed... like murdered?"

Both detectives nodded. Joyce said, "We need anything you can tell us about your neighbor. Even the smallest detail could be important."

The lieutenant edged forward on the sofa. He was smaller than Joyce. For him to get closer to the woman would be less threatening. But getting closer had the psychological effect of being friendly. Trustworthy. "Tell me about your neighbor. Did he have people coming and going?"

She shook her head. "Not really."

"So he did have people, what? Occasionally?"

She didn't answer right away. Then, "I don't snoop."

"Oh, I understand. But...there is a big difference between a...say... a busybody and a casual observance, don't you agree?"

She smiled, slightly. "I try to stay to myself."

Joyce joined in. "I admire that. You wouldn't believe some of the people we talk to. It's like they sit at the window all day hoping to see something they shouldn't...if you know what I mean."

"Oh, I do."

"So tell us, if you can, did your neighbor ever have parties, noisy music. Maybe other things like a ruckus, fighting. General commotion."

Again she appeared to be thinking about the lieutenant's question. "I can't say there was fighting. I heard bumps or banging noises a couple of times. There was music. Not my choice, but sometimes it got loud."

"What kind of music?"

"The kind that kids listen to these days. Not real music, like a melody...more like noise. A lot of bass. Pounding sounds."

"Have you ever heard of rap?"

"Yes, like that."

Joyce went back to visitors. "What type of people would visit? The ones you happen to notice?"

"I shouldn't talk about people. I don't know them and it's not right."

The lieutenant leaned a little closer. "I wish more people felt like that." He paused. "We're trying to find a killer though, and everything is important. I know you understand."

"You think it's okay?" It was her turn to pause. She turned to gaze out the window. There was nothing to see unless she had been standing.

"It is."

She fidgeted with her hands. "Am I going to be safe? I don't want to cause trouble...so they come here."

"Our job is to make sure that doesn't happen."

"How will you know if they come here?"

"We won't let them know we talked to you. It's our secret." The lieutenant sort of waved a hand to her, Joyce, and then himself.

She focused on the lieutenant. He was closest. There was worry on her face. "Have you ever seen something that just didn't seem right? Like mean or mad?"

"Like evil." Joyce's voice was low, not a whisper but hushed, quiet.

She fidgeted in the chair. "I don't want to think about it."

Chapter 57

"Do you think we need to get in the apartment?" Joyce wanted a decision from his lieutenant. The two were sitting in the car still parked at the curb in front of the apartment building.

"I was just thinking, we still don't know if the guy in the apartment is our... your victim. She couldn't ID the photo." He shrugged. "What if somebody else lives there?"

"I know...so, do we let it go, for now, go see the manager, what's your thinking?" Joyce sat behind the wheel hoping something or someone would just take over. Get him out of the entire case. "Did you get the impression she was talking about evil like what we're dealing with?"

"I think she didn't want to talk about it...like something has scared her."

Joyce gazed around at nothing. "I don't think it matters much. If the evil we've seen is in that apartment, I'm ready to leave it alone. At least for now." He looked back up to the third floor of the apartment building. "Think she's safe?"

The lieutenant punched a number into his phone. It rang three times before he heard an answer. "Pastor, hate to bother you, I'm with Joyce and we need some advice."

"How can I help?"

"We think we have another apartment with...well...you know, evil living in it. It belongs to the guy that was beheaded."

"What do you need?"

"There is a lady across the hall. She's pretty tight-lipped, but we think she's seen some things she would have been better off not seeing. We're wondering if she's safe."

"I've heard of this coming...a new warning."

"It's bad isn't it?"

"Had a guy come by. He heard from the Lord...This is probably going to get a lot worse before it's over."

"Pastor, I'm not a warrior like you. I'm a Christian, but this stuff is way over my head."

"Pray lieutenant. Pray. I'll tell the church there is a special need, we'll do it. But you need to be strong."

The lieutenant ended the call and turned to Joyce. "We're good here for now."

Joyce started the car and slipped the lever into drive. "She's okay?"

"Pray that she is, that's the best we can do right now." He looked over to the big man. "But I believe that's enough."

"I'm not convinced...You don't think so either...right?"

The lieutenant shook his head. "I'm going to trust God. I'm all in with the pastor and his team."

"You sure?"

"I don't know how this works, but I'm going to trust it. I have to."

Joyce slipped the gear shift back to park. He was looking straight ahead. He was quiet for a long moment. His head was spinning, wondering how to deal with all of it. At his age, his experience, this should not be difficult. It was. "I had a dream."

"Tell me." The lieutenant tried hard not to show alarm, excitement, or anxiety. He wasn't sure if he was successful.

Joyce stared ahead. He did not trust his emotions to look over to his boss. He took his time. "I don't dream. Hardly ever. Used to. Years ago, when I was a patrolman, I would dream about stuff on the street. But this one really got me." He paused again. His boss gave him time. Then, "I actually woke up scared. I was confused, sweaty and really scared of what was happening." Joyce turned to the lieutenant. "This, all this," he waved a big hand. "It's true... It's real. The evil is here and we're in the middle of it." There was little doubt about the sincerity of what he was saying. He believed it. All of it. And he had dead bodies stacking up everywhere to prove it.

The lieutenant sat for several moments waiting to see if Joyce had more. More to say about his dream. More to say about the case. More to say about the danger. Nothing came. "Let's drive."

Joyce didn't say anything. He slipped the gear shift to drive, and this time, pulled away from the curb. Once moving, the changing scenery allowed the brain to focus on things other than the evil that had captured the attention of both men. Just a few seconds of thinking about anything not a part of the case was welcome.

"You want to stop and see the pastor?"

"What will it help?"

"Might help you. Maybe get another perspective on the attack you're seeing."

"Attack?" Joyce glanced over. "Attack…" He stopped talking.

"I'm just thinking. You know how real all this is. It's not just a bad dream like the one you had. Maybe you...maybe it will help if someone...an authority on this sort of thing will explain it."

Joyce continued to drive. He was thinking. He was trying to put the fear, the uncertainty behind him, and think about the case. There was a solution. He just needed to figure it out. It was his job. He's a detective. He solves things. Puzzles. Murders.

"You ever hear the phrase, a fish stinks from the head?" Joyce glanced over to the lieutenant as he spoke.

"Yeah. Sure...guess it means that if you find the head, you can bury the stink...It's a metaphor."

"There is a head out there... to all this evil. A leader, a boss of some kind. If we find the head and cut it off, well...maybe I'll start sleeping better." He forced a smile.

The lieutenant rode in silence for a while. He too was thinking. He had been a detective...before being promoted, he considered himself to be the stature of Joyce. Good. Tenacious. Clear-headed. He was a homicide guy. "Where are we on the lions thing? Any real chance that's where this is coming from?"

"Maybe it's time we find out."

Chapter 58

When Joyce and the lieutenant returned to the office, Joyce had a message that the M.E. had called. No details, only that there was new information on the shooting victim involving the fortune teller.

In most cases like the fortune teller shooting, Joyce would have arrested and booked the shooter. Self-defense is a valid defense, but it is just as often, an excuse. Making the call is up to the detective. There could be an arrest or, they could be sent home with the instructions, 'Don't leave town'.

"Hey Doc, got a message you called."

"I did...finished the post on your shooting victim. I've got a COD."

Joyce sensed a tone that was not normal. But then, what was normal these days? He shook his head. "Guess I'm about to be surprised yet again."

"I don't know the how, like how this happened, or happens, but the gunshot was postmortem."

"Seriously, she was already dead?"

"You've already seen this detective. The heart was completely destroyed. Burned up, nothing but charred muscle."

"This is like the gift that keeps on giving." He shook his head in frustration.

"I've got your file whenever you want to stop by."

"That's fine Doc. I'm in no hurry. Who knows, maybe I'll wait until everybody in this city is killed by some kind of evil, and get them all at one time."

The M.E. picked up on Joyce's theory. "It's evil that's doing this?"

The case was not a tightly held secret. The number of people who knew that Satan, or an evil force of some type, was involved was growing daily. It was nearly certain that the story would soon break in the paper. Reporters always want the scoop. The ego-driven clicks on an exclusive are far too important to hold a story for the sake of public safety. And there was one reporter who knew all of it.

"Some are telling me that an evil force is hanging over the city. What you're seeing is their handiwork. Thanks Doc."

Joyce walked into the lieutenant's office and dropped hard into a chair. "Well, you can congratulate me." He chuckled.

"You solve something?"

"I made the right call with your gypsy."

"How many times do I have to tell you, she's not my gypsy?"

"Right...anyway, she didn't kill anybody."

"Who's the shooter?"

"Oh she's the shooter, but that's not the COD, the girl was already dead."

"She shot a corpse." The lieutenant shook his head. He didn't need to guess. Whatever the cause of death may have been, the dark cloud of evil that had descended on his city was to blame.

There was work to do. Joyce was acting like a detective. "She was telling the truth."

"How's that?" It was sarcastic.

"She really did see evil, boss. She was telling the truth. The girl she shot....she died just like the girl at the park."

The lieutenant was losing patience. He was frustrated with the idea that evil was taking up residence in his city, and he was determined to do something about it. He knew that the victim from the gypsy's place would also have an apartment, trailer, a home of some kind, someplace. There was certainly a very good chance that demons were there, just like they were everywhere else.

"Tell me what you need. We are going on offense. I know what the pastor said, but we're going to take back these homes, apartments... wherever we find the evil living."

"We need to find this lion's den fast." Joyce was animated. "She told us the truth about the girl being evil, the lion's den angle has to be good. We need to go with it."

"Lion's den...maybe you're right. This is a war, Tommy. We're in a battle. The fight is life and death."

"I'm all for fighting, but where do we find the troops? I don't think we can use SWAT knowing what it's like in those places."

"I hear you. We have to tap into the supernatural. The pastor will be our general in this war. He has a lot of warriors ready to fight."

Joyce wasn't there yet. He wanted to say what his head was screaming...but he knew he would be wrong. The dream with the all-too-real demon told him so. Put that together with the death and destruction that he had seen up close, he knew the enemy was not of this world. It must be destroyed. Joyce knew it was not going to happen without help.

"Okay Tommy, let's go to work. Job one is to take back the two apartments we know of. Next, we need to find the lion's den. You have the plat data and that will translate to an address, it should take no time. With that, we'll take it down as well."

"Gee boss, that was easy." The sarcasm was thick, but Joyce was ready and he knew what to do.

He ignored the detective. "I'll get the assessor's office to give you the file on the Lion property. We should be able to learn the layout. Power lines, gas lines, anything that might affect our plan. I think this takedown needs to be strategic." He paused. "If we get a response from evil like we saw at the porno guy's apartment, we need to be sure we're not creating a giant gas explosion...we can't wipe out the whole block."

"There's not a SWAT guy that'll get anywhere near the place." He paused. Then, "You realize this lion's den lead is based on almost nothing?"

"I know," said the lieutenant, "We need to work it though, right?"

"Yeah, we do...if we're wrong, finding the right place is going to be a problem."

"We'll figure it out."

Joyce was not sure how this would go down but figured the lieutenant had a few ideas. "How...what's the plan going to look like?"

"I have an idea or two. I think the pastor will have a really good take on how it might go down."

"Give me a hint."

"You're not a Bible guy Tommy, It's all in the Bible."

"The Bible tells how evil is destroyed?"

"I think it's better than that, but there's a context. Look, I am no scholar in anything religious. I'm a Christian. I believe in Jesus. I trust God. If God says that he's got my back. I believe it."

"Has God told you he has your back?"

"Yeah, I think so. He's told every believer that 'He will never leave them or forsake them'. I believe that." He picked up the file. "I'll get what we need on the lion's den. You may want to call the pastor. It's time we all got together."

Joyce went back to his desk. His first call went to the fortune-teller. "Hey, Detective Joyce…"

She didn't let him finish. "So am I going to prison?"

Joyce feigned a laugh. "I wouldn't be calling, I'd be there with handcuffs."

"So I'm okay? You believe me?"

"Yes, I believe you. But I need you to stay away from your store...business...at least for a while."

The line was quiet for a moment. "Where do I go?"

"Just take some time off. I'll be in touch. Okay?"

Another long moment, then, "Okay." There was confusion in her voice.

Chapter 59

Joyce and his boss had an on again off again conversation as they drove to the church. Moments of long silence followed by an intense conversation about the impending battle. Both were comfortable with the term. Both had seen the violence of the enemy. Both had seen the death and destruction. Both knew the possibilities. Both understood the incredible risk. Both wanted nothing to do with any of it. Both were ready to do their job.

The lieutenant, Tommy Joyce, the pastor, and a number of church members gathered in the sanctuary. It was the most logical choice for the meeting. It would accommodate everyone.

Joyce looked around. It was the same place he visited the day the jogger lost his head. The atmosphere now was completely different. No laughing, hugging, back-slapping, handshaking. The room was somber. The mood was quiet, sober, serious. The temperature of the room was closer to that of a funeral.

The pastor made the introductions that amounted to little more than polite nods of the head. Joyce recognized the big construction worker. He was a deacon. A church position whose duties were still unknown to Joyce. He only knew it wasn't a full-time job. There was eye contact but little else.

The small group took a seat in the pews. They were for the most part spread out. All were in the first two rows. The pastor remained standing. He was at ground level in front of the raised platform from where he usually gave his sermon.

"I think we all know why we're here. There is an evil in our city and the battle has fallen to the church. Not just our church, but to the Church of Christ." The pastor paused. "I think we should pray first, and then allow the police to explain the task at hand. We are not going to be here long...these men have work to do." He motioned with his hands instructing the group to stand.

A few moments later he prayed. "Oh Lord, how much wepraise you O God. Thank you for being here with us. We know   that you are our strength, our source of power. Especially in this very special time of trouble. Lord, we know that at such a time as this we must, and do trust, in Your goodness. In Your mercy. Gird us up in Your righteousness, O God. Fill us with Your presence that we have the strength to do this. To take on the evil that is going about seeking who they can devour.

"O God, take away our fear, pour out on us Your peace. A peace that surpasses all understanding. We place our lives, our safety in your hands Father. Protect us as we do the work you have called us to do.

"Give us wisdom to know just what to do. Show us where You wish us to be, what actions You want us to take. If we are to engage this evil O Lord, give us an understanding of just how we're to do it.

"Open our eyes, Lord, that we see clearly the work ahead. Open the eyes of our heart, Lord. That we see You in this need and that we trust You. Remove all distractions we may encounter.

"O Lord, this is a spiritual battle. The evil that has come against us is an enemy of Yours. Give angels charge over us...over our city. Protect us Lord, deliver us from evil. We thank You as we pray in Jesus' name. Amen."

The pastor motioned with his hand indicating those gathered should sit down. He waited a bit for all to have the time to reflect on the prayer. This was just the beginning. There was an urgency to take up the fight, but he also knew they needed to wait….wait upon the Lord. It would be the timing of God that would control their actions.

"Some of you here know first hand, have direct knowledge of the evil in this city. We're going to hear from the police now. They will give us a sense of what's happened and what is happening." His eyes scanned the handful of believers. While the building was not highly lit, it was by any standard well lit. When his eyes rested on Joyce he simply nodded.

Joyce was slow to rise. This was a setting completely foreign to him. He was not comfortable. This venue had him, in an odd way, feeling inadequate.

For years he has been routinely called to testify in court. It was common to spend hours, even days enduring questions. Explaining his actions, describing what he found, how he found it, where he found it, and how it proved his belief that the one on trial was guilty. It required the ability to explain what were often complicated fact patterns.

Joyce moved closer to the middle of the assembled group. He took up the position where the pastor stood for the opening prayer. It became immediately obvious to all that Joyce was the biggest man in the room. It meant more than that. His size, his presence had the effect of instilling a sort of confidence. The silent, subtle feeling of most was they had the right man on the job. None save the pastor and deacon knew anything about the homicide detective, but their collective sense was that God knew what He was doing.

Joyce was not so sure. He was the proverbial fish out of water. He had learned the truth of evil. He had seen it up close, and his belief had been confirmed in dreams that evil was just as real as gravity. For those before him, most of them, evil was only a form of intellectual understanding. They had not seen it.

"Let me thank all of you for being a part of this. Over the past days, I have, and the lieutenant..." he gestured to where his boss was seated, "...have had the need to call upon your pastor for protection from an evil....that frankly, I can not adequately describe." He paused and let his eyes scan the group. He used the moment to decide how far this meeting should go. How much did they need to know?

Joyce continued, "The protection we received was nothing less than life-saving. The demons we have encountered are no match for anyone, any human. At present, we are working six death cases. All of them are tied to the evil in our city. I am going to spare you the details of the killings except to say, each of the victims had the evil that killed them, living with them in their homes. We have called on your pastor for protection as we worked to clear the evil from the various apartments, and we know that without your support and prayers, we would likely be victims as well."

Joyce looked to the pastor. "We have identified two more apartments that must be entered. It is our belief that demons live in both. Our first task is to clean them out. My boss here," Joyce pointed, "called it 'casting out the devil' and that is what we must do. I am told..." He now pointed to the pastor, "that as we get further into this campaign, this battle... we will find the resistance multiplied." He stood for a long moment. A sense of emotion was creeping up into his throat. He took his time to get it under control. He was the authority here as far as law enforcement was concerned. His demeanor, his presence is important. Vital.

He continued, "I can not imagine it being worse. I have nothing to gauge what worse could possibly look like. Let me be clear. What you do here is new to me...I don't know how it works...but I know it does...I've..we've seen it. I want to thank you. I am told you are warriors. That's a very good thing. I hope this battle is successful. Based on past experience, I believe it will be." Joyce looked to his boss and nodded and returned to his seat.

When Joyce had finished, the lieutenant rose and took the floor. "What Detective Joyce has told you is all too real. You are only seeing what you must in order to do your work here." As he said it the lieutenant pointed to the floor. "I am grateful for what you're doing." He paused, he too scanned the group of believers who stood ready to wage war with the enemy. "I am one of you. I am a believer. I have been born again and I really try to walk the walk. I trust Christ for my salvation. At times it seems I don't trust Him with much else. I have learned, these past days, that I must. I must trust Him in all things, Amen?"

"Amen." It came from nearly everyone.

"If I were not in this fight with Detective Joyce, I would not have been a part of what you all so eagerly do. I would have, I'm sure, said 'not me Lord, send someone else'. But you have not done that. You are standing up, standing in the gap, claiming the city for Christ. I am so very proud to be a part of you. To be a Christian. Thank you."

The lieutenant stood before them for several long moments. He saw the small smiles cross their faces. He saw them nod.

"Some of you have experience in the things of the spirit. Some have been given the gift of being able to discern spirits. Not all spirits...maybe, but at least some. Others here I am certain, have gifts as well. Some will, I pray, hear a specific word from God about strategy, about how we need to do this."

He waved a hand to emphasize the vastness of what all this really was. "I pray that each of you will be bold, that you will speak what you sense is from God. The Lord uses each of us, but it's up to each of us to do as directed. We will test everything, but we must be bold." He nodded his head.

Joyce was listening to every word. He had no idea his long time friend had such knowledge of these things. Some of the comments were completely lost on Joyce and he knew it. Discerning spirits? He was lost. It didn't matter. The others knew, and that's the important thing.

"Unless we have a special word to change our plans, we will begin with an apartment belonging to a man killed by a demon. We..." He stopped. The lieutenant was about to describe the headless case. To tell it in all its gruesome detail. The details were not important. He started over.

"We are doing the apartment first because we need to protect what may be a witness. A sweet neighbor lady may have seen some of what goes on there. We need to protect her. Your prayers for this battle need to include those nearby."

He looked across the pews allowing the team to absorb what they were told. He continued. "We have identified what we believe is their headquarters. Their temple or church. It is a physical building. It will be our last target....but it will certainly be our biggest challenge...We will likely be back here before that final task." He paused. "We are not satisfied that our knowledge of the temple is complete...accurate. We pray the Lord will confirm our intelligence...or direct us to the real target."

The lieutenant needed to break for a moment. The whole case was spinning in his head. The idea that people with no contact with evil, people of innocence, needed the protection of prayer by complete strangers was nearly beyond belief. He wanted to sit down. He nodded to Joyce.

"When we complete the work at the first apartment, as the lieutenant described, we are going to move to another. The apartment occupied by our latest victim. Killed at the hands of evil. That gives us two jobs to occur over the next several hours." Joyce nodded to the pastor and returned to his seat.

The pastor resumed his place front and center. "The plan for today is to pray for our police. The two detectives specifically, and any others that may be with them when they approach the demons." He turned to the detectives. "I would like to form a prayer circle. We would like both of you in the middle. We will surround you and pray." He paused. He understood Joyce's standing position on things of the church. He silently prayed that the big man would make a decision to accept Christ. "It is a common practice, in times like this, that we lay hands on those we're praying for. Is that going to be okay with you gentlemen?"

The lieutenant knew Joyce would not know what that meant. He told him. "What they're saying is they would like to touch you as they pray. Maybe lay a hand on your shoulder." He nodded expecting Joyce to agree.

Joyce shrugged and stepped forward with his boss while the small group moved to surround them. When they did, the pastor began to pray. Joyce listened to the words and noticed that some were speaking softly at the same time. The group prayer was seen as everyone, or at least most were praying at the same time. Each member expressing what they wanted to say in prayer. For most, they wanted to pray what God was leading them to pray.

The prayer continued for what Joyce considered to be a very long time. He wondered, as they prayed, how anyone could find so much to say when they pray. He had heard people say grace at dinner and it was rarely more than five seconds.

He listened. There were moments when he sensed something unusual. A comforting feeling but he would never use those words. Finally, someone said amen. Joyce didn't know how long it lasted. He considered the pastor's first prayer to be long. He enjoyed hearing the words that seemed to be genuine. Filled with a faith foreign to him. As it was, the group prayer was about two minutes. Similar to the time the pastor used to open the meeting.

Tommy Joyce and the lieutenant took a few extra minutes to talk with the pastor before heading out to the first apartment. Included in the conversation was the construction worker whose secretary was a victim of evil. The conversation was more of a pep talk than anything.

As they moved towards the exit a woman approached. "Detective, could I have a minute of your time?"

Joyce stopped. His reaction was more than just being polite. He understood the effort of the prayer warriors. He had the time. He stopped and smiled. "Certainly."

As she came close she said, "I don't want to be...forward...but I sense you are not a Christian."

Joyce didn't see it coming. He made eye contact. He smiled. He had a fond sense for the kindness, caring, and help she freely offered him in defeating an evil force. "You are right...prior to this....madness, I had no idea what Christians believed."

She had a gentle look. "It's life and death detective. I want to encourage you, strongly encourage you to accept Jesus." She smiled and nodded.

"Thank you."

"A rising tide lifts all boats, so it is with the divine protection we are seeing in your cases. You need to know, detective, that should the enemy gain just one small victory, and people are killed, only decisions made beforehand will save you." Again she smiled. "I am praying for you. Godspeed."

Joyce thanked her again as she turned to leave .

Chapter 60

They sat outside the building. No one had a real sense of how the plan would work. It was easy to think that no one was home, but that was not going to happen.

The idea that a majestically huge creature would be waiting to avenge the evil in the building was a reassuring thought. It was unlikely that even if such a being would show up, none of the team would see it.

"I'm thinking of changing things a little." The lieutenant was talking to Joyce. Both men were in the police Dodge Charger. As was the custom, Joyce was the driver.

"Tell me." Joyce was looking over the three-story apartment building. He was wondering how best to deal with the lady across the hall from apartment 307.

"It should be just you and me." He saw Joyce turn to face him.

Joyce looked at the lieutenant but was not looking at him. He was looking into his own consciousness. He was, in a nanosecond of time, grasping what his boss was really saying.

"You may be right." His eyes went to the two police SUVs and a fire truck parked a couple of hundred feet away. He knew there was an ambulance nearby as well.

"We know our role is simple. To represent the law...not that evil cares about that, but someone needs to be there to at least make a record of what happens."

"We need to protect the lady in 306." said Joyce.

"Let's go. We'll get her out. When she's safe, we'll do what we do."

Joyce understood completely. "Let's take a uniform up with us to escort her out."

"Have you thought about evacuating the building?" The lieutenant knew that in the planning stage, the idea was discussed. In the end, it seemed best to handle it straight up. Just as they did with the girl who worked with the deacon.

At the last second, they had officers check on apartment 207. There was nobody home.

Evil is a spiritual force. It's not temporal. It moves without limitation. Walls, roofs, floors, none of them are obstacles. The lieutenant and Joyce would move in, shake the nest and see what comes out. With the covering of God, and His forces, they would prevail. A simple plan. What must be present for it to work, was faith that God would protect them. The intercessors were working. It was time to move.

Joyce gave him a quick look. Ignoring the question, he said, "Let's do this." He got out of the car and waved to a uniformed officer.

They knocked on 306. "Ma'am, remember us?" Joyce held up his badge.

"Yes." Her anxiety was obvious. "Are you here for them?" She pointed across the hall.

"They're in there now?" Joyce kept his voice low.

She nodded.

"Are you alone?"

She nodded again.

"Okay," Joyce pointed to the uniformed officer accompanying him and the lieutenant. "He's going to take you outside until we have this under control. You'll be safe."

She nodded again. As she came out of the door she forced a smile. "Thank you." She was glad to be leaving, but it was nothing to smile about.

Joyce watched out the window near the stairway until he saw them moving down the sidewalk towards a police SUV. "We're good."

The lieutenant took a deep breath and exhaled. He sucked the air in through his nose and let it out through his mouth. "Ready?"

Joyce nodded.

The lieutenant closed his eyes, turned both palms upward, and began to pray. "Father, give your angels charge over us. There is evil in our midst Lord, and we need Your protection to cast them out. Strengthen us that we are able to stand and do what is right in Your sight. Protect us, be our front and rear guard that this evil is harmless and ineffective against us...Lord, deliver us from evil...this is Your battle, we commend ourselves to you to do what must be done to defeat this evil. Amen."

Joyce was not sure about the next step. His police instinct was to bang on the door, announce who he was and wait. He looked at his boss. They held eye contact for a long moment. He nodded.

"Police, open up." The lieutenant banged hard on the door.

It was not for sure, but both detectives thought they heard a commotion on the other side. Joyce stepped up and banged. He announced who they were. He stepped back a foot or more, raised a very big foot, and slammed it into the wooden door. His plan was to have his foot strike the door as close to the knob as possible. He had done this before and his experience paid off. The door opened.

The detectives moved quickly to either side of the now open door. The action was a trained response. To immediately charge through the door was an invitation to be shot. Getting shot making a forced entry was an all too common occurrence.

As quickly as the door swung open, the now familiar smell of evil spilled into the hallway. It had an effect of slowing the next move. One that was also a part of their training.

It was sudden, powerful. A rush of wind. Not just any wind. Strong, but more than strong. Consuming in an odd sort of way. The power seemed to fill the men as it passed. Like a wind that could penetrate the body, pass through and continue. Not slowed, no sense that it had been impeded. It might compare to a wind hitting a wall, not slowing, and blowing through and over everything on the other side.

The noise was as penetrating as the wind itself. A roar, a powerful engine, like a jet roaring, taking off. Loud with a hint of whining. Thunder but without a concussion.

What followed was not expected. The crashing, the sound of fighting. There seemed to be sounds like steel crashing against steel. The screams seemed proof that great pain was being inflicted. Who, and how, was unknown. But the two policemen, standing, crouching just outside the door knew that whatever it was, they were no match.

What happened next was never considered. An exploding crash. Not like a bomb or explosive. An incredible crushing sound. The breaking glass was obvious, but the amount was alarming. It was not the sound of a breaking mirror or glass table. Breaking wood was included. With the breaking sounds came the shuddering. Vibrations. The building itself was shaking as if an actual earthquake was in progress. The fact that both men were crouching allowed them the ability to remain on their feet.

As quickly as it began it was over. The proof was in the silence. It was a hushed quiet. A form of peace had come over the building. The detectives took their time straightening and moving towards the open door. The smell, the stink of evil was gone, things appeared normal.

Joyce looked inside the apartment. "Holy..." He stifled himself.

The entire wall to the outside world was gone. What was once a typical wall of sheetrock and paint with a double set of wide windows was missing. Whatever, whoever had been in the apartment, went out through the now gaping hole.

Both detectives slowly made their way to the enormous hole and looked out. Uniformed police, firemen, and the lady from across the hall were all looking up. The amazement, the astonishment they showed was obvious, even from the third floor.

"Thank you Lord. Thank you for Your mighty presence. Be glorified in this amazing triumph over evil." The lieutenant was gazing out the hole when he said it. He turned to Joyce. "God is so awesome...isn't he?"

Joyce nodded, shook his head, showed a small smile, and reached for his phone. He had the pastor on speed dial. "Too bad you're not here. Thank you for everything. It's a mess, but everyone is safe."

Chapter 61

The mountain was majestic. Perhaps an overused cliche, but the point remained. It was special, beautifully special. The colors were many, all vibrant. From dozens of species of trees, to even more types of flowers, to snow caps, to lazy streams and winding rivers, lush meadows, everything was majestic. Perfect. Without blemish.

The valley adjacent to the mountain, in comparison, seemed lacking nearly everywhere. Beyond the twisted road descending to the floor, there was little that distinguished this valley from thousands, perhaps millions of others. There was little in the way of wildlife largely due to the limited vegetation. Rocks, crags, steep rocky faces descending hundreds of feet were a bland brown, the color of dirt. It was a place so ordinary that no one would give it a thought. It was there, but nothing more.

The people seemed ordinary. Not the blandness of the dirt-colored valley. But bland due to the vast contrast that there were so many, nothing stood out. Not those wearing threadbare clothing, or those dressed in priceless garments of every style. Workmen wearing the heavy, protective pants and shirts of labor, and city and urban center souls wearing styles and brands of their culture.

The number was beyond counting. Hordes of them flooded the road approaching the fork. At the fork, one path led to the mountain, the other to the valley.

The people, their sizes, colors, and ages covered all spectrums. Every conceivable race was in the swarm of humans. Tall and incredibly short people. Some were exceptionally heavy and labored on the path, others thin as rails without the physical strength to continue. Many were old, seniors for sure. Some were frail, seemingly unable to walk the road leading to the fork.

Many were very old, a century of life had been lived. Those of middle-age seemed prominent, along with large numbers of infant children. The road was full and the line of people was end-less, as far as the eye could see, and the horde kept coming.

When the people reached the fork the separation was shock-ing. None seemed to hesitate. The flow of people continued. It seemed they knew which fork to take. Each made their way as if the choice for them had already been made.

The largest number, far more than a majority, chose the twisted road leading to the barren valley. It was shocking. The mountain, with its beauty, would seem a natural magnet attract-ing nearly all. To forsake the wonders of the mountain for the less than ordinary presence of the valley seemed beyond all un-derstanding. But there it was.

The stream of humanity that chose the mountain showed two prominent traveler groups. First were the very young. Children and infants. The infants were the most young of all the people, and their numbers were huge. These, the youngest appeared as if they had no earthly experience at all.

Second was the wide variety of people from all races, cul-tures, and ages. A widely diverse group of people. Each howev-er could be seen to be happy. They were enjoying the process. The mountain seemed to welcome them to a place that was special. A place seemingly of promise, a place filled with joy.

The largest majority of people were those descending the path leading to the valley. They seemed a steady flow, like lava, moving slowly downhill but always moving. The valley floor was out of sight but certainly, there was a bottom. The idea of a darkness at the bottom, the light blotted out, seemed real.

That's where they were going. There was a large variety of people types. Every culture, every race, every age, people from every social station, and status. All were in the flood of humanity. There were moms and dads, grandparents, and young adults. Conspicuously absent however, from the mass, were the chil-dren.

There came a faint beeping. The sound, as it persisted, be-came louder until finally, it bought Tommy Joyce out of the deep sleep. He laid awake but did not want to move. The beeping continued. He slowly became aware of what happened. The realness of it however would not leave him. Unlike most dreams, this one would not vanish from his memory after being awake for only moments. Not this time. Joyce reached out and silenced the beep. He swung his feet off the bed and sat up.

What? The question would stay with him for a long time.

Chapter 62

The plan for today was to get out early and take down the final apartment. It would be their first visit. When she was shot, It was thought she was a victim. The apartment and its contents were not a part of the case. It would be left to family members to attend to the victim's property.

Only after the cause of death was learned did a visit become important. A security team had been dispatched to the apartment. Instructions were very specific: under no circumstance was anyone to approach or enter the apartment. The security team was instructed to tape off the area around the apartment. They then were stationed outside to watch. They did so from their police cruiser.

For Joyce and the team, there had been plenty of other things to attend to. They were finally ready to see what might be in the apartment. It seemed almost like an eviction process, not what police do, but knowing the dangers of what might be living inside, the job fell to Joyce and the lieutenant.

"You ready to do this again?" The lieutenant asked in a casual tone. Nothing was inferred.

"I was thinking about yesterday. Do you think we might have missed a step?"

"How's that?"

Joyce sat down. "I wonder if we should find a more permanent solution. What's to stop them from coming back once we leave?"

"I don't think anyone will be moving into that apartment."

"Right, but we're doing it again, I was thinking…. Should we be doing more...like holy water or something? Anything that keeps them out."

"Holy water?"

Joyce held his ground. "Yeah, look...I don't even know what that is... I've only seen it in movies. I just wonder how...or if we need to secure the property."

The lieutenant nodded. "Let's go out there...see what we have. If we have to call an audible...we will."

Joyce smiled. "Guess that's why you're the boss."

He had the pastor on speed dial. He hit one button and waited.

"Detective...can I guess that you're about to do it again?"

"We are...should we come by for another session?"

The pastor had a look of concern but Joyce obviously couldn't see it. "I think that call belongs to you. We're here and doing what we do. It's virtually nonstop…. If you want to come by, get 'prayed up' as some might say, you're certainly welcome."

"We might do that, we're getting ready to leave."

When off the phone, Joyce went over a Google map view of the apartment. He worked out distances to adjacent buildings, the closeness of what might be at risk as collateral damage. He had done it before, but a refresher was important.

Then he called the fire station that covered the address of the objective. He arranged to have a unit on location. Just in case.

While Joyce was setting up the fire department, the lieutenant made a call to the head of SWAT. He wanted them to be on location in the next operation. Their role was to watch. To be there. More eyes to see what happens. How it happens. To have a new, different perspective.

"We are not sure what if anything will happen. We want you there to see it. Good or bad."

"Who do you expect to be there?" The tactical sergeant knew his job. He knew how to follow orders. The question was expected. The answer had to be straight up, honest.

"This case is a first, for me and certainly for you." The lieutenant was frank yet polite. Almost quiet in his tone. "Do you have any understanding of evil?"

"Like human trafficking?"

"No...like evil, demons."

Had it not been the commander of the homicide unit doing the brief, the sergeant may have had a different response. "No."

The lieutenant showed him the pictures from the front of the porn shop. "These are real. No photoshop, no tricks. They have killed six...who knows...there could be more we don't know about."

The sergeant was shaking his head, disbelief filled his thinking. "This is real…" It wasn't a question.

"There's more. We have a witness, a very reliable witness who actually saw one of those," he pointed to a copy of the sketch image created with the help of the reporter. "He was holding the head of one of our victims."

"Holy…." the sergeant looked up from the photos. He shook his head. "Tell me what you want us to do."

"I have to ask, are you a Christian?"

There was a long moment of silence. Then the sergeant said, "Not what I should be, but yes. I believe in Jesus. I was baptized about ten years ago."

"You should know, we have a really good prayer team working with us. But the evil is real. And we are going to stop it. The city is at stake."

The lieutenant laid out a few more photos. Some were the crime scene at the porno shop, some were of the dead manager when he had the misfortune of going into a dead man's apartment, and some were from the latest raid that included a now missing apartment wall.

"Okay, you made your point lieutenant. We'll meet you at the scene."

"I think Joyce and I are stopping at the church on the way out there. They have a team of prayer warriors...You may want to pray too." He made eye contact. The look showed this was not a game. "When we get there, your special weapons, your tactics will be of no use against this enemy."

Chapter 63

Tommy Joyce and the lieutenant stopped at the church. When they entered the sanctuary, the scene was far from what they expected. The number of warriors was perhaps twice, maybe more, than what they saw on their previous visit.

There was no large group gathered in a circle. The pastor was not upfront leading the prayer.

Instead, they saw individuals, mostly alone, walking with no apparent destination. They walked all across the sanctuary, each praying. Some could be heard, others not so much. Some walked with their arms raised. There were others seated in the pew with heads bowed. Others sat with their heads up, looking to the heavens. Others had their hands raised, with much animation. No matter one's perspective, it was obvious that there was an abundance of intense prayer. Prayers for the protection of the city, the workers, and for the defeat of evil.

Joyce hoped to see one person in particular. "Give me a minute, I want to talk to someone."

The lieutenant looked at his watch. "We've got time." He knew that while they had work to do, a few extra minutes were not going to change anything.

Joyce had a very brief conversation with a woman during the previous prayer session. He hoped he would recognize her. She had been kind, offering insight into what would happen if he were to be killed.

He didn't have to look very hard. She found him. "Hello detective."

Joyce smiled. "Hi, I was hoping to see you."

"I understand all went well?"

"It did. It's because of what you're doing here." He motioned with his hand indicating the church.

"You're kind to say so detective, but it's God who's doing all the work. We are only asking."

Joyce wasn't sure what to say. He didn't want to sound silly. Uninformed. Ignorant. But he had questions. "Don't stop." His tone was serious.

"We won't, but...was there something you wanted?" There was a gentleness in her tone when she spoke.

"Yes...thanks...you mentioned a rising tide. Decisions are made that make the difference...something like that. Could you explain it to me?" He paused. He was uncomfortable. "It's important." He knew that for a detective, even little things are important.

"If I can be blunt...should you get killed today by this evil, what will happen to your soul?"

"My soul?"

"It's important that you understand that man is eternal. The body dies of course, but the spirit does not. If you're killed, will your soul...spirit...will it, you, go to Heaven or Hell?" There was a soft gentleness to her words.

Joyce looked up towards the ceiling. He exhaled. "I don't know." He looked at her. "I had a dream."

"Oh." She didn't say more. She waited.

It took a moment for Joyce to begin. "There was a mass of people on a road. At the fork, most took the path to a deep valley. The rest went to the mountain."

"Did you see yourself...in the dream?"

"No."

"What does this dream mean to you?"

Joyce again looked to the ceiling. "If people were making a choice of where to go, why would they go down to a valley when the mountain was so beautiful?"

She looked at him with a gentle smile. "You know what the two choices are, don't you?"

"Yeah. I think I do."

"Would you like to choose the mountain, detective?"

Joyce was nervous. Maybe a little scared. "How do I do that?"

"Trust Jesus. Trust Him for your salvation."

"How?"

She motioned to a pew. They both sat down. "In a few words... God wants perfection. To be with Him, that's Heaven...we must be perfect...without blemish. None of us, of course, meet that standard. So God offered His own Son to be a sacrifice."

"A sacrifice? Like on an altar thing?"

She smiled. "You could say it that way." Her gentleness continued. "The sacrifice is Jesus' death, the crucifixion, it took away the sin of all who believe and accept God's gift of salvation. Jesus died so we can live."

"The people going to the mountain have accepted salvation...the others have not?"

"Yes. They confessed their sin, repented in their hearts, and asked God to forgive them."

Joyce leaned forward. His arms rested on his knees. "I have seen enough. There is no doubt that evil is in this world. But I've learned...found that God...I really believe there is a God. He is bigger..." He couldn't find the words. "He is...real. If I'm going to die...I want to be where God is. Whatever it takes."

"It takes trusting in His Son...trusting Jesus. Jesus died to pay for your...my sins. Trusting in that sacrifice saves us from going to Hell."

He lifted his head to face her. "How do I do that?"

She reached over and rested her hand on his. "Pray with me. Father, this man wants to know you. He wants to trust in Your Son Jesus for his eternal salvation. He wants to be saved and become one of Yours." She looked at Joyce. "Do You trust Jesus as your Savior? Do you believe in your heart He is Lord?"

"Yes."

"Would you like to ask God to forgive you...? To wipe away your sin?"

"Yes." Joyce was emotional. He was afraid his voice might break. It didn't matter. He wanted this.

"Oh Lord, I want to thank you for my brother. Thank you for giving him your gift of salvation that comes from Your Son and our Savior Jesus. We praise You Lord, and thank You as we pray this in Jesus' name." She squeezed Joyce's hand.

"That's it?"

She was smiling as she nodded."Welcome to the family, detective."

"Am I a Christian?"

"You are indeed. Do your work, detective. As you do, know that you belong to Jesus. No matter what happens, you're his...forever."

Chapter 64

Joyce and the lieutenant were back in the car. The next stop was the apartment of the lady shot by the fortune teller.

"You find who you were looking for?" The lieutenant was sure he had. He saw him sitting in a pew. He was talking with a woman. It was easy to see they were praying.

Joyce looked to his right. His look was somewhere between a grin and a smile. "I'm a Christian." He made a firm nod. The inference was, that's for sure.

"Welcome."

"Thanks."

After a few moments in silence the lieutenant turned to Joyce. "Do you feel better about going after evil?"

"Do I feel better, like safer? I suppose, but the risks are just as big."

"Had any thoughts about our plan? Do we need to make any adjustments?"

Joyce was under no illusions. The lieutenant was a veteran detective. He was good enough to get promoted. Good enough to supervise the conduct of some of the city's most important cases. If changes needed to be made, the boss would say so. "We're good."

Overnight security reported no problems. No one had come or gone. Joyce accepted the report at face value. They were advised of the seriousness and danger of anyone going into the apartment. There were two officers. Joyce trusted that had naps been taken, at least one of the officers was always awake, watching. Joyce told them to stand by. They were not relieved.

Someplace in the back of his mind, Joyce considered if it would be a good idea for the two officers to see the value of their work. It was known that the assignment of watching a building could be considered demeaning. Below the status of a patrol officer.

The SWAT team was waiting when they arrived. The firetruck and ambulance were also on the scene.

It probably looked like a huddle. The homicide men called everyone to gather around. "This case is different than anything you've ever seen. If you have questions, ask them before we start. We're working six death cases. The killer or killers are evil.

194

Not just evil people, but demons." The lieutenant paused when Joyce approached a fireman.

Joyce saw the reaction of a firefighter. He took the few steps and held out a nice 5x7 glossy photo from the front of the porn shop. Then he showed a photo of the headless victim. "This is real."

He decided to show the pictures to anyone wanting to see them. They were part of the file shown to the SWAT sergeant earlier.

"If you believe in the power of prayer, I suggest you take a moment to pray. The evil that we believe is living in that apartment," Joyce pointed, "is deadly."

The apartment building was the nicest they had seen working this case. Upscale or luxury were words used in marketing. The style was a garden type. The unit, like the others, was ground level.

It included a wide patio door that gave access to the brick patio. No ordinary concrete for this high-end apartment. A brick patio with a matching planter surrounded two sides. It was designed to have flowers accenting the private space. The planter showed no sign of life. Not even weeds were growing.

The lieutenant continued. "We have no illusions of fighting this evil. We have learned that the fight belongs to God." He paused expecting a snicker or two. If there's a trait common to police, it's being cynical. "Our job is to ferret the demons out of the building. Once out they will likely flee. The warriors from the Lord will be here. Some of you will see them, others will only see what happens...last time, an entire wall of the building was destroyed. Gone. Only a pile of bricks on the lawn." He waved an arm for illustration.

"The fire department needs to be ready. Fire is possible. Maybe likely. You guys," he pointed to the SWAT team. "will go door to door and get the neighbors to safety."

The building was such that only four units were under the roof of the victim's building. That meant only three units would be evacuated.

"Once the building is cleared, SWAT will stand by just in case there are mere mortals in the building." It sounded silly but there was nothing silly about the tone. The seriousness of the lieutenant was clear. "For the most part, our weapons are useless against this enemy. Just the same, be ready." He pointed to the EMTs. "I hope we don't need you."

Chapter 65

Joyce was grateful that these operations were done in the daylight. All too often police work, the worst of it, happens in the dark of night. Evil is associated with the night. Evil does its work in the dark. The darkness of evil is far more than a metaphor.

It of course was not always the case. Evil killed a runner on a Sunday morning. But the theory seemed to be well-founded. The devil does his best work in the dark.

The lieutenant stood with Joyce. "This might be a good time to pray."

Joyce nodded, "I'm new to this, but I'm with you."

"Lord, again we come here needing Your presence. Your protection. Evil dwells in this apartment. Help us Lord, cast out the evil. We pray that You are our front and rear guard. That as we do the work, you have given angels charge over us, to protect us, to take up this fight and destroy the works of the devil. It is by Your most powerful hand that this enemy can be destroyed. We pray that it is Your will to cast out evil. Free this place of the darkness that consumes it. Protect Your people. Gird us up in Your truth and do this...In Jesus' name...Amen." When the lieutenant opened his eyes he nodded to Joyce.

They stood at the front door. It was the popular steel exterior door that is filled with foam for insulating purposes. Beyond a deadbolt lock, security was not considered. The plan was to act like the police. Knock on the door, announce their presence, and wait. If it went the way they prayed it would, evil would be angry.

They would stir up everything inside the apartment. Then the power of God would take over and evict the evil. There was no known police tactic outlined in a manual. This was 'do as you must, pray for the best'.

Joyce banged on the door with his closed hand. It may as well have been a hammer. The door frame shuttered. "Police, open up." His voice was a shout, loud, and filled with authority. Even those standing by the parked vehicles knew things were starting.

Nothing happened. The detectives heard no noise coming from inside. Joyce repeated the demand including three power-ful blows with the base of his fist. They waited.

"Should I kick it in?" He motioned to the door.

"Try the knob."

Joyce reached out, took hold of the chrome-colored knob, and turned. His eyes widened. He slid his body against the wall away from the door. The lieutenant watched with the same sur-prise Joyce showed when he realized the door wasn't locked. The two men exchanged a look. Police everywhere know it as acknowledging the next move. Joyce nodded. Then pushed.

The door swung open. The response was swift, violent, and frightening. Whatever, whoever it was inside, their strength was great. The door more than slammed shut. The violent force from inside sheered the door from its hinges, sending it several feet into the grassy area along the sidewalk leading to the parking lot.

Police tactics train on where to stand when knocking on doors of potentially dangerous people. The tactic paid off. Any-one struck by the flying door would have been hurt. A fatal injury was certainly possible.

The door was just the beginning. As it made its way across the front lawn, a terrorizing shriek came from the apartment. And then a second. Similar yet different. It was louder, more menac-ing. The sounds, the screams that were meant to terrorize were working. They were frightening. Especially for the two standing just outside the open door.

It wasn't intentional. Joyce had warned others that guns were no match for the evil they came for. He slumped a little, his back tight against the building. He pulled his .40 caliber Glock 22 and stood waiting for evil to make a move.

Nothing happened for several long moments. The lieutenant and Joyce exchanged looks. Then the lieutenant pulled his own pistol, nodded to Joyce, and moved.

Instinct says to move quickly, the element of surprise. Enter the room fast, get the drop on what, who, was there. The lieutenant didn't. He edged to the door, made a quick look, almost bobbing his head in then back out. He didn't see anything. He leaned his head against the exterior wall of the apartment. He tried to think of what he saw.

The apartment, while considered upscale, was actually like any other apartment once inside. He had seen what was a short hallway. There may have been a door to the right. Probably a coat closet. The place women might keep a vacuum cleaner. The hallway opened to the living area. The large glass patio door would be to the right. He thought he saw a counter with stools on the left several feet inside the apartment. The only thing he knew for sure, was the patio door was to the right. It had to be. He had seen it from the outside and knew where it was.

The two detectives again exchanged the look. The lieutenant looked up and whispered a prayer.

Joyce couldn't hear the words but when his boss lowered his head, he uttered, "Amen."

The lieutenant then made another move. Similar to the first. This time, after pulling his head back out of the open doorway, he slipped sideways past the threshold. He didn't raise his gun, but he was ready.

There was movement. Only a glimpse but he knew something was there. If air can be seen, just a glimpse, that would describe what he saw. Fear began to creep into the equation.

Fear is an interesting concept. A phenomenon that is almost alone on its own scale of human emotion. It can be a good thing, and it can be bad. When just the right amount is present, it can create a healthy respect for danger. It was that fear the lieutenant was feeling.

He had three decades of police experience. Over the years he could recall multiple times when being scared was just plain smart. Searching a business for a burglar certain to be hiding comes to mind. Before canine units, slowly moving through unfamiliar spaces in the dark was scary. Frightening. But the fear created an edge. A vigilance.

It moved again, not in the same place as before but he was certain it was there. "Help me Lord," he whispered the words. The volume didn't matter. It was only important that God heard.

Joyce had edged around the doorjamb and past the threshold. His eyes moved. He was not seeing the movement noticed by his boss. He didn't even know there may be movement.

Suddenly the lieutenant stood erect. "In the name of Jesus, I command you to leave. Jesus is Lord of this city and you are commanded, by the authority of His holy name, to leave." The command, it was a command, was loud, bold, filled with authority.

Joyce snapped his eyes towards where the lieutenant was looking. He hoped, he wanted to see what was happening. The lieutenant was pointing his gun at something. He had no idea what, and he knew even less about what prompted the command. He liked it though. He felt emboldened to hear the words.

"Praise God," Joyce said the words without realizing he had.

The rush of wind was unexpected. It came from behind. The force caused Joyce to brace himself. A smaller man may very well have been knocked over.

"In the mighty name of Jesus, I command you to leave." It was the lieutenant again. He was louder now. This last command came just after the wind blew in through the apartment door.

Suddenly it was there. They were there. Three in all. Joyce could not believe what he saw. In an instant however, he knew what it was. He had seen them.

Two were just as he had seen in the photo. Not exactly the same, but yet the same. Different clothes maybe. They were huge, ghoulishly ugly. They were in the living room only a few feet apart. One had a gigantic sword. Joyce thought it might be the one that took the head off his victim.

The third was from God. There was no question the giant was an angel sent to protect them. He was not a picture book image. He was a man. Huge. A comforting sort of big. Maybe ten feet tall. No wings. He appeared like what one might think a soldier of ancient times would be like. His sword was bigger than the demon's.

When the swords met, sparks could be seen flying from the steel blades. Being a spectator was not a position to be envied. The violence was beyond what anyone had seen. Certainly not in sports. Even the ancient games of Rome did not see the deadly intensity of the fight waged before the two detectives.

At first, it did not seem the fight would be fair. Two giants against one. But that thought was soon dispelled. The warrior from God was superior. The fight raged for only a few moments. It seemed longer but it wasn't. Finally, the demons knew they were beaten and retreated.

Maybe it's the nature of evil, but the demons would not just turn and run. They first made a statement. Nothing verbal, but a statement just the same. It is like a disgruntled party on the wrong side of right taking one last action out of spite. Like flipping a giant evil finger at all things good.

The two demons appeared to make their way to the closed patio door. Eight feet of glass leading to a brick patio and open space. They turned, and as they did they produced fire. From where or how, neither detective knew. But fire is fire and the results were quick.

What started as a handful of fireballs resulted in a brutally violent conflagration. The room was consumed. Not just a few flames and smoke, but a continuing eruption of fire. Each piece of furniture. Each decorator item, everything in the room individually and simultaneously burst into an intense, volcano type inferno.

The scene outside the building was beyond any belief. There was a silent agreement in the minds of the witnesses, that what they saw was not of this world.

It began when they heard Joyce pounding on the door. Then, in a rapid chain of events, they heard death-defying screams. The sound came from the apartment. It was not what either the lieutenant or Joyce would make. The assumption was, it came from the evil. An evil that was mad and ready to fight.

When ordinary people see or hear what is not ordinary, all manner of ideas come to mind. Such was the case for those outside. In the end, none of them would report the same story. None saw or heard everything the same.

Collectively, however, they heard the sounds of evil. Then they heard the sounds of a great fight. For some, the sounds were foreign. Unknown. For others, it was breaking of furniture and windows. Then would they say an explosion of sorts, but not an explosion like that of a bomb. Not a gas leak. But a force that blew out the large patio door and window.

Some saw what came next, but they saw it differently. Some did not see it at all. It was a force, a being perhaps, a burst of something. Smoke, a giant plume was one thought. Another saw something large. Not living, but something. It was big, and it seemed to give the impression of something bad. The word evil was used but they didn't see evil. They knew evil was in the apartment so it made sense to attach that description. But that's not what they saw. One said he felt it.

When the final explosion came, all feared for the two detectives. The likelihood of them surviving the horror show was nearly non-existent. If the two men were in the building when it went, they were surely going to be names on a wall someplace. Fallen in the line of duty. Only a miracle could have saved them.

The firemen were quick to act. None had expected it. None believed that a fire would consume a building as this one did. But they were there and they acted as expected. The building wasn't saved but it could have been worse. So much worse.

Joyce and the lieutenant were standing in the middle of the room when everything erupted. One deep breath and the lungs of the policemen would be consumed by the heat. Death was a certainty.

As quickly as the fire started, the angel of the Lord covered the men with his presence. There were no angel's wings this time. There was however divine protection. A force, a presence, an angel enveloped both of them. They were safe in the care of the angel, in the arms of their Lord.

The sudden attack was quenched by the warrior sent for that very purpose.

Chapter 66

"Hello detective," There was a sound of excitement in his voice.

"Hey, pastor, I only have a second but I wanted to report all is well here." Joyce's voice, his tone, sounded tired. Exhausted. "We can talk about it later but your team really came through. Thank you."

"Glad we were able to help, but all the praise goes to God. He is awesome, He will never leave us or forsake us...Oh, and welcome to the family. I can't tell you how happy I am."

A small smile formed on Joyce's face. "Thanks."

The clean up at the scene took time. The fire was the biggest task. Once the fire was out, firemen went through the apartment, just to be sure. There were no bodies.

Explaining to the assembled team what actually happened filled the time as the firemen did their work. Many of those who witnessed what had occurred were unable to fully understand the seriousness of the evil driven out by God. Not who they were, or that God would actually do it. In the end, Joyce invited everyone to the church on Sunday. The complete unabridged version would be told.

"Detective." One of the firefighters was shouting.

Joyce turned towards the shouts. He saw the man waving an arm, indicating he was needed near the patio.

"Found something." The fireman was wearing a white helmet.

"What?"

"You may not like it...the men found a head."

Joyce let the words sink in. He didn't need an explanation. "Have they touched it, moved it?"

The chief raised his radio and asked.

Joyce heard the response. It was graphic, but no one was about to touch it.

Joyce nodded, he understood. He pulled out his phone and called the medical examiner. It would likely be a wait, but they needed to do this right.

"You guys take pictures?" Joyce was talking to the chief.

"We're not on vacation."

Joyce shook his head. "Is it safe for me in there?" He pointed.

The chief looked first at Joyce's shoes. He then looked at the floor of the apartment. There was an inch or two of standing water just inside the patio door. Both men stood on the other side of the now missing glass sliding door.

"It's safe but you don't want to go in there. It's a mess."

"I need a photo of the thing." He looked inside, then to the chief. "It's my job."

The chief reached inside his heavy turnout gear and pulled out a cell phone. "I'll get you one."

"A couple...thanks." Joyce was pleading.

It didn't take long before the chief was back at the patio. "What's your number, I'll text them to you."

A few moments later, Joyce had his results. "It's him." Joyce was talking to the lieutenant. The chief had taken a total of five pictures and texted them to Joyce.

"Still had his beard." It was charred, but there was little doubt they had the missing head.

Finally, the lieutenant was convinced their work was done. The medical examiner had collected the head. The fire was out. The scene was secure. He joined Joyce in the Dodge Charger and they headed for the office.

"I think we need to make a detour." Joyce looked to his right.

"Okay," the response was casual.

Joyce drove in silence. The idea had suddenly popped into his mind. It was not a conscious thing. It was not something that had been lingering in his mind and only now was getting action. As he considered this move, he questioned why he had not thought of it earlier. Seemed like a natural act. Something a good detective would have done sooner.

When he wheeled the car to the curb the lieutenant realized what Joyce was doing. "You thinking what I think you're thinking?"

Joyce nodded. "Can't believe it took me so long."

The lieutenant silently agreed. He too had missed the obvious. "Think she's here?"

"Part of me says I hope so, another part says I hope not."

The two descended the steps. The space was crowded when the two of them stood shoulder to shoulder. The neon light was off.

Joyce turned the knob and pushed. Nothing. The deadbolt kept the door from opening. He placed his face close to the glass and looked in. What he could see looked normal. The lighting in the store was subdued when open. The few inside lights appeared to be off. The only light helping to see inside came from the small front windows. The only thing Joyce could be sure of, was the business appeared to be closed. He knocked just in case she was in the back.

"Ever been around back?"

Joyce shook his head. "I'm not even sure there is a back." The comment seemed odd. Certainly, there was a back to the building. What Joyce meant however, is he didn't know if the business had any access to the back. There could be space but not accessible to the fortune teller.

The lieutenant climbed the steps back to the sidewalk. He looked left and right. Neither he nor Joyce had ever paid attention to the adjoining businesses. The one to the left was a small antique shop. It gave every appearance that it was old. As if the business itself was antique. He took the few steps down to the front door. It was unlocked. The place was open.

Joyce watched. He was halfway up the steps from the fortune teller's door. He watched the boss go in. The inquiry did not need them both. The other adjacent business was a tattoo shop. The door was standing open. Joyce approached the steps leading down to the door when he heard the faint music. He knew it to be Alan Jackson. He guessed he would fit in.

"Hey there big guy." The voice belonged to a fiftyish man with two full sleeves of tattoos. Joyce guessed he was bald. He had a red and black Atlanta Braves baseball cap.

"You the boss?" Joyce spoke a little louder than what was needed. It was a personal strategy he used on occasion. Coupled with his size, it seemed to neutralize some people. You never know when somebody thinks they're smarter, bigger, tougher than they really are.

"I'm it."

Joyce looked around. The place was small. There were two stations for the artists to do their work. A mirror consumed much of one wall. Photo albums were scattered across a countertop just below the mirror. There were three chairs along the adjacent wall. With chrome legs, they looked like something that came from an old-style diner. One might easily get the opinion that the business could double as a barbershop.

"What do you know about the lady next door?" Joyce made a slight gesture towards the fortune-teller's.

"The gypsy?"

Joyce grinned. "Yeah."

"Think she's in jail."

"Really?"

"Yeah," He was sitting on a stool. It matched the chairs. He straightened up. "She shot a girl."

"Have you seen anyone coming or going?"

"No...it's pretty much like it is since the cops left."

Joyce considered the comment. It occurred to him that the door had no notices. All the yellow tape was gone. It seemed odd. It was his case. Had the scene been released, it would have been him to do it. It's standard procedure to paste a Do Not Enter notice on the door. It's an active crime scene. Who took it off? Who cleaned up the place? His mind continued. While things were dark inside the fortune teller's business, he should have noticed trash left behind. Every crime scene has it when the police leave.

"Is there access out back, to get in there?" Joyce pointed towards the fortune-teller's again.

"You mean, like a back door?"

"Yeah."

"Are you a cop or something?"

Joyce nodded. "Yeah...so what's back there? Is it parking? Your place obviously doesn't go all the way to the back. The building is bigger than this." He motioned around the space.

"Let me show you." It was clear that his only task at the moment was listening to Alan Jackson. He talked as they walked. "The building is over a hundred years old. I have no idea what all has been in my space. I know there are two stories above me that are apartments."

"Do you live up there?" Joyce pointed to the ceiling.

He opened a door. "I live right here." The space was small, but neat. Like a studio apartment. It included a bed against one wall. The kitchen was a small set of cupboards, a microwave, a refrigerator, and a sink. There was a door that Joyce guessed was the bathroom.

In the very back of the space was the exterior door. Joyce looked towards the front. He considered the building, from outside, seemed to be bigger, deeper. When the rear door was opened, it made sense. It was an old space, abandoned from its original use. There was a car parked in what was now a converted space. The tattooed man used it as a carport.

Joyce smiled, "I get it now. What was this space for...originally?"

"I'm not a historian, but I've been told this was the boiler and coal room. The apartments upstairs are still there." He pointed up. "Here, let me show you."

When they walked out of the parking space Joyce found they were standing in the alley. Looking at the back of the building he saw the windows on the second and third floors.

Joyce walked over to what should have been the back of the fortune teller's space. "Is hers like yours?" Joyce pointed to the back of the building.

"Never been in it, but I suppose it is."

The space was enclosed with a sliding door made of heavy wood slats. It was reminiscent of something found on a barn. It hung on an iron track and slid sideways. Joyce grabbed the large steel handle and pulled. The door slid easier than he expected.

"Oh...no..." It was a low, moaning sort of sound. "Stay away." Joyce had turned to the tattoo guy. "You don't want to see this."

"You're really a cop." There was surprise in his voice.

"Where are you?" Joyce had his phone to his ear.

"I'm in the antique shop."

"Get the car and come around to the back door. I'm in the alley." The urgency in Joyce's voice could not be missed.

"What happened?"

"I found her." Joyce hit the red button on his phone and called another. As soon as he heard a voice he was talking. "We have another one. She's in her office...business...we're going to have to go in."

There was no response for an uncomfortably long moment. "Trust God...I'm here...there are others...we aren't stopping. You have Him with you detective. Pray and believe. You've seen it, you know it's true."

"Okay, I have to go, thanks."

When the lieutenant pulled up in the car Joyce was just getting off the phone. "I called for backup. I want the street blocked off just in case we have a replay of this morning."

Joyce turned to the tattoo guy who as yet, had no idea what was going on. "We need to evacuate the building. I need you to get in your car and leave, or walk up to the corner and wait. Either way, lock up your place and leave." Joyce was polite but firm. There was no room for discussion.

The patrol sergeant pulled up. The lieutenant gave the instructions. He wanted uniformed officers to evacuate the building. Get everybody out of the rentals above the three businesses. He was told the tattoo shop had been advised, but the lady in the antique shop had not.

"You think they're in there?" The lieutenant could hear the fire trucks in the distance as they made their way through traffic.

"Actually...." Joyce turned his head towards the open garage door. "I can't imagine them not being there." He turned back to his boss. "It was plain stupid to open that door." He gestured with his hand. "I should have known better...rookie mistake."

"Don't be so hard on yourself." The lieutenant softened his tone. "You have a covering Tommy. You're okay because God wants you that way."

"Why?"

"You have things to do. God has a plan."

"Guess we should pray."

"Yeah."

"You're the expert."

The lieutenant took a minute, maybe a little less, praying quietly. The idea that anyone other than Joyce would hear was unlikely. It didn't matter.

When he finished Joyce had a question. "This morning, you said...commanded the demons to leave in Jesus' name. What's that about?" Joyce's voice was low, subdued, searching.

"I learned...a few years ago that...where there are devils, a believer can cast them out in the name of Jesus. I think it's from the book of Mark."

"Mark?"

"Mark is a book in the New Testament. It is one of the four gospels. Matthew, Mark, Luke, and John. You've heard of them...right?"

"Does everybody know this stuff but me?"

"You're fine. You'll learn about the Bible, the Word of God."

"So tell me about casting out demons."

He looked at Joyce. There was eye contact. "I don't know Tommy, I've heard about it...This is new to me too...I just had the urge to say it. I don't know where it came from. I wasn't thinking about it."

"Do you think it helped?"

He shook his head. "It didn't hurt...that's what's important." He paused. He saw the patrol sergeant headed their way. "Most people will think we're crazy just talking about evil...demons." He pointed to the partially open garage door. "Can you imagine what they think when we actually try to do something about it?"

Chapter 67

This was new for her. She was out of her comfort zone but she needed...she wanted help. She had no idea where to turn, so here she was. As she stood in the front entry wondering where to go, a young man came through a set of double steel doors. He seemed in a hurry. The doors crashed as he pushed the bar and made his way into the entry. The noise from the doors was amplified by the vast amount of tile and marble. It startled her.

"Excuse me...can you help me?"

He stopped abruptly. He had not expected to see anyone as he made his way out. He was young. She judged him to be the same age as her son, but perhaps he was older. Thirty tops was her best guess. He was dressed like he worked there. Coat and tie, shined shoes.

"Oh, hi, how can I help?"

"Are you the minister?"

"Well, no...yes...I'm an assistant minister...are you looking for our minister?"

"I guess I am...I need..." She paused, she was afraid she would cry. Tears were forming, her voice was about to fail. "I need to talk about a funeral."

"Oh, I'm sorry." He sounded like he cared. His smile turned to a look expressing concern. "The minister is in his office, do you know him? Are you a member?"

"No."

He allowed a small frown to cross his face, then smiled. There was a moment of hesitation. "Come with me, I'll show you to the office."

She waited in what she considered an expensive chair in the reception area of the business office. She knew it was the business office because of a sign just outside the door. She squirmed. The idea crossed her mind that such an expensive item should be more comfortable. But she also knew she was nervous. The wait was longer than she hoped but she understood that she didn't have an appointment.

"Hello..I believe you're waiting for me." He was a nice looking man. Neat, wearing a grey suit coat and red striped club tie. Probably close to her own age.

"Yes, thank you for taking the time to see me."

"Let's step in here," He motioned with his arm to a door that likely led to his office. "You can tell me how we can help."

She took a seat in a red leather, straight back chair, part of a pair placed in front of a large wooden desk. She looked around, attempting to get a feel for what the church was like. It was her first visit, not only here, but to any church. She had been to weddings and a funeral, but never to a service where a sermon is preached. She knew preaching, but never in a place like this.

She was struck by the art on the wall. There were three prominent pieces. She did not recognize them as famous. The images were of things she didn't understand. She was expecting a painting of some type depicting Jesus. There wasn't one. Nor was there a cross.

"How can we be of help...a funeral I understand?" The tone was what she expected. He seemed kind, gentle.

"My son..." This wasn't going to be easy. Her voice was shaky, she didn't know if she could trust it to get through this. She knew she had to be quick. "My son passed away...I need someone to do his funeral and don't know where to go."

"I see, I am sorry for your loss...I understand this will be a very hard time." He saw the need and slid a tissue box to the edge of the desk. "Are you a church goer?"

She took a tissue. "Yes...no...I'm a Christian. I go to church all the time, but I do it on TV." She wiped her eyes. "I love them so much...but I know they can't help me with the funeral...they are praying though, I know that."

"That's nice..." There was a slight pause. "Tell me about your son."

"Oh..he was such a good son...I'm afraid he had...he had some problems over the years. He struggled. He made some really bad decisions. But he was trying, really trying to do better."

"I am so sorry....how did he die?"

"He was killed."

The minister wasn't sure if he should continue. He wanted her to know he really was saddened by her loss. He wanted her to know it made a difference. "Was it a car accident?"

She struggled to answer. She began by shaking her head. "No, no...he was killed...murdered. He didn't need to die. It was cruel...evil."

"That's sad." It was genuine. He had never met a family member of a murder victim. He had never done the funeral of a murder victim. He had never known someone who was murdered. When it came to murder, they were only stories on the news.

"Tell me what you are looking for."

"I'm not sure. I just don't want him gone, his dying to be without someone to at least pray for him." She paused, her head was down, and she was looking at her hands in her lap. "I do...have...of course...but someone...from the church should at least show respect for the loss of life."

He looked at her for a long moment. "I understand."

And he did. He had more grieving family members sit right where she was sitting than he could count. Each of the loved ones had something special they wished for. The usual list included a chance to tell how wonderful the person was. How much they cared for others. But there was one overriding desire that nearly every grieving family wanted. That is, that others know who died. That others would hear their name. The name of their son, daughter, mom, dad, their loved one who died. They are gone now, forever. But maybe others won't forget. At least for a while.

The idea is understood, but not often expressed. Each day on the news people hear of famous celebrities, politicians, athletes, and actors who die. The average person wishes that the same attention is given when they have a loss. When their mom, or dad, or family member dies.

"Can I ask," he began, his voice soft, caring, "was your son a Christian?"

She couldn't hold it back. The knowing was wonderful, but the grief was overpowering. Between the two, all she could do was sob. A broken-hearted grieving that mothers have. Others too, but mothers more than any. She took several tissues before answering.

"My son had a very dark side...but a week ago, I don't remember the day, we were talking...I asked him if he believed in

212

Jesus." She wiped a few more tears, wiped her nose and continued.

"He told me he wanted to...he said he didn't know how...that something was stopping him...we prayed...I prayed with him...and he asked Jesus to come into his heart." She lost it. Her sobs were deep, heaving sobs. The grieving tears seemed endless. It continued for several minutes.

Finally, she looked up at the minister. "I gave him a Bible. He told me... he promised me he would read it."

The minister needed to figure out the schedule. There were a number of details that needed attending. He wasn't sure if the grieving mother was ready.

"Are you up to making arrangements...now?"

She nodded.

"Where is the body?"

"The coroner has it...him."

"Have you spoken to a funeral home?"

She shook her head. "No...I wouldn't know where to go."

He nodded that he understood. "Will you...have you thought about a viewing...at a funeral chapel...anything like that?"

"We can't do that..." She took a deep breath and then found the words. "He was burned...burned up...not cremated but that's what I'll be doing...a cremation." She gave the minister a look. It was a combination of seriousness and sadness. "I haven't seen him...I'm told I don't want to."

"I think I understand."

She nodded.

"Let's do this. I'm going to call some people who can claim the remains from the coroner's office. They will do the cremation for you and we'll have a small service here." He paused, his tone was amazingly gentle yet businesslike. He made decisions so she wouldn't have to.

"I may not be the one to do your service, but I have some wonderful assistants. One of them will give your son what he deserves." He ended with a nod and smile.

Chapter 68

"Ready?"

Joyce looked at him. They were both standing in the middle of the alley. The patrol sergeant was there. They advised him that he would be better off standing behind the tattoo shop. The more distance from the victim, the safer he would be. He had no idea what they were talking about.

The back of the fortune teller business and the tattoo shop, while similar, were not the same. The tattoo shop had an open space used as a garage. More of a carport. The wall to the alley was open. The roof was the floor of the apartment on the second floor.

The victim was in an enclosed garage space of her business. The large sliding door was sufficient to allow a car to drive into the space. Whether the fortune teller used it as a garage was unknown. When Joyce looked in after opening the door, he only saw the body. There was no car.

"I guess it's now or never." There was no humor in Joyce's words.

"Protect us Lord, we're trusting you for our safety. Give Your angels charge over us."

"Amen," Joyce started towards the open door. He had moved two or three steps when he stopped. Abruptly. "Holy….what…?"

"What?" The lieutenant snapped a look at Joyce in time to see him pointing to the garage.

"Oh God, save us…" He had stopped. He held his eyes on the garage. "You see that?"

"No...see what?"

"I don't know. It's there. The whole garage is filled with it...him...it."

"Oh God...this battle is Yours. If this is the enemy Lord, only you can defeat it. Send us Your angels." He was not loud. Joyce heard him but only because he was listening. The lieutenant didn't see what Joyce did, but knew who would help.

Joyce searched for the words to describe what he saw. At first, he thought it looked like a hologram. An image like something from a movie, *The Matrix*, or something. It filled the space. Floor to ceiling. Side to side. The space was wider than the sliding door, and the image filled what Joyce could see. The top middle of the thing was a face. Weird, not so much ugly, yet it was a type of ugly. A deformed, horribly deformed human face. The eyes, nose, and mouth were in the right place, but they were not right. They were deformed, irregular, weird, and maybe ugly.

The thing was a gray color. All of it was gray but some places were darker than others. Joyce didn't see arms or wings or other appendages he would expect from a demon. He had some experience now, with demons, but this was different.

Where the arms should have been, he saw what appeared to be a wall. A wall of bricks, or maybe stones. They were on each side of the face and descending down to the floor. There were no legs. The center of the image was a garment of some type. It too was gray. Dingy, not at all appealing. The very top of the head looked as if it were obscured by the roof of the garage.

"Help." It wasn't a shout but Joyce thought it may have been. He said more. "I know I'm new, but please God, do this."

As soon as the words came out, everything began to change. Fast. The sky started churning. Clouds, thick and black formed in what seemed like seconds. Joyce remembered the force earlier. The apartment was just hours earlier. This looked to be worse.

Joyce turned to the patrol sergeant standing yards away by his cruiser. He yelled, "Tell everyone out front to get away. Move away from the front of the buildings."

The sergeant seemed confused. He watched as Joyce closed the distance. His strides were big.

"Get on the radio...now...Tell the men out front to get away. Tell them the buildings are going to explode." The sergeant had a blank look. "NOW."

Joyce turned back to the lieutenant who had been watching. The sky was swirling now. The wind had picked up, blowing hard, like a storm was growing. The scene looked like a tornado was about to hit.

When Joyce was back at the lieutenant's side he asked, "Can you see it?"

"No."

"It's there, It's huge." As the words were spoken an incredible rush of wind struck both men. It was as if there was a twister. It had been building in the swirling black clouds and now descended into the alley and they were in the way. As fast as wind, the force arrived, both men were thrown to the ground. Violently.

The sensation compared to football. It was a feeling of being struck by a player running into you at full speed. No pads, no protection.

From his position on the alley's dirty asphalt, Joyce saw it. The power that laid out both he and the lieutenant. As quickly as he looked up and got a glimpse, the giant gray image, the hologram, was enveloped by the force. The force, the thing that sent the two detectives to the ground was not a linebacker. It was not a tornado. It was just what both men had prayed for. The appearance of it was sure. Certain. It looked as the wind would look if you could see it. Joyce saw it.

"Oh my God." It was a whisper, but Joyce didn't even know it was that. It seemed more like a thought. The force, the warrior sent by God was easily twice the size of the gray thing in the garage. The realness of it was overwhelming.

It sounded like thunder when the angel crashed into the demon. The noise did not stop there. Joyce was certain that there was a scream, more than one. He expected it came from the gray thing. An explosion followed. Not from a bomb. Not a gas leak, or some other accelerant. The explosion was the sudden and complete destruction of everything. Splintering wood, crushing brick and concrete, shattering glass. All of it became little more than dust. Or so it seemed.

The force, the God warrior, the angel the detectives prayed for, continued through the garage. The gray demon would have become the tip of his spear. But the angel did not have a spear. He was power, strength. An energy, a force like no other. Like that of a tornado, but not a tornado. It was focused destruction. The brutal, ferocious, righteous force of God.

When it finally burst out the front of the building, those who witnessed it had no idea it was coming. The sounds from the alley had not reached them. When it did, everyone, all of them fell to the ground. It was a reaction. Natural. Wrapped in fear, and shock. No one was knocked down. They all ducked down. Some were prone. That was a good thing. The amount of flying debris would fill countless trucks when the demolition team arrived with trucks and tractors. None of it hit or hurt the police, the firefighters, or the neighbors who were probably closer than instructed. The protection was absolute. Complete.

It ended as quickly as it began. The lieutenant and Joyce were still laying in the alley. The patrol sergeant was huddled behind his car. The clouds were gone, the wind was calm. Any evidence that a storm had come was gone. The dust was settling.

"Praise God."

Joyce got up slowly. He wondered if he had pulled something, like every muscle in his body. "Amen."

The lieutenant looked at him. "You're getting the hang of this Jesus business Tommy."

Joyce smiled. "I am amazed that I missed it all this time." He pointed to the garage, or where the garage once stood. When the dust had settled, it was possible to see the people out front who were now moving around. "Let's see if she's still there."

They slowly approached where the building had stood. Their eyes searched the floor of what they believed was a converted space now used as a garage.

"She's gone." Joyce tried to gauge just where the body would have been. Nothing.

"Gone?"

"Yeah."

The lieutenant looked around. The floor was swept clean of whatever had been there. Even if they were not looking in exactly the right spot, it didn't matter. The floor was clean. Nothing. "I guess...as I think about it...I'm not surprised."

Chapter 69

"Tommy, your favorite reporter's on line two." The lieutenant nodded. A sarcastic gesture of good luck.

Joyce shook his head, "What...you can't handle it...her?"

"Your case, you deal with it." He chuckled, turned, and went back to his desk.

"Joyce." Dealing with reporters had always been something he left to others. There were plenty of detectives who liked seeing their name in the paper.

"Sorry to call like this," She sounded sincere.

"Right." He sounded annoyed.

"Seriously detective, the last thing I want to do is get involved in all this again."

"What do you want then?"

"The story is going to break."

"Why would you do that?"

"I'm not."

"Tell me why you're calling, then."

"My editor wants a story. You're creating a stir, a really big stir and it's time for a story."

"What have you said?"

"Look detective, last time we talked...that was the worst day of my life. There is no way I want anything to do with your case."

"So why call?"

She hesitated. She called from her cell, away from the office, but somehow felt like someone was listening. "They want a story. What's been happening, people dying, the story's coming out. The paper wants something...fast...they want it now, ahead of the online reports."

Joyce thought he had a lid on things. He had slow-rolled the reports, kept things sketchy, avoided the obvious connections between the dots. There was a part he couldn't control. It, of course, was the most important. Dozens if not more were aware that a spiritual attack was being waged against the city. They were the prayer warriors that made his work possible. They were also likely, if unintentionally, a source of information.

He considered it would only be a matter of time and some Facebook user would post how God saved the city. How the devil was cast out, and believers were delivered.

As a new believer, the whole idea was actually exciting. It was easy to understand a misguided post on social media. Except for a few of the warriors, the details of how serious the attacks had been were virtually unknown.

Joyce was done thinking about it. "Here's the deal. Write your story, be fuzzy, use images anyone can find on the web." He paused. "Sources close to the investigation are saying that there have been four deaths that are extremely rare as to the cause of death. The four deaths, at this point, have not been declared homicides. A party of interest in one death may have been killed in an explosion at a trailer park."

"That's it? That's the scoop?"

"You're a witness...you want to tell your readers what you saw?"

"Of course....of course not."

"I gave you an idea...you're the writer, be creative." He paused. "That seems like it's natural in your line of work."

"What about the apartment fire this morning?"

Joyce didn't answer right away. He didn't want to lie. "What about it/"

"Did you know you were on TV?"

He shook his head. "How'd I look?"

She ignored him. "What happened?"

He wanted to tell the truth, just not all of it. "It belonged to a victim. We thought there might be a friend there." He was thinking. "She died of a heart issue...but we don't know everything. When we went in, the place went up. It just burst into flames."

"Like a booby trap?"

"Yeah, like that."

"Was the friend there?"

"No, no one was in the apartment....no, we didn't get hurt...it was close but thanks for asking."

The little jab was sharp. She didn't think she deserved it. She let it go. There was a lot more. She knew that much but, in the grand scheme of things, the people didn't need to know any more. Those at risk have no idea they are, and those who are not, well, they're not. "I've got a dumb question."

"Shoot."

"Can I quote you?"

"Yeah sure, my name is 'a source close to the investigation'." He smiled.

"I'll make it work."

"Can I give you one more tip?"

She was a mix of frustration and confusion. "What's that?"

"Come to church Sunday."

"Sounds like you'll be there."

"I will."

Chapter 70

Tommy Joyce and the lieutenant were in early. When working a case, a new, fresh, or big case, working on Sunday is no different than any other day.

Today was different. The two men were going to church. For Joyce that was different. For his lieutenant, going to this church was different. But there was more. They weren't only going to church for all the usual reasons believers go, but because it was a part of the case.

"You see the paper?"

Joyce smiled, "Yeah...don't know about you, but I think she did okay."

The lieutenant dropped the paper on the desk. The headline was all the way across the top. The story was above the fold.

EVIL SWARMING IN CITY, 4 DEATHS POLICE SAY, the sub-headline read. *SOME REPORT A SATANIC CONNECTION.*

"I'm cutting her some slack. Reporters don't write headlines. The story shouldn't hurt us. She did the best we could hope for.

"We'll see..." The lieutenant wasn't so ready to dismiss it.

"What have we accomplished...exactly?" Tommy Joyce wanted to change the subject. His tone was low. The question was serious.

The lieutenant looked at his detective for a long moment. He understood. The past several days had created a bond of sorts. The kind of thing common with police partners. But they were not partners. The lieutenant understood. "We know that evil kills, and it's having a field day."

"But what have we done for the victims? Our job is to find justice for the victims...isn't it?"

There was a long silence as both appeared to be reading but were actually thinking. Finally, "We know the killer...killers won't find justice. At least not in this world. The victims have seemingly picked their fate."

Joyce raised his eyes from the file. "Are we sure?"

"You have a different take." It wasn't a question.

Joyce turned in his chair to face a portable whiteboard. "Let's talk this through again."

"Okay." He looked at his watch. They had time.

"Victim one burned to a crisp but not his heart...why? Victim two. No trauma but her heart was burned to a crisp."

"Yeah, exact opposites...we talked about it."

"Victim number three lost his head. No other trauma."

The lieutenant knew the case. "And?"

"We went to the trailer park, right?"

"Right."

"We never figured out who lived there. The neighbors told us the guy was a skinny meth head. The vic was anything but."

"Right."

"We need to know why. How did the car get attached to the trailer?" Joyce got up and made a note on the board.

"We got the head Tommy. We know that evil did it."

"So why was it at the girl's place...? Not his?"

The lieutenant was watching, listening but felt the review was busywork. "Okay, so the fourth vic is collateral damage. The manager of the apartment our...your first victim rented."

Joyce continued, "Number five is the girl shot by your gypsy." He smiled as he said gypsy.

"Number six is the fortune teller." The lieutenant finished the list.

"Six dead. What's the common denominator?" Joyce raised both arms. Like a sign of searching.

"Fire."

Joyce turned back to the board. The first victim was incinerated. The second victim had a burned heart. The third. "Hold on, the third was beheaded. No fire."

"Sure there was, the trailer." The idea came to the lieutenant out of nowhere.

"And his head was in a fire...right?"

The lieutenant nodded, "Right."

"Okay, let's go with that." Joyce looked at the board. "The apartment manager died in a fire. Then the girl shot by the fortune teller, she had a burned heart. And finally the fortune teller herself."

"The fortune-teller. We don't even know if she's dead."

Joyce knew but he couldn't swear to it. But he knew.

"Not having a body is a big deal." The lieutenant wanted to say yes. But couldn't.

"There was a body in the garage when I pulled the door open. I saw it." Joyce pointed to his eyes. "With my own eyes." He was emphatic.

"So who did you see?"

"I was guessing. Assuming."

"There's more...there has to be more."

Joyce sat back in his chair and rolled it close to his desk. He spun to face the lieutenant. "When I was talking to the tattoo guy I realized that the scene at the fortune teller's was wrong."

"Wrong how?"

"It had been cleaned up. The yellow tape was gone. There was no seal on the door. When we looked through the glass there was no trash. We always leave trash. It's like a calling card. The place had been cleaned."

"And she would be the one to do it." The lieutenant finished the thought.

"So she was likely the one I saw in the garage."

"But we don't know...like...know for sure."

Joyce was thinking. "The dogs found nothing in the debris. The body was there and then gone. We both know it was her...and she is with them."

"Let's go to church."

Joyce didn't stand up. He watched his boss getting ready. "I have a take you should hear." Joyce's tone was serious.

"Okay."

"Think I have an understanding of how the hearts get burned up."

"Really?"

"Bear with me...I had a dream...It scared the....It was frightening. Scary. I had the feeling that if it didn't end, my heart would...burst...into flames."

The lieutenant was quiet. This was no time to be cute. With all they had witnessed, it is...was...very likely the dream came from God. The lieutenant knew at least in a small way, that God uses dreams. He recalled one Scripture. *'Young men will see visions, and old men will dream dreams.'* Joyce would qualify. More likely as an old man. He wasn't going to tell him that.

"Tell the pastor."

Chapter 71

When they walked into the sanctuary things were just as Joyce remembered them. Today was Sunday. The members were assembling. They had come to hear the preaching.

For Joyce, the pastor had transformed his faith and earned his respect. He avoided the hugs and back-slapping.

The two detectives were together. Some from the prayer team recognized them and took a moment to say thank you. Joyce and his boss knew it was those same warriors who needed to be thanked. It was their hard work and faithfulness that allowed them to find success.

One prayer warrior summed it up nicely however. "Thank you for having the courage to stand. Praise God for His faithfulness in protecting all of us."

The music was loud. Louder than Joyce remembered it, and louder than the lieutenant was used to. The church he attended was subdued in comparison.

Joyce wanted to be in the back. He somehow sensed his recent conversion meant that's where he belonged. He compared it to a football season ticket holder. The first year usually meant a nose-bleed seat. As time passes, they slowly move closer. Maybe, after years of faithful attendance, they'll find themselves on the fifty-yard line right behind the bench.

Joyce motioned to an open row of seats and he and the lieutenant sat down. There was a book rack in front of them. Joyce remembered the books to be a Bible and a hymnal. Both of which he had no knowledge. The loud music seemed more of a jam session than a service. Joyce listened and watched. Both were skills he was good at.

The music stopped and a man Joyce thought he recognized approached the podium. Joyce figured there was a name for a podium unique to church but didn't know what else to call it.

"Good morning everyone." There was happiness in his voice. "Let's all stand and worship the Lord." He raised his palms upward.

Everybody stood, including the lieutenant and Tommy Joyce. When the music started, the words appeared on two giant TV screens on either side of the stage or dias where the band was. It was more than a band. It included an electric keyboard, brass, strings, guitars, and a drummer who was tucked away inside a glass cage. Joyce counted the singers. Seven. Each held a microphone. They all appeared to be having a good time.

As before, when he first came to a service, the people, those assembled, seemed to do their own thing. Some raised hands, some swayed, others stood singing and looking around. Some were focused on the TV screen so they could read the words. Joyce had a passing thought. *If the words are on the screen, why the hymnal?*

Worship was a new experience. As a new Christian, he was still learning. But one thing was certain. Joyce felt he belonged. Somehow, as new as a baby, he seemed to sense he was in the right place. The feeling was good. He liked it.

The music stopped. A collection was taken and announcements were made. "Let's pray." It was the pastor.

Joyce listened. He had his head bowed and his hands folded. Some of the words were lost on him. He knew, he understood the tone, the message. The pastor was expressing everything he and the lieutenant experienced, felt, and thought. They were grateful. God was awesome. The pastor continued to pour out his praises for the works of God, His protection, His mercy, and His grace.

The pastor paused. He looked out at the people. Joyce had opened his eyes to see. The pause made him curious. "May the words of my mouth and the meditations of my heart be acceptable to You my God..my Redeemer."

For the next several minutes the pastor laid out the attack of darkness that was being waged against the church. He commented several times that the powers of evil, the devil, were at work in the city. He cited the fact that the deaths of at least six people had been directly tied to the work of Satan.

As he continued, the pastor cited the amazing work of God's people. He commented that the prayers of the righteous availed much from the power of Heaven. The church of Christ had taken up arms to defeat the enemy and that victory upon victory had occurred. God was gracious in His infinite power to protect His people and quench the fires of the enemy.

Then came what Joyce would call the pivot. The pastor moved from the works Joyce had personally witnessed, that he had been a part of, to what all hoped, prayed, would be the final chapter in the defeat of evil.

"We have, in our prayers, been successful in every endeavor to defeat Satan. Our biggest challenge is now upon us. We..." he passed his hand across the entirety of the people.

"Now we will take the fight to the seat of Satan's power. Our friends in the police have identified the church of Satan." He paused.

Then, "Yes...Satan has a church right here in this city. He has filled it with demons determined to kill and destroy. We know because we have seen it. But more so because God, in His Word, has told us. So...there is work to be done. It will require each of us to take up arms against the enemy. It will require each of us to give ourselves to prayer, and to fasting. It will require that our faith will allow us to make known to each other everything God chooses to share. When you're in prayer and God speaks, tell us. If you're in prayer and you see something...in the spirit...share it with the church. Everything God does is vital. We can...we will find victory. But we must do it God's way."

The pastor gave an illustration that was new to Joyce. He reminded the people of a Bible story. The walls of Jericho. God made it clear that he would deliver Jericho into the hands of the Israelites, but the victory had to come from His battle plan.

Joyce listened. He was shocked that a nation would walk around a walled city. They did it every day for six days. The priests carried the Ark of The Covenant. Joyce had no idea what that was.

They would parade around the city once a day for six days. Finally, on the seventh day, they circled the city seven times. Then, with the sound of a trumpet, all the people gave a shout. When they did, the walls came down and the Israelites went in and were victorious.

The pastor made the point. The Lord is in charge. Do it His way and He will protect us. "People, we do this as God tells us."

Then he closed. "In conclusion be strong—not in yourselves but in the Lord, in the power of his boundless resource. Put on God's complete armor so that you can successfully resist all the devil's methods of attack.

"For our fight is not against any physical enemy, it is against rulers, principalities, and powers that are spiritual. We are up against the unseen power that controls this dark world, and spiritual agents from the very headquarters of evil.

"Therefore you must wear the whole armor of God that you may be able to resist evil in its day of power and that even when you have fought to a standstill, you may still stand your ground.

"Take your stand men and women... then with truth as your belt, righteousness your breastplate, the Gospel of peace firmly on your feet, salvation as your helmet and in your hand the sword of the Spirit, the Word of God. Above all be sure you take faith as your shield, for it can quench every burning arrow the enemy hurls at you. Pray at all times with every kind of spiritual prayer, keeping alert and persistent as you pray for all Christ's men and women."

The pastor walked out from behind his podium. He walked a few feet across the large dias. He motioned to the worship leader. When he did, some of the worship team reassembled. The music ministry was fairly high-tech. Lights, a natural part of their worship, began to change. When the keyboard player was in place, the music started.

The pastor wasn't done. "We are in extraordinary times. We are actually seeing the workings of evil. You need to know that this war has always been here. It has only now become so obvious. If you are here and have never accepted Christ as your personal Savior, there will not be a more urgent time." The pastor paused, pacing the dias. "We are told Jesus is the way, the truth, and the life...that no one comes to the Father except through Him. If you want to ask Christ into your heart...you can do it now. Everlasting life is a free gift of God. If you are being called, if you know you need Jesus, if you don't know for certain, that if you died tonight that you would go to Heaven...come up here now and give your life to Christ....your eternity depends on it."

The pastor turned to the worship leader and nodded. He turned back to the assembled. "Come now as we sing."

Joyce heard the invitation. He wished he had known about Jesus sooner. He wondered how much he had missed.

The music was similar to what was played earlier. Joyce looked at the lieutenant with a smile. Both were enjoying the service. That alone was surprising for the big detective. The idea of being a part of so many people committed to God was truly life changing.

"Come on everybody, let's stand and praise the Lord. He alone is worthy." The worship leader was all in. Praise and worship were his strength, and to Joyce, he seemed good at it.

In between songs the leader would make proclamations, thanking God for what He was doing to protect the church and the people of the city. When Joyce heard the word about protecting the people, he remembered what the wonderful woman told him. 'A rising tide lifts all boats.' Joyce knew there were unsaved souls going about their business without any knowledge or concern about the evil wreaking havoc in the city. He wanted to pray for them.

Then the music stopped. Everybody was standing. The worship leader faced the sanctuary and all those assembled. "Now to Him who by His power within us is able to do far more than we ever dare to ask or imagine—to Him be glory in the Church through Jesus Christ forever and ever, amen!"

Chapter 72

She was uncomfortable. It had been that way since the day she became a witness. She prayed it would just go away. She knew it wouldn't. Going to church was a good idea.

She believed something special would happen this morning. The fact that Detective Joyce had recommended she be there was another good reason. That she was a Christian would have been reason enough.

She guided her Toyota into the parking lot. She followed the directions of the lot attendants. Most people did not have trouble finding a parking place. The attendants were not needed, but their service was a welcome convenience.

Being uncomfortable, unsure, uncertain, had become all too frequent. Now, sitting in her car at church, the feeling showed up again. Fear was not far behind. She took a deep breath, closed her eyes, and prayed.

When she opened them, she gasped. "Dear God." Her instinct was to believe it was a miracle. Seconds earlier she whispered a few words, *give angels charge over me*, then...there it...he... was.

Before the demon with the head, she had no experience with things of the spirit. After that day she convinced herself it was punishment. God was not happy with her casual approach to her faith. She knew her prayer life, her attitude to things of God, had waned.

"Thank you Lord." It was only a whisper. It didn't matter. God would hear. He was the only one she was talking to.

All the usual words did not, could not, describe what she saw. Majestic, beautiful, glorious, amazing, huge, resplendent, none of it expressed the overwhelming goodness of God's angel. She watched for several long moments. She marveled at his sereneness, as he sat upon the portico over the main entrance to the church.

He was masculine. Male...that was certain. Dressed all in white, bright, crisp. He was wearing a robe of sorts, but yet not a robe. The wings were there. Bigger than she might expect, but that was not a conscious thought. She was certain he was watching her. She was the focus of his attention. She was sure of that. "Oh Lord, thank you so much."

It was after she had stepped out of her Toyota that she saw it. She was facing away from the church. Looking over the top of her car towards the main road. The same road she used to access the parking lot. Her thought had been how wonderful it was that so many were coming to church.

He was at the top of a tree. An old tree. The largest, tallest of those lining the road. He was the opposite of what had appeared on the portico. She only saw it for a moment. The shock caused her to look away. Her eyes went to the church entrance, the portico covering, and the angel. He was gone. She didn't want to look but couldn't stop herself. Her head turned back to the tree. It was gone.

She put her head down and walked swiftly towards the safety of the church. As she entered, the sounds of praise and worship assured her that she had come to the right place. She was safe.

She quickly found a seat near the back. Emotions are not always a dependable signal of one's feelings. This morning, the highs and lows of witnessing the best and the worst of the spiritual realm, had the reporter not knowing if she should shout or cry. She bowed her head and prayed.

The music transitioned from the opening jam session to a popular contemporary song from *Hillsong*, an amazing group of Australian believers. She stood and joined the others in singing, praising and worshiping God. It has always been her habit to do so with her eyes closed. Only when she wanted to read the words on the giant television screen would she have her eyes open.

Today, that was not the case. For reasons unknown, she opened her eyes. When she did she saw it. Him, them. They were above the dias, directly over the worship team. They were not the same, but they were similar. A giant smile crossed her face, "Praise God," slipped from her lips.

She watched for several long moments, believing that one of them was the same as her angel in the parking lot. He was her angel. He had come to her, for her, from God, an answer to prayer. She believed it.

Chapter 73

Joyce spotted her near the back of the church. He had the sense she was headed for the exit. He wanted to talk. He had read her article. Both he and the lieutenant considered it a piece that would work for them.

He caught her before she slipped outside. "Read your piece."

She recognized the voice and turned. "How'd I do?" She smiled.

"Good...didn't care for the headline." He smiled back. "I know you don't write 'em."

She had stopped and moved out of the flow of people leaving. "So...there is something coming?" The reference to the sermon.

Joyce nodded. "It's got to end...I think we have a plan."

"Feel like sharing?"

He looked back towards the sanctuary. "Why don't you join us." It was an invitation rather than a question.

An expression formed on her face. Questioning.

"We're making plans. Maybe you want to be a part of what we're doing."

She considered it for a minute and thought she should pass. She shook her head. "I don't think you need me."

"On the contrary." Joyce looked serious. "You're a witness." He smiled. A gentle look formed. "You, better than most, understand. You're a Christian. I think you're the sort of person to help us."

She shook her head. Then she cocked it a little, giving a signal saying please...no.

Joyce waved an arm. "Come on." He began walking.

She shrugged and followed the big homicide detective back into the sanctuary.

The lieutenant was alone near the dias when he spotted Joyce walk in. He was surprised to see the reporter was with him.

"What a pleasant surprise." The lieutenant was serious but not convincing.

"I didn't think you came here." She showed her best smile.

He returned the smile. "You did a nice job on the article."

She nodded. "Glad you liked it."

"Where is everybody?" Joyce was looking around.

The lieutenant motioned towards a door. "They're waiting for you." He led the way into the fellowship hall.

"They're all waiting for us?" Joyce was surprised when they entered. Even with all the contact he'd had over the past days, this crowd was unexpected. They were seated at three large round tables. Some were drinking coffee. A plate of pastry was on each table. "So this is called fellowship."

The pastor had his back to the three when they came in. He turned when he heard Joyce's voice. "Hello detective...detectives...and...?" He was smiling. Happy to see them.

"I found a new warrior wandering in the back. Invited her to join us."

The pastor recognized her. "Nice to see you again."

She forced a smile. "I enjoyed your sermon pastor."

He nodded. "You know how important this is, don't you?" He saw something, felt something, understood something...he just wasn't sure what it was.

She almost fell into a chair. Her entire person, face, body language was screaming. "I saw them." She went from a wide smile to a painful frown. The change was faster than she could speak.

"She was a witness in the park." Joyce was filling in the blanks.

"No...I saw them today...here." She was emphatic.

The pastor grabbed a chair and sat down facing her. "Tell me."

She related her experience. What she saw. Where they were.

"I saw them. They're here all the time. I saw them too." It was the amazing lady who took the pictures. The warrior who proved early on, that the attack was demonic. She was at one of the other tables.

There was a lot of talk. Everyone talking at once. Excitement filled the fellowship hall. The idea of angels sitting in the sanctuary was more than some could believe. With two witnesses, they were ready to.

"Praise God...praise God." The pastor stood up. He scanned the people seated in the room. "We have work to do...but praise God we're not doing it alone."

Joyce waited. He had questions. This type of fight was new. He had never seen anything like it, never heard anything like it. The Jericho story was in his memory. He waited to hear what a plan would look like.

"Let's pray." The pastor raised his hands. "Father, we praise You, You have given us the protection You promise in Your Word. Thank you Lord. We know the fight is not over, but we know the fight is Yours. We stand ready to do the work You call us to. We are ready to hear from You. We will wait. This battle belongs to You. Tell us Lord...tell us what to do. Give us clear orders. Your will be done Oh Lord, our God. Sovereign, glorious, loving, and faithful. In Jesus' name, Amen."

The pastor looked over the group. There was no doubt he was in charge. He was their leader and he was willing to be exactly that. As the Israelites had Joshua to lead them in defeating Jericho, this Christian body had their pastor.

After a long moment the pastor continued. "I believe the Lord will tell us exactly what to do. We will hear from the Lord." He stopped, looked to the floor, and then to the ceiling. It was not a scripted moment. He did not realize what he was doing. He was listening. He was sensing a leading.

The Holy Spirit was moving within him. "What we have seen...here, today, is unprecedented. What we see is the Lord's presence. To reassure us that He is here. He is working. He is having His way. God will finish this. When he wants His church to act, we'll know. Stay in prayer. Open the eyes of your heart. Stand ready to serve the Lord. Don't be afraid."

The pastor turned to the detectives. "Where are we?"

Joyce hesitated..for only a moment. "We think we know where their church is. The place they use as a headquarters. We have the details. Not only the location but the floor plan, the infrastructure. Gas, electric, what they need for services." He paused, "What we don't know is...if our information's right. We had a single source. That source is now theirs, with them. At least we believe they got her."

The lieutenant added to the report. "If the location we're working with is correct, we're blind as to what's inside."

"God knows." It came from the deacon.

"He does." A lady at another table was firm.

"He'll tell us...what we need to know." Another warrior was speaking up.

The pastor was hoping, almost expecting that someone would hear from the Lord. That one of the warriors would receive a word.

"Hallelujah," one of the team shouted.

Several turned to her. She had been sitting at a table but was now standing. She raised both hands, extending her arms to the ceiling and shouted again, "Hallelujah." Her eyes were closed.

"Hallelujah." She opened her eyes as she shouted again, she saw the others watching. "You hear it?" The excitement was beyond expression.

"No." A lady was excited. She sensed she was missing something.

"Yes, Hallelujah." Another shouted.

Then another, followed by more. More were hearing it.

"Great and amazing are your deeds, O Lord God the Almighty! Just and true are your ways, O King of the nations!" There was singing. A wonderful, beautiful sound.

The singing continued, "To him who sits on the throne and to the Lamb be blessing and honor and glory and might forever and ever!"

Joyce heard it. He considered the music of the worship service to be wonderful, emboldening his newfound faith. What he now heard was beyond anything he had heard, anywhere.

The pastor heard it. He was overcome with a joy that could not be expressed. The origin of the singing was hard to pinpoint. He looked across the room. He had the sense the singers were there, in the room. As if he were in the midst of the singing. "Praise God...Thank you Lord." He knew it was the voices of angels."

The fellowship hall could easily accommodate a couple of hundred people. Today there were about half that. Various groups seemed to congregate together. A casual observer may have thought the clusters were determined by age, family size, the age of children, or some other identifiers.

The warrior group was about thirty strong. That left about seventy other church members present in the hall.

The excitement of the warriors as they became aware of the singing was soon noticed by the others enjoying fellowship. They did not understand. They had no idea that the warriors were warriors. Most only assumed it was a large collection of friends.

It was quickly becoming obvious that something special was happening. It was the first time anyone could remember that such an outpouring of praise had occurred outside the sanctuary. The group of warriors were now fully engaged in rejoicing in the presence of angels.

Then a lady on the other side of the hall got a glimpse. Her arms went straight up as she shouted with joy.

It didn't stop, one after another. Christians were getting a glimpse of God's presence. The pastor had just preached an amazing sermon on the spiritual warfare raging in the city. He preached the truth of how the battle belonged to the Lord. That believers would be called upon to follow as God directs.

The experience was real, tangible. It swept across the room. Children were there. One suddenly yelled, "Grandma...look...an angel!"

Chapter 74

Waiting is not easy. The police, almost by definition, are people of action. When a call goes out for help, the police respond. The action is usually swift.

Most citizens have never had the need to call the police. For many, when the need comes to dial 9-1-1, it's not because of crime. It's usually the result of an accident. Car crash, falling off a ladder, cave in on a construction site, the emergencies are many and varied. In each case however, the swift action by the police is needed.

Joyce had found things to do. The paperwork for the police was never-ending. He used the time since Sunday's amazing service to catch up. He meticulously went through his notes, photos, and memory to accurately record, in report form, the events that began one dark night in a blighted shopping center.

His thinking continued to return to the concept of waiting. Had he done what he always does, Joyce would have taken on the evil at the lion's den by now. The details of his assault against the enemy were fuzzy. He never actually drew up a plan. He continued to wait on the Lord.

As he pecked away on his computer, he wondered just what a plan might look like. What God was planning. He was a new believer. He had little to go on. He had not read the Bible. He had never attended a Sunday school class. His knowledge of things involving God came from Hollywood.

Over the years he had seen movies about the parting of the Red Sea, the crucifixion, the birth of Jesus in Bethlehem, and some other stories. He knew that Noah built an ark. He knew that Sampson was killed when Delilah cut his hair. All of his knowledge came from movies.

Joyce had learned first hand since this case came to him that there is a very real evil in the world. It kills. It will kill anyone, anywhere. He also learned that God is just as real. God is bigger and more powerful than evil. Joyce was convinced that God would defeat Satan. When the time is right, God would reveal a plan to finally and completely defeat evil.

The big detective stopped what he was doing. The idea came to him without prompting. Several times since he became a Christian, he'd had the sudden and emotional reminder of what God did for him.

The knowing, the knowledge of how he had been shown the greatness, the realness, the love of God. All of it was beyond description. The truth of who Jesus is and knowing Him, accepting His gift of salvation, being on the path to the mountain and not the valley, consumed him.

Then came the inevitable question. What about those who have not seen evil and good? Those who never see an angel or have the dream of choosing beauty over despair. How do they learn about Christ? About the path to eternal life with Jesus?

The desk phone rang. "Homicide, Joyce,"

"Hey Tommy, I just heard something you might want to know." Joyce recognized the M.E.'s voice.

"Really, what's that?" Small talk was rare with the medical examiner.

"I got a call from a church minister. He said he had spoken to the mother of your...what are you calling him...? Porno store clerk?"

"Wow, I'm guessing you have the contact info?" Joyce took down the information and thanked the good doctor for calling.

Once off the phone he leaned back in his chair and considered what he had learned. A church minister was reaching out on behalf of the victim's mother. If the mother was talking to a minister, she was likely a Christian. The idea of her son dying at the hands of evil as he did had to be like losing him twice. He called the minister.

"I'm Detective Joyce, homicide." He told the minister why he was calling. He learned the minister was doing the funeral of his burn victim. Joyce explained that from the perspective of the police, the case was a homicide. Finally, he got to his real interest.

"Was he a member of your church?"

"No detective, nor is his mother."

"Do you know if she is a church person?"

"Actually, I think she is quite active, but she does everything online and through television."

"Do you have a sense about her son...my victim?"

There was a pause. As if the question was either confusing or inappropriate. He finally answered. "I have no information other than he has been a troubled soul for a while. His mother told me...but she also said he was a new believer...or at least wanted to be."

Joyce was thinking. The condition of the heart had become a focus in his case. "We have some things going on...in this and other cases. I think if you're handling the funeral you should know it."

The minister asked for details. Joyce deflected the questions. Instead, he gave him the contact information for the pastor. He explained it would be better if he learned about the case from the church's perspective and that the two could explore the risks and options in handling the funeral.

"Oh, one more thing...do you have the contact information for my victim's mother?"

Joyce decided it was better to talk to her in person. The case, the details were too personal to handle on the phone. The address was not far. He could be there in no time. If it turned out she was not there, he would lose about fifteen minutes out of his day. A day that was committed to waiting.

Upn arriving, Joyce saw the interior door was open. Only the screen door was keeping out unwanted pets and bugs. He tapped lightly. Not his official police knock. As he did he noted music, soft, pleasant.

"Yes?" It was a woman's voice. It sounded kind. Joyce could not see who it belonged to.

"Police...ma'am." He answered with his nicest, kindest voice.

"Police?" She appeared at the open door from the side. "How can I help you?"

"Ma'am, I'm Detective Joyce. I'm here to talk about your son."

She appeared as if she would cry. She pushed open the aluminum screen door. The invitation was obvious. She turned and retreated to the living room of the small two bedroom bungalow. The house was old but neat, well maintained. The same could not be said for all her neighbors.

Joyce motioned to a chair, nodding. As a policeman, it was his job to size up people. Try to evaluate just who he was talking to. In this case, it was a tender woman, probably his age or a few years older. She seemed healthy, well groomed. No evidence of being prosperous, rich, privileged.

"Please, yes...have a seat detective...Joyce, was it?"

Joyce nodded as he sat. "Yes."

"You know something about my son?" She was anxious.

Joyce's tone was the same as the one used by police when notifying family members of a tragedy. Gentle, caring. "Yes, ma'am...I am the detective assigned to his case. I'm investigating his death."

"I see," She stopped but it was obvious there was more. Then, "You saw him..?"

Joyce remained sensitive. "Yes...I did."

"Was it bad...as bad as the coroner said?"

Joyce knew that only the truth would be acceptable. "I am afraid it was." He waited before asking, "You know where he worked, don't you?"

She nodded. "I know...we talked about it...he was changing, detective. He wanted to stop what he was doing... Change his life."

"I was told by the minister that you are a lady of faith?"

"I'm a born again Christian."

Joyce smiled. Before this case, he would have thought such talk was silly. "So am I." It was almost exciting to say it.

She liked hearing it. She nodded with approval. "My son was too."

Joyce hoped he would hear those words. His reason was twofold. He wanted those who died to enjoy eternal life with Christ. A Christian dying, even at the hands of evil, has that assurance. Second, he knew it would advance his theory on the burned hearts.

Joyce asked, "His heart belonged to Christ?"

"Yes, we prayed right here just a few days before he died."

"You prayed with him?"

"Yes."

"That's wonderful...then you know he's in Heaven."

Joyce wanted to know more. It had nothing to do with his case. He wanted to hear how people, seemingly lost, broken, hopeless, find Christ. Become saved. "How did it happen?"

She smiled again. A gentleness came over her. "Prayer...I prayed for him. I would suggest he change. And I loved him."

"When he actually decided...how did it happen?"

"You're new to Christ...aren't you?"

Joyce looked at his shoes. Then...a moment later looked up to the mother of his victim. "I had no idea. None of it...until I saw the evil...I mean really saw it."

"So then someone told you about Jesus?"

"Generally, yeah...it got a little complicated...but yes."

"Isn't it interesting how a simple decision seems so complicated?"

Joyce smiled. "I am only glad I made it."

"Let me show you something." She turned on her television and turned on what Joyce thought was a saved video of some sort. "We...we were talking and I was trying to help my son make a decision...to accept Christ...I showed him this."

Joyce watched. It was like a music video. A group of largely young people were in a concert setting, the band playing to a packed arena. The song was similar, in a way, to what he had seen and heard at church.

Joyce watched and listened.

Who am I that the highest King would welcome me?
I was lost but He brought me in

It didn't take long listening for him to understand the importance of the lyrics. The message was overwhelming.

Free at last, He has ransomed me, His grace runs deep
While I was a slave to sin, Jesus died for me
Yes, He died for me

The singers, the music, the lyrics, the crowd of thousands worshiping. It was inspiring. Moving. He had to take a deep breath to keep the tears from showing. He watched quietly to the end.

"Is this the thing...is this the one thing that caused him to accept Christ?" Joyce pointed to the TV. He knew his voice was betraying him. He was emotional. More so than at any other time on the job. He was okay with it. She understood.

"Yes, he even cried. He wanted to change. He knew he was on the wrong track...he hated that job...he wanted to change and he knew that he was in trouble... if the things he was doing...who he was doing it with...it could get him killed." She stood up and walked to the window. She stared out at nothing. She was thinking about her son.

She turned to Joyce. "I'm not the only one he had. He met a Christian guy who was trying to get him to change. He was witnessing." She sat down. "I think he lived in the same building."

Joyce felt it. He couldn't describe what it was, but he felt it. "Was he the manager?"

She shook her head. "I don't know. Could have been I suppose. I only know he lived in the same building."

Joyce didn't remember exactly how the manager died. Only that he died in a fire in the son's apartment. The manager had been considered collateral damage.

"You are working on funeral details?"

"I talked to a minister, he...his staff..they're setting things up. He is having a mortuary claim my son's body."

Joyce had a decision to make. Did the grieving mother know what her son had gotten into? Would she want to know? Was she in danger? Would those at the funeral be in danger? What, exactly, were the risks?

"How much do you know about his...other friends?"

"He was into some dark things...I got the impression it was really dark."

"What do you know about demons?"

She took a deep breath. Then after a moment exhaled deeply. Joyce understood. "Would you consider yourself a prayer warrior?"

She looked at him in an odd way. "I'm a Christian, detective. I pray all the time."

"I have some people you need to meet."

Chapter 75

The pastor was alone...not something common in recent days. There were others in the sanctuary praying. The attack was real. The defense was more real. The prayer warriors of Jesus Christ were doing their work.

A tap at the door. "...Pastor...do you have a minute?"

He looked up. "Of course." He motioned for her to come in.

"I want to ask you about something." She wasn't nervous as much as unsure if she should be bothering the pastor. There was a lot going on and he was busy.

He pointed to a chair in front of his desk. "What is it?" His natural tone was soft, reassuring, kind.

She was talking even before settling in the chair. "I don't know if this is important...I have been in there praying...I think...I feel I was prompted to read a Scripture." She gestured in the direction of the sanctuary.

He listened. He did not know this woman. He'd seen her but had not had personal contact. "You think it's about the battle?"

She nodded. "I do, but it doesn't make sense to me. I don't want to bother you but maybe you'll see something I don't."

"I'm glad you did...you know how the Lord works. He uses us...all of us for His good."

"I was praying. I know the police are working to take down the...their church. I sense that they may be going to the wrong place."

"Really?" He was not showing surprise, but curiosity. "Tell me what you think."

"Well, I was praying for protection for the assault against Satan's church, when it happened." She gazed back to where the warriors were doing their work. "I sensed that I was hearing that they have the wrong place."

"You think the Lord was telling you that Satan is not where the police are planning a raid?"

She nodded.

He smiled as a way to reassure her. "What else?"

"I had the sense to look up 1st Peter, chapter five, verse eight."

The pastor opened his Bible. Finding the Scripture he read, "Be sober, be vigilant; because your adversary the devil, as a roaring lion, walketh about, seeking whom he may devour." He looked up. "That the one?"

She nodded.

"Did you have a sense about what it meant?" He read it again, looked up. "Was there an emphasis?"

"I had the feeling we are all stuck on the lion...I got the idea that we should be thinking about the adversary."

A sense of amazement formed on his face. He smiled. Nodded. "Isn't God good?"

She smiled, almost a grin. Then nodded.

"Thank you...I'll call the detectives. This may be big."

244

She didn't linger. With the message relayed, she quickly returned to the sanctuary.

The pastor bowed his head and quietly prayed. He asked the Lord about the word given. He asked, prayed for understanding. Wisdom as to how he should handle the message. He knew the police had at least some concern that their information on the lion's den was weak.

He re-read the verse given to the warrior. The idea, when taken in a fleshly context made little sense. But God is greater, wiser.

"Detective Joyce?"

"Hey pastor, to what do I owe the pleasure?"

"I'll be brief...I just talked to one of our warriors. She thinks the lion's den info may not be correct."

Joyce shook his head. "Why should I be surprised." It wasn't a question.

"I know. I don't have an answer...but there is a clue." He paused waiting for Joyce to comment. There was none so he continued. "The focus on lion may be wrong."

Joyce had no idea how it all worked. He would listen expecting direction that would come from God. "Tell me what you believe."

"I believe the Lord has told a warrior that the lion den you're looking at is wrong. That you should look for something that includes adversary instead of lion."

"Adversary?"

"Right...there is a Scripture in the message. The lion of course is the devil...he is also called the adversary."

"So I'm looking for a place with that in the name?"

The pastor took a deep breath. "I don't know...I believe the information, but I don't know how to apply it."

Joyce was thinking. "I'll check some things...maybe the word will pop up." He waited a moment and added. "We can only pray."

"I know...let me know if I can help...in the meantime, if I hear anything else, I'll call."

Chapter 76

Joyce walked into the lieutenant's office. "Tell me how this plat book works." He dropped the Lion's file on the desk.

"Do I see a problem?"

"That may not be our target." He pointed to the file. "The pastor called...said a warrior heard it's not lion but adversary."

The lieutenant picked up the file. "I'm guessing they got a word." He looked at Joyce and knew he needed to explain. "Somebody was praying and God impressed on them a certain Scripture. A word. From the word...the Bible."

"I thought the lion den idea was from the gypsy, not the Bible...how did we get to the Bible?" Joyce sounded perplexed.

The lieutenant continued to read the file. He looked up to answer. "Lion made sense...actually it still does because of Scripture describing the devil as a roaring lion."

"How did we get to adversary?"

"I think it says adversary as well." He typed something into his desktop. After a moment he said, "Yeah, here it is, I was right," he looked at Joyce, "again." He laughed.

Joyce didn't think it funny. "You have a Bible on your computer?"

"I just Googled the phrase, it's here. 1st Peter chapter five, verse eight."

"What does it say?" Joyce hadn't thought that Google would have the Bible, let alone a phrase.

The lieutenant read it off the screen. "Be sober, be vigilant; because your adversary the devil, as a roaring lion, walketh about, seeking whom he may devour. There are several translations. This one uses the word adversary with the word devil."

"So where do we go from here?"

The lieutenant still had the file open. As if a light went on, he slid the file to Joyce. "Read through this for anything that could connect the lion's den to another property." Just as quickly, he started tapping keys on his desktop.

Several minutes passed. For Joyce, reading the legalese of a real estate document seemed cumbersome. He understood the words, their meanings, but it took effort. Reading and re-reading everything to be sure he understood.

He sat for a moment thinking. The pastor used the word clue. They had a clue about the real target. How would adversary be a clue? What does it mean?

"What does adversary mean?"

The lieutenant turned away from his screen. "Opponent, I guess."

Joyce waved his hand. "I know that, but what I'm wondering...are we looking for adversary or a word that means adversary? Didn't you say there are several translations?"

"Let's see." The lieutenant went back to his desktop and started typing. "Here you go." He started reading synonyms. Then, "Nemesis, I like this one."

"Why?"

He shrugged. "I'm thinking of a name. A company that would own a building."

"So nemesis is a name?"

The lieutenant went over the synonyms again. "Anything jump out at you?"

"We need to do better than this. We can't guess."

"I'll print all these words out. We'll research the assessor's files for names that match any of these...It's not perfect, but it's a start."

"How long will that take?"

"A while, I imagine."

Joyce was anxious. He wanted action. "Can we do it on our computer?" He pointed to the lieutenant's desktop.

"Don't know." He picked up his phone and made a call.

Chapter 77

The minister took Joyce up on contacting the pastor spearheading the campaign. From Joyce's perspective, the pastor was the general, the leader, the warrior in charge of keeping the prayer efforts going. Making sure all were engaged in the war to defeat evil.

When the two men of the cloth met at the epicenter of the war against evil, the pastor welcomed the minister to see firsthand the plan to defeat the works of Satan.

They sat in the pastor's small office and exchanged pleasantries. Finally, "Tell me about this evil."

The pastor was not sure what perspective the minister held. "When you talk about spiritual warfare, what comes to mind?"

"I'm not certain..actually...but...I generally think of people struggling with sin...addiction, anger...you know."

"Your right, those are all too real...and far too common. What we are fighting now, however, is a matter of life and death."

The minister seemed surprised. "What does that mean?"

"The battle is all over town now. People are dying. Deaths are mounting up. The man...the son of the lady that came to you...he's one of the victims."

"I'm not sure I follow."

"Satan is killing people. It's that simple. Demons...evil...the evil cast out of Heaven by God at creation, those demons are going around killing people right here in our city."

The minister wanted to scoff but respected his colleague enough not to. Finally, "How?"

The pastor spent the next several minutes explaining the case. He cited the known death toll and the two homicide detectives who were working day and night to root out evil and lessen the deaths. The pastor explained how fire and destruction occurred in several dwellings where demons had set up housekeeping.

The pastor came to the issue of locating Satan's church. A place that had to be destroyed if evil was to be cast out once and for all.

"We are praying day and night. Asking God to reveal to us His plan. A plan that we can act on. Then He can do His will and destroy this evil."

"How do you think this will work?"

The pastor smiled. "I've been thinking about that. I sort of have the sense it will look a little like it did in Sodom."

"Really?" The minister sounded serious, but his head was not going there. It all sounded...crazy.

The pastor understood. He had lost count of the various denominations, churches, types, and styles that comprise the church of Jesus Christ. All were the body, the Bride of Christ. Many had a particular focus. For some it is salvation, others it's feeding the poor, and for others the Sacraments. None are wrong.

All seemed right in their thinking, but not all were right in all things. The Revelation of John, the last book of the New Testament proved the case. John was instructed to write to the seven churches. The scroll cited the various shortcomings of those seven churches, yet each was a church belonging to Christ.

"We have a fairly active group of believers when it comes to things of the spirit. I learned...during this battle, that some of my members, here...see angels, routinely, in our sanctuary."

"Angels...in your church?"

The pastor shook his head with a smile. "I know, how wonderful is that?"

"And you have seen the demons?"

"Not me personally, but others have."

"And you believe them?"

"I do." He looked the minister in the eye. He smiled. "It's real. God has shown His people so that we can do His will."

"What is that?"

"His will is that we drive them out...His angels protect us, they do the heavy lifting...it's all to glorify Him. God receives all the glory." The pastor pointed to the ceiling as he said it.

"I've always, since seminary, thought of evil as a metaphor. That sin was evil. That evil came from the devil, but not that the demons were actually present."

"I think you're in good company with that. Most who hold that view are sincere. They are, unfortunately, sincerely wrong. What we're seeing now is not a metaphor. The detectives I mentioned, they have witnessed the works of the devil. They have also seen what the angels of God can do."

"Can it really be?" The minister didn't say it to doubt the pastor. He said it in astonishment.

"Would it help if you saw it with your own eyes?"

The minister sat for a moment. Then, "I don't know if I want to."

"A dear lady here saw demons and took a picture." The pastor gave the minister a serious look. "It's real...I'll show it to you if you want."

The minister looked at his shoes. "This is frightening."

The pastor nodded and waited.

After a long moment. "God is in this, isn't he?"

"Yes."

"If God showed this to a believer...then He wants us to know."
He nodded. "That means I need to know."

The pastor took the photo from his drawer and slid it across the desk.

It was a silent gasp. The minister dropped his head and prayed. After a moment he raised his head. "What can I do?"

"There was a concern, from the police, that evil may want to visit you during the funeral. That you would be in danger. Unprepared."

What's your take?"

"I think," the pastor paused a moment. "I believe that the darkness can not comprehend the light. The light of Christ in your church is your protection." He added, "It's outside the church that they do their deeds."

"So the church is safe."

"That's right. The working theory, from the detectives, suggests that the man you're doing the funeral for was a victim. He was completely burned up. There are details but you don't need them now. The man was a new Christian, only a day or two. The autopsy showed his heart was perfect. Untouched by fire."

The minister sat motionless. Thinking. Listening. "His heart belonged to Jesus."

Chapter 78

The search to find the correct lion's den was going nowhere. The papers from the assessor's office only offered more opportunities to guess. Murders are not solved by guessing.

"I need to do this the old-fashioned way." Joyce had walked into the lieutenant's office and dropped into a chair.

"You're old-fashioned, that's for sure." He grinned. "What are you going to do?"

Joyce gave a long uncertain look. "I'm going out to the lion's den and I'm going to see what happens."

"You just going to walk up and ring the bell?"

Joyce turned serious. "I'm going to stake it out. Wait. See who comes and goes."

"Do you have a plan?"

"Right now...not really. We're not making progress sitting around here."

"Want company?"

Joyce stood up. "Tell you what. I'm going to do a recon. Check out the place and see what's there. Businesses means people, and people see stuff. Maybe we'll get lucky. I'll call if I hit something."

When Joyce pulled to the curb across from the address dubbed the lion's Den he was a little surprised. The surprise caused him to criticize himself for not doing this sooner. The fortune-teller had given him the lead. The warrior had a word that the lion's den was not this building. But that was no excuse for not at least checking it out.

He rationalized that if this building was connected to the evil, then perhaps there may be a clue in or around it that would lead him to the real lion's den.

It was a simple single story brick building. A guess would suggest it was new about twenty years ago. The actual date was in the file. Joyce didn't care. He sat at the curb and watched. He allowed his eyes to slowly move over the building. His hope was that something would jump out at him. He wanted to see something that told him what sort of business was conducted inside. The only clue was a relatively small sign set in a steel frame with an image. An artist's conception of a lion. Joyce shrugged when he saw it. It did, in a way, confirm the lion's den theory. It was consistent with the assessor's file.

His eyes then began a scan of adjacent buildings and businesses. He was parked just across the street from the lion's den looking towards the end of the block in front of him.

On the corner was a tire shop. An older building, certainly here longer than the brick building with the lion sign. Next, working back toward him was a Subway sandwich shop. Then a thrift store of some type. He didn't know a lot about that industry other than they were often connected to a church or charity. Then a greeting card shop.

Joyce then turned to his right. What he saw would have qualified as a miracle a few weeks ago. Today he would call it providence. The ATM was a wonderful tool for nearly any case. This one belonged to a credit union whose name was unknown to the veteran detective.

Joyce walked into the credit union. He showed his badge to a lady sitting behind a desk. "Detective Joyce, homicide."

She looked surprised. The word homicide does that to a lot of people. "How can I help?"

"You have an ATM on the sidewalk out front. I'll need access to the video." He smiled and nodded. He wanted to be liked. His size and appearance often had the opposite effect.

She picked up the phone and punched a couple of numbers. Then "The police are here. They would like to talk with you." She set the phone back on the desk set. "It'll be just a minute." She tried to smile.

The wait was no more than a minute or two. A young man, probably not long out of college approached. Joyce gauged him quickly. He was walking fast. Not a run but his gait was hurried. He had a serious look. This would be his first time dealing with the police. Joyce would have his way.

"You're from the police?"

"Joyce, homicide." He flashed his badge. Between his size, his tone, and the manager's youthful inexperience, Joyce was in charge.

"How can I help?"

"You have an ATM on the sidewalk...I'll need the video card for the camera."

The manager was quiet. He wasn't sure what the rule was for protecting the video. He knew that the card was replaced weekly, it was his job. They were stored in a file. He wasn't sure who would get access. "I'm not sure."

"I understand, you probably haven't had to deal with this before. Be assured it's okay."

"You're from the police, FBI?"

"Police, homicide." The tone coupled with the word homicide has a unique effect.

"Homicide?"

"Yes, I'll need the card that's in there now, plus the past two weeks. I'll sign whatever you need. I'll need them now...please."

The manager had a confused look. He stood in the lobby giving the impression he was not sure what to do.

Joyce pulled a thin leather wallet from his inside coat pocket and showed his official police ID. He then showed the manager his badge again. He handed him a business card with his name, title, and phone number. "How many days on each card?"

The manager was still reading Joyce's business card as he answered. "Seven."

"Great, I'll take the one in the camera now, plus the last two." He paused and waited, the manager didn't move. "I have six murders to solve so I would like you to get moving." His tone had changed. He was using his police authority voice.

Chapter 79

"How do you spell detective?" Joyce walked into the lieutenant's office unannounced.

"Let me guess, J-O-Y-C-E."

"We've got a winner!"

"So what case did you solve?"

Joyce set the three video cards on the desk. "I may be overblowing this, but we have almost three weeks of video for everything coming and going from the lion's den."

"Where did that come from?"

Joyce smiled. The idea of providence was still on his mind. "There's an ATM right across the street."

He picked up a memory card. "How many months did you get?"

"I asked for three weeks' worth." Joyce turned serious. "I wasn't sure exactly what we should look for. I figure at the very least we would get license plate numbers."

"Three weeks? Who has the time to watch?"

"Isn't there a pool of guys for this sort of thing?"

The lieutenant was shaking his head. "I'll work on it."

Joyce picked up the most recent card and headed for his desk. He wanted to get started. With no idea how long it would take to view all three weeks, he knew getting started was important.

On the drive back to the office, a few ideas were considered. Knowing the ATM camera would run twenty-four hours a day, he would have pictures and video of any movement in and out of the lion's den just across the street. What he didn't know was the quality of those images.

Evil loves the dark. The best evidence of evil being present in the building would be what happened at night. The license plate numbers could be a treasure trove. Joyce was particularly interested in two cars. The leased car used by the headless victim, and the Honda belonging to the girl who died in the parking lot at the park reserve. To see either or both would advance the theory that the LDI building was more than a tip from a missing fortune-teller.

How long it would take to view the videos was a guess. Joyce hoped that scanning would work. Speeding up the video two or three times normal speed was a thought. An idea he hoped would collapse the time needed to find anything pointing to the real lion's den to the adversary.

"God...I'm new at this, praying...new to You, to faith in what Jesus has done for me. But I know it's all real. You are God. Help me find what we need...what we need to do our job...to do our work. The warriors have been faithful to ask for Your protection...I pray that I can ask for a solution to find the church of evil. You know where it is...You know everything. Help me find it. Allow me to find the evidence to prove where to go. Oh Lord, I need Your help. Help me...please. Amen."

Joyce raised his head. He glanced around the homicide office to see if anyone had noticed his sudden prayer. The idea of prayer was new. The events in the case however had shown him that God does hear, and He does act when people of faith pray, asking for help.

What he had seen, witnessed, the evidence for the value of prayer had been overwhelming. That did not stop him from thinking about what others might think if they saw him pray. He was frustrated by the thought.

The project was going to take some time. Joyce settled into his undersized desk chair and loaded the first video card. It appeared from the time stamp that the card was new in the camera six days ago at 8:12 A.M. As he watched the screen he realized just how tedious the job was going to be. The image quality was not bad but he had seen better. He had the thought that maybe a credit union has less to spend on security than a bank.

He started at the beginning. Patience was not his best suit but he knew the job. It had to be done. He figured out how to speed up the footage. It was like watching an old-time movie where everything moves fast. The concept of speeding helped the patience thing.

As he watched he learned that when a customer was standing in front of the camera, extra care was needed to not miss what was happening behind the ATM user. A vehicle entering or leaving the LDI's parking lot would easily be missed. Screened out by the credit union patron.

The mind wanders when doing tedious work. The places it may go are wide and varied. One thing that nagged at Joyce was the time it would take to watch the entire card. Six days, times twenty four hours is one hundred and forty four hours. At double speed, he would be watching this video card for seventy two hours.

Rather than stop watching, Joyce called his boss on his cell.

"You getting too old to walk across the room?" The sarcasm was obvious.

"Sorry," Joyce was serious. "I'm watching the video card. Didn't want to stop."

"What's up?"

"I was thinking. Each card is going to take seventy-two hours minimum. That means three shifts, for three days...per card. Maybe the crime lab techs can help...just thinking."

"I'll check."

He continued to watch. The credit union ATM had more visits than he would have guessed. His mind continued to work. He considered that those who worked at the various local business-es would use it. Even if it meant extra fees if they were not a member. He wondered if anyone from LDI would walk across the street and insert a card. He watched.

Joyce maintained a log of license plate numbers. He decided to only log those coming and going from the lion's den. He added any that parked at the curb in front of the business. He had a post-it note at the top of his screen with the two plate numbers related to his case. They were not yet a consideration. The video card he was watching was recorded after the two deaths. Both cars were still in the police impound lot.

He had done the math on how long the review was going to take. He knew the time would likely be longer. Each time a car turned into his targeted parking lot he had to stop and enlarge the image to correctly read the plate. It wouldn't be a lifetime of extra hours, but it would take time. And time was of the essence.

His mind wandered as he watched. For the most part, he remained focused on the case. That included moments when he would think about the warriors giving of their time to pray. He knew better than most the value of the selfless act.

Joyce reviewed in his head the facts of each death. He knew there were details, things in the file he had recorded but had forgotten. It was those things he tried hard to recall. Something was in the file that could help. An unseen or forgotten fact. A clue.

He had the thought to pray. "Lord, I know there is something I am missing. Help me find it. Tell me Lord what I need to know. What is it, where do I look, what have I missed. Help me Lord...Amen."

The sun had set. The images of the video were now in darkness. Joyce paused the video to get a better look at a license plate on the back of a car turning into the lot. As he zoomed in, the license number remained a blur. The idea of finding evidence of demons and those who worship them was becoming less likely. He took a screenshot in hopes that the crime lab would be able to enhance it.

The detective allowed the video to continue. If the business was like most, there would be no traffic in and out of the lot in the late-night hours or the early hours of the morning. Only watching would tell. With no traffic, the LDI building would become less likely the church of evil he was looking for.

When a car turned into the lot Joyce again paused the video. He zoomed in on the license. The numbers were not readable. He zoomed until the plate was so pixelated that it was hard to know if it was a license plate. What he saw however, was a word. He didn't know what the letters were, but they were not numbers. He took another screenshot.

He resumed the video. His thinking went to the vanity plate. What could a single word do to help find evil? "Oh crap..." Joyce couldn't believe he hadn't thought of it.

He rolled his chair to an adjacent desk. It was late and the office was empty. The guys on the night shift were out on the street. A few clicks of the mouse and he had his answer. He rolled back to his desk and picked up his cell and called the lieutenant.

"Tell me you found something."

"I did...can't believe it took this long."

"Something on the video?"

"No...I just thought to run Adversary as a vanity plate." Joyce was both mad at himself and elated he finally thought of it.

"No!"

"Yeah."

Chapter 80

Tommy Joyce and the lieutenant sat in front of what appeared to be an all glass two-story office building. The building was modern, contemporary style, with sharp angles forming corners that were not the customary ninety-degree turns. There was a prominent section in the front that jetted out forming a triangle component. A small loading dock was in the rear as well as a parking lot.

"That's the place." Joyce nodded towards the building. It was the address listed for the vanity plate, Adversary. The plate belonged to a company called Dragon. Nothing else. No extra words like company, incorporated, or other identifiers.

"So..." Joyce paused. He was thinking, wondering, hoping it was the building they were looking for. "This could be it."

Both men had played with the name Dragon. The first idea came from the lieutenant when he suggested the building was a dragon's lair. A natural transition from lion's den.

"We need a break."

"I actually prayed for one."

The lieutenant turned to face Joyce. "I like the sound of that." He turned back to the building. "Want to drive through the lot and see if the car is here?"

Joyce shook his head. "I don't know. They know we're after them. They probably know we're sitting here. I don't feel like picking a fight...at least not right now."

"We need to know if this is the place." He paused. "We need to know for sure, Tommy."

"We know Adversary is a real name. Right?"

"It came as a word, from God...that's pretty strong."

Joyce nodded. "Won't get a warrant on that though."

The lieutenant grinned. "You aren't going to be asking for any warrant." He pulled out his cell and hit a number on speed dial. "Need a favor."

"How can we help?"

"We're in front of a building We call it the dragon's lair. If this is the church we would like to have a covering to drive into the parking lot and get a look around."

"Sure...we're still here...will be until there's an all-clear."

"Thanks pastor." The lieutenant punched the camera button on his phone and selected video. He pointed to the driveway and nodded.

Joyce slipped the lever to drive and made a hard left turn, crossed two lanes of traffic and drove into the driveway. The building was on their right. The lieutenant held the phone up recording the building. They rolled past the loading dock into the parking lot. Joyce made his way around the lot looking at license plates. When they were done, they had nothing new to support the concept of a dragon's lair.

Once back on the street Joyce asked, "Now what?"

"The office," he paused, looking out the window but seeing nothing. "Guess we need to keep watching videos."

"We?"

260

"I know, but I'm working on getting help. Tomorrow Tommy, we'll have help in the morning."

Upon returning to the office, Joyce watched the videos. He was thinking and praying. He needed an answer. Something they could, as they say in the business, hang their hat on.

The lion's den continued to offer nothing helpful. By 9 P.M., the ATM was seeing no business. Cars were no longer entering the driveway across the street. Joyce wondered if there were any left in the lot. He watched.

The idea came from nowhere. He looked at his watch. Maybe, just maybe...He stopped the video and checked the internet. It'll work, he thought. "It's got to work," he whispered. The office was empty, the whisper didn't matter. He took his gun out of the drawer, snatched his coat off a chair, checked its pocket for the car keys and headed out.

The street was all but deserted. An occasional car would pass but nothing that could be called traffic. The lot in the shopping center across the street was empty except for two sedans parked near the entrance to the bookstore.

The bus bench was typical. A plexiglass structure with a single metal bench. There were advertising posters on all three sides. Joyce could only read one. A personal injury lawyer promising big settlements.

He had checked the schedule before leaving the office. The bus was due in about fifteen minutes. He figured the witness would arrive a few minutes before the bus.

His wait was less than he thought. A middle aged woman wearing a light jacket carrying a large shoulder bag approached the bus stop. Joyce knew he could easily frighten the lady if he just climbed out of the car and approached her. She was alone in a less than great neighborhood. She would be wary.

His plan was to sit with the car running and the lights on. He turned on the dome light so she would see who was in the car. He waited until she entered the bus shelter.

"Hello ma'am, police." He held up his badge as he leaned towards the open right side window. "Could I talk to you? Please."

She stooped to look into the car. She was several feet away but would easily see the big hand holding the badge. "Police?"

"Yes ma'am, Detective Joyce."

When he said his name it clicked. Now she recognized him. The big detective that had been to her church. "Detective Joyce...is it really you?"

"Yes," he laughed. "It's really me." He looked in his mirror. No traffic. He opened the door and stepped out. "I was hoping I could catch you here."

She looked surprised. "Why would you be looking for me?"

"Well," he said as he walked up to her. "I need your help. I know it's late, but you may be the only one I know that can help me."

Her eyes widened. Her look was less than a smile but she didn't seem shocked. "How can I help you, detective...besides praying for you?"

Joyce saw the bus coming. "Would you mind spending a few minutes with me...? I'll drive you home."

She glanced at the bus, now about a block away. She nodded. "Sure."

Joyce opened the car door and she got in. By the time he was behind the wheel, the bus was waiting behind him. He flashed the hidden blue lights in the back window for a moment, a signal to the bus driver to go around.

"I've never been in a police car." She seemed relaxed.

Joyce got serious. "I would like you to help me find the source of the evil you have been praying about." He watched her.

"How would I be able to do that?"

"You don't have to help. You may not be comfortable doing it. It could actually be dangerous. If you say no, I'll understand...I'll drive you home and that will be that." He nodded. He held his eyes on her. Not threatening, but hoping.

"I don't understand."

"Of course you don't...let me explain. You have a very unique gift...something God has given you. Frankly, your gift is something completely new to me." He paused, gauging just how to ask. "We've found a building. I think it's the one used by Satan as a church."

She was getting concerned and it showed. She began twisting a piece of the strap to her bag. "I don't like this."

"I know...I understand. It bothers me too. But I was hoping we could drive over to the building. You would have a look. Maybe you'll see something to confirm it's the right place...the place we're looking for."

"What are we looking for?"

"Actually...with your gift, I'm hoping you'll see one of them." The conversation had gotten progressively more awkward.

She looked him in the eye. "It doesn't work that way."

He didn't flinch. "How does it work?"

"God decides what to show me."

"Do you pray to see things?"

She gazed out the window. "I pray to see God's angels."

"Do you see them?"

"Yes." Her voice was low, soft. She was nodding her head.

Joyce wasn't sure if he should say what he was thinking. He was too new to the Christian way of seeing things. If he said what he wanted to, she might think he was simply trying to talk her into something. She might think he was lying.

She stayed quiet for a few moments. Joyce wondered if she was praying. From his perspective, it looked like she might be. He waited.

"I have a special interest in this case detective. It scares me. I know we should not have the spirit of fear, but I'm afraid." She stopped for a long moment. "My son may have gotten involved in this. He may have somehow... gotten into all this evil."

Joyce didn't see it coming. He had no answer. He was speechless. He reacted. It was nothing learned in years of police work. It seemed new but natural. He laid his huge hand on hers. "Oh God, be here now with this dear woman." He squeezed gently. "I am so sorry. I had no idea. How can I help?"

"I'll help you, detective. It may save my son."

Chapter 81

Joyce dropped the prayer warrior at her home. A small house in an old part of town. It appeared neat, well-maintained. He guessed it was new in the 1920s. Like every other home on the block, it was a two-story house. A dormer jetted out on the second floor. Every house had one, but they were all different. No two alike.

He got out and opened the door for his favorite warrior. They had begun a friendship. He considered her an amazing woman with an even more amazing faith. Her courage in the face of danger rivaled that of any police officer Joyce had known.

He walked her to the door. "I can't tell you how grateful I am for your help."

She worked her key into the lock. Then she turned to Joyce. "I think we're a team. Warriors against evil...but both of us have a special interest in defeating this evil." She smiled and went inside.

"Thank you," Joyce said the words as she showed an unsure smile while closing the door. "Protect this woman of Yours Lord. Let her angels be with her...protecting her, giving her peace in her home. Thank you Lord."

He had said the words. It wasn't something he thought but rather something he felt. His voice was low as if a whisper, but his heart was screaming to God for help.

Joyce fished his phone from his coat. "We found it." His voice was excited.

The lieutenant's reaction was slower than Joyce was expecting. "Great...something on the video?"

"No...nothing like that," he paused. "Sorry if I woke you...but you need to know."

"What happened?"

"It's a long story. I can stop by now or tell you in the morning. Either way, you're going to love it."

The lieutenant was waking up. He was scratching his head as he listened to his detective. "You found the dragon's lair?"

"Yes...positive...absolutely. It's the place."

"Wow. How can you be so certain?" He stopped talking as a thought came to him. "Did God give it to you?" He sounded excited.

"Better than that...well maybe not, but yes... God was...is working to help us."

"There's more, isn't there?"

"You won't be able to go back to sleep. I'm coming by. See you in a few." Joyce hit the end button, pulled away from the curb a little faster than he was accustomed to.

The lieutenant went to the bathroom, unlocked the kitchen door to the back yard, and brewed a cup of coffee from his Keurig. He had hardly gotten settled at the table when he saw headlights fill his driveway. Moments later and Joyce was coming through the back door.

"Coffee?" The lieutenant pointed to the Keurig.

While the coffee was brewing, Joyce slipped off his coat and draped it over a chair. Then with coffee in hand, he took a seat and started talking. His excitement was like that of a rookie. A case that had him on the verge of retirement now showed a form of life and enthusiasm for his job that had disappeared years ago.

"It was the most amazing thing."

"What?"

Joyce explained how he had the thought to track down the warrior who had taken the pictures at the adult book store. He explained what the lieutenant knew. She had a gift. Joyce had learned it was the gift known as the discerning of spirits.

"I met her at the bus stop. The place she was when she took the pictures."

"A bus stop?"

"Yeah, it's in the report. She takes the same bus every night."

The lieutenant nodded.

Joyce went on to explain how he talked her into helping. He told the lieutenant about her very personal need to find and defeat the evil.

"So I drove us over to the dragon's lair. The building you and I saw today." He checked the date. "Yesterday."

The lieutenant raised his eyebrows. "You mean you confirmed that building is the one?"

"Right, the one we drove by, you shot a video of it as we drove in and out."

The boss sipped his coffee. When he raised his head again he said, "How did you...how were you able to confirm it? You know...absolutely."

Joyce somehow felt he should be more reverent. God was working in him. Through him. But he was excited. Almost like a kid. He knew the seriousness. He did not have to remind himself of the death he had seen. But he had also seen the works of God. Angels in battle with evil.

With the help of the prayer warrior, he had absolute proof that the dragon's lair was in fact the very building where Satan's minions were operating. A church of sorts. He wondered just how many people had been drawn into the death and destruction that evil promises all who venture in.

"It was the most amazing thing." Joyce was serious but the joy he felt was obvious.

"She told me how she sees angels. It's really a regular thing for her. She is truly blessed." He looked his boss in the eye. "If there is one thing I have learned, it's that God blesses people."

"I hear you Tommy. I know I've probably missed a lot because I've been so casual about Jesus."

"So I had asked her to watch for anything...good or bad. When we pulled up to the building I looked at her. Her eyes were like saucers. I knew she saw something. Then she looked behind us. We were parked. Almost where you and I sat." Joyce smiled as he shook his head.

The lieutenant didn't say a word. He knew the story was coming. He too had seen, up close and personal, what Joyce was likely to share. He knew the truth of spirits. Good and evil. It was, after all, what the battle was about. A fight between good and evil.

"I asked her what she saw. She didn't answer right away. She kept looking at the building and she would turn and look behind us. Finally, she asked, 'you see them?' I told her no."

"I watched her for what seemed like forever. Then she told me there was a huge, evil being sitting on the front roofline of the building. She described it. It was similar to what we already know. When I asked where... exactly, she pointed to the triangle portion that was jetting out from the front of the building. I asked if she was afraid. She said no. She smiled and turned to look out the back. She said we had protection. I asked her if she saw an angel."

"Did she?" The lieutenant was sure he already knew.

"Are you ready for this?"

The lieutenant laughed. "Yes...tell me."

"I thought she was looking out the back window. But she was looking in the back seat."

"You had an angel riding with you!?"

"So I asked her about it...I think she was surprised I couldn't see it. So she asked me if I could smell him. She said the angel was a 'him'. I actually sniffed a little. I wanted to. You know, smell something. We both know the stink of evil. I hoped I would get the scent of...I was thinking...I was hoping it would be the smell of heaven."

Chapter 82

"We found it." Joyce was still excited.

"Good morning detective...yes, I heard you took a field trip last night." The pastor was equally excited.

"She called you?"

"She did. I think it may have been the minute you dropped her off." The pastor's voice became more solemn. "She, more than anyone I know, has a need for this to end."

"Yeah...you're right. We talked about it." Joyce was quiet for a moment. "She's an amazing lady. Her son is very lucky to have her as his mother."

"I pray it works out, detective."

"I do too."

"So have you received a plan?"

Joyce hoped the question was rhetorical. "That's your department pastor. I'm waiting to hear what it is."

"I'll keep you up to date." The pastor didn't want to leave false hope but believed what he had to say. "I don't think it will be long."

Joyce made the report to his lieutenant. They discussed what would be their next move as they waited on God. The CSI techs had been approved and were currently working on the video cards. They, for the most part, were computer geeks and would likely see things the older detective might miss. It was an admission Joyce would not make.

Joyce settled back into the small desk chair and rolled it up to his desktop computer. He was ready to organize a crime file that would never see the light of day when the case was closed.

Closing a case, especially a homicide, offered three choices. The one most preferred at least in the early going, is a case closed with the arrest of the suspect. Even should the killer be acquitted in a trial, the case is closed.

Next is when a case is found to be something it is not. A homicide that is later found to be a suicide is closed as unfounded. It was not really a murder. The last choice is when a case is closed for exceptional reasons. It is known as an exceptionally closed or cleared case. An example is in a murder case where the killer themselves are killed. There is no one to charge with the crime. The case is over, closed.

It would likely be the third choice in the death cases Joyce had sitting on his desk. The results would be welcomed. End the killing, stop the deaths by eliminating the killers. That would be those who came seeking whom they can kill and destroy.

Exactly how that would happen, how evil is destroyed, was not clear. At least not to Joyce. In conversations, he was given the idea that mortals, like he and his boss, could not stop evil. Their weapons are harmless and ineffective against the powers of darkness. But God can and does overcome evil.

What happens to demons when they are vanquished by the angels of God? Joyce thought they were banished to Hell. He was told the Bible supports such an idea. The fact was, he did not know.

What he did know was he wanted it to end. To end sooner rather than later. As each hour ticked by, he wondered if new victims were falling to the works of the devil.

Chapter 83

The minister was alone in his office. His assistant was with the grieving mother conducting a funeral for her son. The funeral was in what was once the church sanctuary. It was now a chapel having been converted after a new, larger sanctuary was recently completed. The chapel was now used for occasions such as the funeral of the burn victim.

He appeared. He did not enter. There was no notice or announcement. The secretary was at her desk in the business office and did not inform the minister of the visitor.

He was a man, tall, big. He held the presence of authority. His hair was dark. Not well groomed, but not long. His complexion seemed dark as well, tanned. He was dressed in a manner that did not seem normal. Exactly what was different was missed by the minister. The man now in his office, how he arrived, was what captured all of the minister's attention.

Even before he could speak, the minister sensed a fog, a mist in the air but not moisture. It wasn't smoke but it was like smoke. It was faint, light. The thought of an aura came to mind.

"Don't be afraid." The voice was low in tone. A deep, resonating voice. The words crisp and clear.

The minister was tempted to talk. Ask a question. Ask who he was. He didn't. He knew. The events surrounding the funeral, currently ongoing just a short distance from his office, coupled with his conversations with a fellow pastor were sufficient.

"The God of Heaven has given you a word. You are to write on a tablet and run. Take it to the one who knows what to do."

The minister did not hesitate. He retrieved a yellow pad from his desk and took a pen from his shirt pocket. He began to write all the words from the visitor.

"The high priest, the one who knows what to do, is to assemble the church of Christ Jesus. The assembled shall be seven witnesses, a herald, an assembly of singers who sing the songs of angels as those before the throne of God, and Christ Jesus who is seated on a throne at the right hand of the Lord God."

The minister was writing. He was taking down every word. The fog, the aura had now enveloped both the visitor and the minister. In the fog, the task of hearing the words and recording them seemed effortless. The cadence of the visitor's message, while normal, was easy to manage when writing. The minister was able to keep up.

"The witnesses shall be the high priest and the priest. Two guardians of the people, peacemakers, men of God sanctified, pure and holy for and by the Christ which is Jesus the Lord. Two women belonging to the Church of Jesus Christ. One grieving and one praying. And a holy man of God given to the works of the Bride of Christ and in assistance to the high priest. These shall be the witnesses as chosen by the Lord God."

The minister wrote. Recording each word as they were given to him by the visitor. His mind did not wonder, nor did he even speculate on the words or the meaning of the words. He only wrote them on a tablet as directed by the visitor.

"The witnesses, the high priest, and the priest, the two guardians of the people, peacemakers, men of God sanctified, pure and holy for and by the Christ which is Jesus the Lord. The two women belonging to the Church of Jesus Christ. One grieving and one praying. And a holy man of God given to the works of the Bride of Christ and in assistance to the high priest, along with the herald and the singers who sing the songs of angels before the throne of God, shall find themselves in prayer and in fasting beginning at the next middle watch and remaining in prayer and fasting until the Lord has accomplished the work. The work shall be like that of Sodom, and shall be accomplished by the Lord."

The minister continued to write. Each word as spoken was written on the tablet as directed by the visitor.

"At a time, after the tenth hour following the time of prayer and of fasting, and before the first watch, the seven witnesses, the herald, the singers who sing like the angels before the throne of the Lord God shall assemble before the Dragon's lair, a place the Lord God has revealed.

"There and at that time, the singers who sing as the angels who are before the throne of God, shall sing continuously. And then, because of the prayers of the saints, those righteous in the sight of God, delivered unto salvation by the sacrifice of the lamb of God, being Christ Jesus. The Lord God of Heaven shall rescue from the snare of the Dragon, those in the midst of the Dragon who belong to Christ Jesus the Lord who are righteous having surrendered their hearts. It shall be as in the day of Lot. The holy angels of God shall be the rescuers. The assembled will witness and give testimony to the wonders and works of the Lord God of Heaven."

The minister had not given thought to the words. He recorded them as they were spoken. Taking down each word without errors or omissions. He wrote them on a tablet. The aura, the fog that enveloped him and the visitor had grown thick. It surrounded them like a cloud.

"Then, when the rescue by the angels of the Lord, as ordered by the Lord God is complete, and with a sign from the angels of God, the singers who have been singing continuously, without ceasing, shall stop. And then the herald with his trumpet shall sound the trumpet a shofar, a ram's horn. And then the angels of the Lord God of Heaven shall cast down on the Dragon's lair fire and brimstone as in the days of Sodom, and the Dragon's lair and the dragon and the demons and the other evil inhabitants of the Dragon's lair shall be destroyed and the evil shall no longer dwell in the city."

The minister wrote the words. As in a cloud, all other things, the business of the church and the people were as if they did not exist. He wrote as if the words were the most important thing under Heaven.

"Be ready, people of God and of the Lord Jesus Christ. For when the fire and the brimstone are released from Heaven, the Lord God will protect His people. For the seven witnesses, and the herald, and the singers who sing like angels before the throne of God, and the saints rescued from the Dragon will, in an instant, be delivered to the sanctuary, the place of the high priest where they are to praise and worship the Lord God of heaven, in spirit and in truth, giving thanks to the Savior, Jesus Christ their Lord.

"Then, the high priest and the priest shall, in their sanctuaries, for seven sabbaths, testify and give witness to all that occurred, giving praise and glory to the God of Heaven. The high priest and the priest, in their testimony and their witness, shall make an invitation to those who have not accepted the gift of salvation, to come forward and surrender to Christ and receive the gift of eternal salvation. And then the high priest and the priest shall baptize with water those who come forward, baptizing them in the name of the Father, the Son, and the Holy Spirit.

"When the high priest and the priest obey the word of the Lord God of Heaven and make a testimony of these events for seven sabbaths, then they will witness a one hundredfold return of people who come to the altar for salvation. There shall be a revival in the land.

"Thus says the Lord."

The minister had not looked up to the visitor the entire time he gave the message. When the final words were penned and he had set the pen on the desk, the minister looked up. He was alone. The cloud had lifted and the noise of the busy office was again obvious.

The minister prayed.

Chapter 84

"We have to talk."

The pastor was surprised but happy to hear from the minister. "Did you want to come by, meet somewhere...or just talk now...on the phone?"

"No... I mean yes, I must come now to see you." He was uncomfortable. This was completely new to him. His denomination discouraged the gifts of the Spirit. While they recognized them, they believed they had been reserved for the early church. They believed the gifts of old had passed away.

"Are you coming now?"

"Yes, I'm leaving, right now..." He was anxious. It showed in his voice. "I have received what I believe is a word from God."

"I'm here. Come as quickly as you can." The pastor had been waiting. He knew, deep within him, that a message was coming. He did not know how or from where. He was ready.

"It's a miracle." They were the first words spoken by the minister as he came through the door.

The pastor was not surprised. "That's exactly what we're waiting for...waiting on." He smiled.

"I know, but it's even more. I have no words." He opened a small valise and removed the message.

The paper was an exquisite work of art. An old piece expected to be of antiquities. "Where did this come from?" The pastor's voice showed amazement.

"I just received it...it was given to me...but it's a miracle. A gift from God...I have no explanation." He looked at the paper, the print was precise. Letters as if drawn. Art.

The pastor looked up in wonder. "I don't think I understand. Where did you get this? How did it come to you?"

The minister explained what happened. He began with the visitor appearing, the direction of 'to write on a tablet' and then how the visitor spoke the words. The minister told him about the cloud that filled the room around him and the visitor.

"I wrote it down. Word for word on a yellow pad I had in my desk. When it was over, this is what I had." He pointed to the message.

"Praise God." The pastor stared at the single oversized page that held the message. "What did you use to write this?" He pointed to the page before them.

"This." The minister pulled an ordinary ink pen from his shirt pocket.

"What does it say?"

The minister had a blank look. His eyes went from the pastor to the message and back to the pastor. "I don't know." He looked at the message. "I just wrote. I don't know what he said. I only wrote it down."

The pastor was quiet. He did not know for sure what to say, or how to receive the message. He turned to the minister. "Let's pray." He didn't wait.

He placed a hand on the minister's shoulder and began to pray.

The pastor prayed for several long moments. He praised God for His faithfulness. He asked for understanding and that they would be given a clear sense of what the Lord was saying in the message. He thanked the Lord for protecting them and showing the way to victory.

"Let's read this together." The pastor did not lift the paper but centered it on the desk. Both men stood over the message. The pastor read it slowly, out loud. The minister followed along reading to himself while listening to the words as they were spoken by the pastor. They read the message slowly. Each word was read. The reading took nearly five minutes.

"Do you understand?"

"Yes, I do," said the pastor. "I understand."

The minister was quiet for a moment. Then asked, "Do you know who these seven witnesses are?"

"Yes, I am sure I know each of them." The pastor looked at his colleague. "You're one of them." He nodded and smiled.

"Tell me."

"You are the priest. A Godly term for a leader in a fellowship of believers. I believe the high priest is me. I am the first to lead the effort and I am the one who helped you to understand how important the work is."

"What's our plan? I'm not sure I understand the time table of the message."

The pastor was staring at the message. As he did, the words became more clear. "We start right now."

Chapter 85

The pastor went to work. He began by contacting those who would be hardest to assemble. It began with his worship leader. He quickly briefed him that the worship team needed to assemble in the sanctuary at midnight. That it was going to be a long night of prayer and fasting. The team could easily be busy for twenty hours.

Next, the pastor called Joyce. "Good news detective. We have the word...the message of how to proceed."

Joyce smiled to no one. "Awesome. What's next?"

"Both you guys need to be here by midnight. Our instructions are to be in prayer and fasting for several hours."

"Wow." Joyce wasn't sure what that would be like, just what it meant, but he knew it was something that needed to be done.

"I would like you to pick up your favorite warrior at the bus stop again. Bring her with you to the church."

The pastor was brief. He had a lot to do. "I'll explain everything to the whole team when we're all together."

"Okay...I'm...we're in."

"Tommy, this is the real deal."

Joyce wasn't sure he understood the point. He knew, probably better than most, how big this was. He smiled to himself. He was glad that he had learned God was bigger. "Thanks."

The pastor called his deacon and gave him the heads up to be in church at midnight.

The last of the witnesses was left to his new friend and colleague. The minister would contact the grieving mother whose son's funeral had been held at his church.

The first to arrive were members of the worship team. Some were alone and others carpooled. One set of singers were a husband and wife. Tommy Joyce arrived with his prayer warrior. The lieutenant came in a few minutes later having come from home. The hour was late and the night would be a long one. The deacon was the first to show up and spent the time with the pastor in the office. The minister arrived with the grieving mother. She was happy to see that detective Joyce was at the church. He had been a comfort for her in the time they spent together.

As they settled into seats in the first couple of rows, they spoke quietly about the coming event. No one actually used that word, but everyone knew something special was about to take place. God was about to show them that all their prayers were working.

The minister was new to the group. Being a stranger lasted only minutes. They received him warmly and knew God had him there for a purpose. Some churches have trouble accepting outsiders. The reasons are many. Nearly all are petty and not worth wasting time over. This church was not one of them.

"We are here tonight for a very special purpose." The pastor was standing in front of the pew facing his team. "God has called us here. We are his tool in defeating evil. The prayers you have been so faithful to send to the throne of grace are going to be fulfilled."

The pastor had prayed at length as to how he should manage the team. How to explain what was about to happen and what was expected from the warriors. The actions would dictate what the Lord would do to defeat evil. He was led by the Spirit to first read the message. Each of those assembled would then know exactly what God would do if they did as God directed.

"Blessed are those who hear the word of God and obey it." He stopped and watched his team.

Then he moved to the dais and stepped behind the podium that was in the center. He had placed the message on the podium in preparation for this moment.

The pastor held the message as a holy word from God. He was careful to treat it with great respect and handled it as little and gently as possible. It was late, the lighting in the sanctuary was low. He turned on a small light on the podium.

"Prepare your heart to hear the word of the Lord."

The pastor began to read. He had the sense that the words held a type of reverence. They were not Scripture, but they were from God and given to the church for such a time as this. He read the words with that in mind. In the reading, he maintained a pace that not only respected the value, the truth of who gave them, but that also ensured an understanding of their meaning would be possible. The purpose of the message could not be overstated.

When he finished, he lifted his eyes to the team that in essence had been chosen by God. "This message was received today. It was given to our brother in Christ. He is the priest referenced in the message." He paused a moment. "There are details I sense I should explain. The message makes it clear that we are to be in prayer and fasting, beginning right now. This is the watch, the midnight hour that the message instructs.

"For some, the idea of praying all night, not eating all night and into tomorrow will seem difficult. I want to encourage you that as you pray, ask the Lord to help you. To sustain you. I think you'll be amazed at how the time will fly by, fatigue will not be the problem you may expect, and you won't be hungry. Really." He nodded his head.

"Let me clear up the who's who in this word. I am the high priest. Don't get hung up on the name. My colleague here, who received this message is the priest."

He pointed to the deacon. "That guy you all know is the assistant to the high priest." The pastor was smiling. The seriousness of their purpose was pleasing. God was working and it was a joy to be a part of it.

"The two guardians, the peacemakers are our friends from the police. We all know the risks they have taken in finding evil. I am so grateful we have been able to go to battle with them." He nodded to the detectives.

"The mother in prayer is our wonderful warrior who has been instrumental in getting this whole battle against the powers of darkness on the right track. We are going to, this very day I pray, see the rescue of her son."

The pastor looked fondly at the mother who had lost her son to evil early in the battle. "We have a grieving mother joining us. A powerful woman and lover of Christ. Her son, a born again Christian was lost in the war. Today she will see the Lord avenge his death."

One of the warriors shouted, "Amen." The pastor nodded in approval.

"I imagine that it's obvious that our amazing worship team are the singers. They sing as if angels before the throne of God. We are truly blessed to have them." He smiled. "And the herald? That is our worship leader. He will be there, but not one of the singers. He will sound the trumpet, like that of the shofar."

"Now, as to the timing, we are officially in the third watch. We are to stay in prayer as we fast until the time we assemble at the Dragon's lair. The message instructs that we do that after the tenth hour, which is three in the afternoon. We will be finished before the start of the first watch which is six in the evening. That is today."

He had more. "This is a unique occasion. God has instructed us to do this in obedience to Him. Over the course of the next several hours, some of you may sense the need to share...a word, or a Scripture. I want you to do as you're led. It can be done by simply reading or proclaiming as you are led." He considered if there was more. "This is an informal assembly, but it is a very solemn one. Be reverent. Honor the Lord in all that you do."

Chapter 86

The warriors assembled on the sidewalk across the street from the Dragon's lair. It was the building discovered by the two detectives, and then confirmed by the warrior. A praying mother who, when she witnessed the evil at the adult bookstore, had the courage to photograph them.

The pastor was meticulous in the setup for the team. He had studied the message. He knew the instructions. He understood what must be done. He envisioned what the outcome would look like.

Every team member was important. The singers were vital. God had made clear their role. They were to begin singing as angels before the throne of God. They were well suited. The weekly praise and worship were often compared to just that.

The worship leader was not a part of the singers. While he was prominent in church singing, the role of the herald today was singular. He was to sound the trumpet, the shofar. He was the herald, that was his only role.

Joyce looked over the setting. The sidewalk appeared different. He remembered a bus bench and two newspaper boxes. None of them were there. The sidewalk was a clear span of concrete. All the space the singers, the herald, and the witnesses would need. He also noticed that the businesses with access from the sidewalk were closed. Each of them had signs stating so.

The singers formed an arching line, a form of a semi-circle. One end at the corner. The line of singers then extended to the portion of the sidewalk directly across the street from the far end of the Dragon's lair. Where the driveway gives access to the parking lot and loading dock. The semi-circle was an inspiration of the pastor. He had sensed it during prayer.

The herald was positioned on the curb at the center of the line of singers. An equal number of singers extended to both his left and right.

The witnesses stood near the curb. They were not at the edge. They each were a pace from the edge of the curb, standing on the sidewalk directly across the street from the Dragon's lair. The herald was in the middle. The witnesses lined up just behind him, but in front of the singers.

To the herald's right was the pastor, the high priest. To his left was the minister, the priest.

The detectives, the guardians, peacemakers, were next. Joyce stood by the pastor, the lieutenant stood beside the minister. Next were the mothers. The mother that was grieving stood by the lieutenant. The mother praying was next to Joyce. The final witness was the assistant to the high priest, the deacon. He stood two paces behind the herald, in front of the singers.

Precisely at the tenth hour, the singers began. The sound was overwhelming. Joyce, standing in place at the curb, closed his eyes and imagined what the music must sound like in Heaven. He was new to things of faith. His belief in Jesus being the Savior of mankind was new. But it was exciting. God was real.

Angels were real. He had seen that truth up close and personal. The idea that the Creator of all things, God, would take on flesh and be a man was incredible.

The lieutenant was deep in prayer. His heart held a sense of aching. He prayed for forgiveness. He had prayed that prayer many times since the case turned toward evil. He felt guilty for not being the Christian he had intended on being so many years earlier. Then he praised God for allowing him to be right where he was at that very moment.

The pastor, the high priest of the message, continued in prayer. The knowledge that the God he served was about to put His power on display for the body of Christ to witness was beyond anything he could ever ask or imagine.

The minister, the priest, and the receiver of the message found himself in a place that did not exist. Not in his seminary training, not in the liturgy of his denomination. But he was here. God eternal, the Holy one of Scripture was allowing him to witness a miracle only God could do.

The mother praying was doing exactly that. Her heart was filled with the excitement that angels sent by God were going to rescue her son. She knew the story of Lot, she knew what happened at Sodom. She knew how Abraham had prayed for his nephew Lot, and bargained with the Lord to save Lot and his family from destruction. She knew the story of how God poured out his wrath on Sodom for its sin.

The mother grieving would be eternally grateful for being allowed to witness a great work of God. Her heart held deep scars from the loss of her son, but she knew God understood. He too had lost a Son. Today she would see justice. A justice only the Creator can exact.

The priest's assistant, the deacon, stood in his place. He was overwhelmed with the need to pray. His personal faith had been under attack in the early days of the battle. Now he was to see the power of his Lord on full display as the minions of Satan would be cast out and cast down into the very depths of Hell. He knew Hell to be a real place, a punishment allowed for those who rebel against the King of kings.

Chapter 87

Time stood still for the singers, the witnesses, and the herald. Those assembled before the Dragon's lair had no sense of how long they had been there. But it wasn't only time that stopped. The traffic, cars, trucks, and buses had stopped. There was no traffic or people coming or going around the Dragon's lair.

It started before the first watch. The singers began singing. The witnesses were standing. Ready to witness the power of God as directed in the message.

There was a sound. Not loud but not faint either. It came from the Dragon's lair. The two story lair was a modern structure with glass windows extending the full width and height of the building. A prominent element was a triangle section jetting out from the front, the tip of the triangle pointed directly at the witnesses, the herald, and the singers.

The sound changed. Its volume increased. The singers were loud, clear, and crisp in their worship. The singing was the dominant sound before the Dragon's lair. But a second sound, the new sound, was growing.

The witnesses were unable to discern the source, only that the sound came from the lair. Then it happened. A popping. A section of glass in the triangle cracked. At first, it was a small twisting line. In moments it grew. A spiderweb effect was spreading across the glass on one side of the triangle.

Then there was a ringing. The sound of metal, like a cracked bell, became clear. The witnesses watched. They listened. Then the ringing turned to clashing. Metal on metal. Like the sound of swords. The sound was familiar to two of the witnesses. They had heard it before.

Next came the screeches. Loud, piercing, terrifying sounds. The sound of pain. The screams joined in the noise. Horrible. Sounds of torment.

Glass was breaking. It was in the area near the back. Near the loading dock. They were not cracks but rather large shards of window glass all smashing to the ground near the parking lot.

The witnesses watched. They had the impression that the glass had been blown out by an explosion. They did not hear an explosion. But they heard the screeching, the horrible, almost insidious sound of anguish. More glass, more breaking and crashing.

Next came the sight of what appeared to be the dragon. Not the whole dragon, but its tail. A long grayish form, like a giant snake or serpent, extended out the door of the loading dock.

The dragon's tail twisted and turned. Flipping and flicking. It, the tail, appeared as if it were searching for something to strike, but there was nothing there.

More glass crashed to the ground on the side, near the rear, by the loading dock. The giant shards struck the dragon's tail but they did not pierce it.

More screeches, more wails of anguish came from the building. There was a war raging inside. The sounds of war are not pleasant. They are terrifying. They are once in a lifetime sounds that none should have to endure.

The witnesses watched. They endured the sounds and sights of the battle being waged across the street. The mother praying found that only her prayers were sustaining her. She wanted to lay down, to faint. Her heart screamed the words, 'How long O Lord?'

More glass was breaking, shattering, and crashing down around the building. There were more shrieks and howls. The sounds of torture, cries seeking pity. Then more sounds of war. Swords crashing, smashing steel on steel. The terrifying image of the battle of good and evil raged on.

The thought that any life inside the building might prevail, that life could endure the violence, was unthinkable. The hearts of the witnesses said otherwise.

The singers sang as the singing of angels before the throne of God. The angelic sound gave power to the witnesses to watch and hear the violence as it continued.

The sounds grew, the pain and torment increased moment by moment. The time of anguish was not calculated. Time had stopped but the battle of good and evil had not.

Flesh and blood were there to be a witness. The powers and principalities of God and of Satan raged on in a deadly battle. It's an eternal war. This is but one battle. The witnesses waited. The message was clear. The battle would be fought but the victor was preordained.

Inside the scene was different. The sounds, the cries, the clashing of swords, were not the same as what was heard.

A rite was being conducted. The supreme dragon was exacting privilege. He was an odd looking figure, like a man, but with a face that did not seem like a man. Two assistants, equally ugly yet different in appearance, were tending to the altar. A fire was being prepared. There were more. A balcony of sorts overlooked the altar where a number of spirits, minions of the dark, had assembled.

There were two disciples who did not comprehend the purpose of the ritual. They were standing in the midst of the altar watching.

A follower, a disciple found to be unworthy was on the altar. Her spirit was in her but all life had departed. The brightness of her robe, a symbol of royalty had been removed and was used as a rag before the altar. The rite would not allow any appearance of virtue. The rite was not a sacrifice, but the final act before eternal suffering.

The dragon and the assistants appeared agitated. There was a presence stirring. Unseen, but a presence was felt. The spirits in the upper level began to screech. A loud noise. A sound of fear.

Two fighters, warriors dressed in the battle garb of the throne were there but had not yet appeared.

"You are in great danger." The words were spoken by a fighter.

The two disciples, the only mortals, did not understand. They did not comprehend the purpose of the fighters. The two beings had suddenly appeared. They were tall, swift in movement. Mighty in strength, and filled with the knowledge of war.

At first glance, the fighters appeared frightening. "No, we're supposed to be here," said a disciple.

"Come with us." The voice was clear, crisp. "You have to leave." The authority in the voice demanded compliance.

The two fighters and both witnesses moved towards the front of the lair. An area that was a part of a pentagram. Outside it appeared as a triangle.

The dragon was changing. No longer a figure of a man, it became a reptile. A dragon by any description. It seemed to have the body and wings of a bat. It grew, consuming much of the space around the altar. The dragon saw the fighters. His rage spilled out, expressed with ear-bursting screams. Screeches that could cause hearts to stop beating.

"Wait." The fighter said to the disciples. "Stay behind us or you will die." It was a command. Loud. Clear.

Both fighters suddenly grew to a size twice what was first seen. In an instant, each had swords. As quickly as they grew another change occurred. Both fighters now had a face on both sides of their head. They wore a helmet, a silver skull cap type covering, and an iron breastplate. The fighters could see both front and rear.

The battle began. The dragon's weapons were long, sharp talons that appeared to be iron. The points were dull in finish but sharp as a sword. In addition, he had a tail. Large, bigger than either fighter. The dragon caused the tail to sweep across the space. Candle stands, ornaments, and other furnishings, anything in its path was sent flying.

The two attendants joined the fight. Both changed in their appearance. They became animals of some sort. The body of a man yet a head of a beast. Each had a sword.

The attendants proved to be harmless and ineffective. The fighters quickly vanquished them with a single long wide swipe of a sword decapitating them both. Their cries of pain and anguish lasted long after the heads were separated.

The dragon went on offense. Wild swings of his giant foreclaws missed as the fighters worked in tandem to split the dragon's attention. A wild fury erupted. The giant and deadly tail continued to sweep the large space. The building interior was being destroyed. Windows were breaking, the sounds of destruction unremitting.

The dragon made an attempt to escape. It appeared the plan was to flee out the large rear door. From there he would take flight and be gone.

The dragon backed toward the loading dock. The tail was flailing. He was making long sweeping motions with the dangerous talons. Screeches and howls were continuous.

The fighters would not allow the escape. A swift and sure strike of a fighter's huge sword struck a foreleg. It did not separate, but the wound was severe. The leg rendered harmless. The dragon continued to thrash. Windows shattered. The sound of the crashing blows was terrifying. The violence of evil was beyond what the disciples watching were able to understand. They both made a dash for the front exit.

The dragon had powers, weapons that the disciples knew nothing about. The fighters had warned them. But fear was the one thing that would drive them to run. The dragon raised, turned his giant head towards the ceiling two stories overhead. He then jerked the head down casting a fireball towards the running disciples.

With a full face on both sides of their head, the fighters saw everything. The fireball was deadly, but the fighters more so. Moving like light, a fighter stood before the disciples to deflect the weapon. The ricochet sent the fire back to its source. The dragon coughed. A wind, like that of a hurricane, caused the fire to fall harmlessly to the floor, sizzling as it expanded the last of its power.

The dragon was crippled. Movement was limited when compared to the skills of the fighters. The fighters danced around the enraged enemy striking it again and again with their giant swords. The loading dock had a chain used to raise and lower the door. A fighter recovered the chain.

With the skills learned in warfare, the fighter worked towards the dragon's neck. The second fighter stayed engaged in the fight. He was able to make a wide swipe at the remaining front claw. The blow found its target. The dragon was crippled. The fighter with the chain secured it to the beast and then chained him to his own altar.

Both fighters and the two disciples left the building to the outrageous screams and howls of the chained dragon.

Chapter 88

The two disciples stepped out the front door of the Dragon's lair. Following them came the two fighters. The fighters were big, majestic, and had the image of men. Their size was now like that of a big man. Their faces as of men.

The singers who sing the songs of angels as those before the throne of God and Christ Jesus who is seated on a throne at the right hand of the Lord God, were singing. The music was glorious, beautifully loud.

The disciples appeared soiled and worn. They were unkempt. Their faces, unshaven and covered in soot, showing fear. The sunlight was bright and they shielded their eyes with their hands from the light. They stood still on the sidewalk.

The fighters stepped up alongside the two disciples. One on the right and one to their left. They stood tall. Their authority was understood. Fighters, centurions sent from God for such a time as this.

The fighters remained motionless for a long moment. Then the fighter to the right of the disciples raised a giant sword. When he did, the singing stopped.

Everything was quiet.

Then the fighter lowered his giant sword. He pointed with an extended arm directly at the herald.

The herald had been waiting. Patient. Waiting for the moment described in the message when the angels of God would come from the Dragon's lair, make a signal calling him to sound the trumpet, like that of a shofar, a ram's horn. The full time he stood he held his trumpet at his right side.

When the disciples and the fighters emerged from the lair, the herald felt a change in his hand. The thought was he had dropped the trumpet. When he looked, he saw a miracle that only God could do. The trumpet was gone. He now held in his right hand, a long twisting horn. A ram's horn. A shofar.

The herald raised the shofar and blew it as directed in the message. With the sound of the shofar, a cloud formed. Not a storm, but a cloud, up high. It was heavy, thick yet billowing white.

The witness, the mother in prayer, had a clear view of the disciples and the fighters. Her interest was in the disciples. Those rescued by the angels of God from the Dragon's lair.

When the sound of the shofar was complete, she raised her hands to Heaven and shouted.

"Hallelujah!" She felt as if she would fall but a force sustained her. She waited for the disciples to cross over.

The disciples moved towards the witnesses, the herald, and the singers. As they did, the two fighters, the angels of the Lord, vanished. A wind began to blow.

The attention of the witnesses, the herald, and the singers were drawn to the forming clouds over the Dragon's lair. Suddenly an image appeared. Visible but not clear. Not all saw it the same. The high priest, the pastor saw a rider on a white horse. The priest, the minister saw a majestic being as if he were a member of Heaven.

Then the clouds turned dark, rolling, lightning flashed. Then the sound of thunder. Then, a giant ball, like fire, came out of the dark and rolling clouds high over the lair.

Then it was quiet. The clouds, the lightning, the thunder, the images, the fireball. All were gone. The witnesses, the herald, the singers, and the disciples were suddenly, in the twinkling of an eye, in the sanctuary. The place where prayer and fasting took place on the third watch.

There was no prompting. When the singers realized that they were in their sanctuary, as described in the message, they began to sing. Loud, clear, holy, majestic music.

The mother who prayed was however, the first to respond. She located her son standing near the singers. He was looking around, obviously bewildered.

She called his name, shouting, "Thank you, Jesus. Praise God." She made the few steps to his side and embarrassed him in a hug only a mother can provide.

His eyes filled with tears. That last time he saw her they were praying that Jesus would accept him. Save him. "Oh Mother, I'm so sorry. I'm so sorry." His sobs overcame him. He did his best to cling to the only thing keeping him from falling to the floor. His mother, a woman of God who refused to give up. He truly was a prodigal.

A second mother, one who was grieving, instantly understood the need of the other disciple. The man, hardly more than a boy was alone in the sanctuary. He was unkempt, dirty, hygiene an apparent afterthought. His face was dirty but also bruised. A closer look would reveal multiple bruises on several areas of his body. It was unclear if he had been in a fight, or physically abused.

She approached the confused disciple. At first, he was standing. But overcome with fatigue, he dropped into a pew at the front of the sanctuary. She smiled, nodded, and gently sat beside him. "You're safe now." Her voice was that of a mother. Gentle, caring. She watched, waiting. Praying quietly.

Finally he spoke. "Where am I?"

"You're safe, you're with friends. We'll help you...whatever you need."

He sat up, more erect. His head was turning, looking. The singers were still singing. They had the sound of angels. He saw the giant cross above the altar. "Is this Heaven?"

She smiled, "No dear, you're still alive."

"Oh, thank God."

Tommy Joyce looked around the sanctuary. It was only seconds ago he was standing near the curb watching the sky. Clouds were beginning to boil overhead and a storm was nearly certain. He remembered hearing one of the other witnesses say, "Praise God."

Joyce saw the lieutenant. Not next to him but there, in the sanctuary, just a few paces away. As they made eye contact, the lieutenant settled into the pew, exhaled heavily, and bent over. His forearms rested on his knees. He closed his eyes.

"Dear God, holy and glorious God of creation. Thank you for your goodness, your mercy. Praise be to you, my God, and to Jesus Christ my Lord and Savior."

"Amen." Joyce sat down beside him.

The worship leader was in front of the singers who stood on the dias. Their singing continued out of desire. They truly loved worshipping. Even without the events of the past twenty hours, worship was enjoyable. Since seeing the mighty works of God, being present in the midst of His great miracle, their desire to sing was magnified.

The pastor, sitting on the lower step leading to the dias watched his worship leader. "I see you got your trumpet back."

The worship leader looked down to see the brass instrument hanging at his side. "I can not explain it." He raised his eyes to meet the pastor's. "When the time came, the shofar just appeared. The trumpet was gone and the horn was in my hand." He smiled, shrugged, then nodded his head.

"God's timing. It's always perfect." It was the minister. He was only a few paces away and heard the conversation. "God knows what we need. He sees to it we have it when we need it." He shrugged. "His timing."

"Amen." The pastor nodded.

"You know...I've preached that message. Today I understand. Before...well, I'm not so sure I really believed it." He looked at the pastor. "Know what I mean?"

The pastor bowed his head. He had a thought but wanted to get it right. Then he looked at the minister, then his deacon. "It's vital, more than vital, that we remember the last part of the message."

The minister looked up to the ceiling. He didn't see any angels. But he wasn't expecting them. He had seen the image in the cloud just minutes ago. The spiritual realm became real. New sights would always be welcome, but his belief did not rest on future experiences. The doubts he held evaporated. He had accepted God by faith years ago. That faith was cemented in all the events since a grieving mother entered his church seeking help for her son.

"I think," said the minister, "there are more than a few who sit in the pew each Sunday thinking they are going to Heaven. I have come to believe they might be uncomfortable sitting there over the next seven weeks."

Joyce sat down next to the pastor. "Thank you."

The pastor gave him an odd look.

"Without your faithfulness, I would not be saved. You saved my life."

"Jesus saved you Tommy, He just used us to guide you to Him."

" have spent a lifetime fighting what most call evil," he paused and looked up. "Now I see what real evil is like." He turned to the pastor, "And it's in the world."

The pastor nodded.

"Maybe, over the next few weeks I'll be here...to see many more come to know what I've missed all my life."

The End

I hope you have enjoyed reading this story. More importantly, I hope that it has helped you in understanding the Love God has for you. For all of us.

"For God so loved the world that he gave his one and only Son, that whoever believes in him shall not perish but have eternal life." John 3:16

I have another novel, *Kinderhook, "The Essence of Evil."* in this same Spiritual Warfare Genre. You are sure to enjoy another wonderful story. It is available on Amazon.

Made in United States
North Haven, CT
08 April 2022

18050040R00163